2

RAGTAG TEAM

SLAMDOWN TOWN

TOWN

★ ★ ★

RAGTAG TEAM

AMULET BOOKS · NEW YORK

by **MAXWELL NICOLL**
and **MATTHEW SMITH**

Library of Congress Cataloging-in-Publication Data
Names: Nicoll, Maxwell, author. | Smith, Matthew, author.
Title: Ragtag team / by Maxwell Nicoll and Matthew Smith.
Description: New York : Amulet Books, 2021. | Series: Slamdown Town ; 2 |
   Audience: Ages 8 to 12. | Summary: When Tamiko is transformed into Game Over,
   she and best friend Ollie, as Big Chew, team up to face Slamdown Town tag-team
   champions the Krackle Kiddos, but will their friendship survive?
Identifiers: LCCN 2020019061 | ISBN 9781419745942 (hardcover) | ISBN 9781419745959
   (paperback) | ISBN 9781683359456 (ebook)
Subjects: CYAC: Wrestling—Fiction. | Best friends—Fiction. | Friendship—Fiction. |
   Brothers—Fiction. | Magic—Fiction.
Classification: LCC PZ7.1.N536 Rag 2021 | DDC [Fic]—dc23
LC record available at https://lccn.loc.gov/2020019061

Text and illustrations © 2021 Abrams
Jacket illustrations by Christian Garland
Book design by Brenda E. Angelilli

Printed and bound in U.S.A.
10 9 8 7 6 5 4 3 2 1

Amulet Books are available at special discounts when purchased in quantity for premiums and promotions as well as fundraising or educational use. Special editions can also be created to specification. For details, contact specialsales@abramsbooks.com or the address below.

Amulet Books® is a registered trademark of Harry N. Abrams, Inc.

ABRAMS The Art of Books
195 Broadway, New York, NY 10007
abramsbooks.com

To Ryan, Olivia, and Lindsey,
our original tag team partners

CHAPTER 1

TAMIKO

100,000 points.

That was the high score Tamiko Tanaka was trying—no—going to beat today.

Bionic Unicycle Racing II, *The Quest for Dinner*, *Porcupine Heist*. She held the high score on every game in Slamdown Town Arena's decrepit arcade room.

Except for one.

Brawlmania Supreme, the retro eight-bit wrestling brawler, was Tamiko's greatest gaming challenge. Being the only wrestling-focused game in an arcade set in a wrestling arena naturally made it popular, but the game was *infamous* for being extremely difficult. There were rumors that it was unbeatable, like the video game version of a claw machine.

Tamiko had no problem wrestling her way to the game's final opponent, the dreaded and diabolical Buff Boss. After years of practice, she could even get there with one quarter.

But the problem was actually *beating* the eight-bit menace.

She strolled across the stained, mildewed carpet, past beeping machines, clacking air hockey pucks, and screaming kids. With each step, she prepared herself for today's victory.

Nothing would get in her way. That is, except for the fresh-faced fourth grader who had the audacity to be playing *her* game when she arrived.

"Get out of my way, newbie!" she yelled.

The boy's eyes went wide when he saw her. "Sorry," he squeaked, and scurried off.

He hadn't even finished playing, but everyone knew *Brawl-mania Supreme* belonged to T-A-M, the three letters that held every place in the top ten list except for number one.

That belonged to D-E-V, the game's original developers. For years, she'd climbed the ranks, creeping closer and closer to the first-place position. She'd grown to despise those three letters and the sinister creators behind them who knowingly made a game that would eat your quarters and ask for seconds, all while dangling victory in front of your face.

As Tamiko planted her sneakers in front of the game, a familiar greeting flashed across the screen:

ARE YOU READY FOR BRAWLMANIA SUPREME?

"You bet your pixely butt, I am," she muttered.

The sounds of retro music and the murmurs of the other gamers in the room faded away. As was tradition, she pulled up her lucky sock—the only one she was wearing—and blew a strand of tangled hair out of her face. She took a quarter out of her oversized pocket and placed it in the machine. The coin landed with a satisfying *clink* in the bowels of the arcade cabinet.

A list of playable characters filled the screen. Tamiko yanked the semi-functional joystick over to her preferred choice, the mysterious masked wrestler Miss Creant. She wore all black from head to toe and boasted a high-flying, high-energy move set that allowed Tamiko to control the ring. Tamiko slapped the worn attack buttons, gritted her teeth, and readied herself for action.

Quick maneuvering and intense button-mashing tapped out her first-round opponent, the commander of the ring, Staff Sergeant Stryker. She pinned the jokester Hyena—whose constant laughing fits crackled out of the speakers—with a flashy animated combo. And the letters K.O. flashed on-screen after she hit the heroic Sammy Slamdown with Miss Creant's special attack, a Heinous Hangman, by spinning her joystick and tapping both buttons at the same time.

The text on the screen issued a warning that sent goose bumps up her arms:

PREPARE FOR FINAL MATCH!

Her skills had brought her, once again, to the big, bad, pixelated champion.

"The Buff Boss," muttered Tamiko under her breath.

He was big, he was buff, and he wore a suit and carried a briefcase.

"So the boss of the game is a literal boss?" asked a voice from behind her.

Tamiko whipped around, ready to tear into the person responsible for ruining her concentration. Instead of one culprit, she found a dozen onlookers surrounding her.

"Of course the boss of *Brawlmania Supreme* is a literal boss!" said Tamiko.

She used to be able to game in peace, but not since she, her best friend Ollie, and his brother Hollis saved Slamdown Town from closing a few months ago. New fans continued to flock to the arena ever since, and that meant having to deal with fresh-faced newbies hogging her game and gawking bystanders messing up her focus.

"Stand back, everyone!" she said, raising her hands in the air. "Professional gaming is serious business. I wouldn't want any of you to get *hurt*."

Tamiko grinned as the onlookers took two steps back. Part of her liked having a crowd. But the other part of her realized she needed to focus and forget the annoying onlookers.

GAME ON!

On-screen, Miss Creant bashed Buff Boss with a Corrupt Chokeslam that left her opponent dazed and confused. Tamiko yanked the joystick back to avoid the Buff Boss's Briefcase Beatdown before leaping forward and attacking with a Monstrous Moonsault Combo. A siren wailed as Buff Boss trapped Miss Creant in a Business Meeting Hold. With her sweaty, aching palms, Tamiko smashed the attack buttons to escape. She twirled the joystick, tapped both buttons simultaneously, and rammed an Enraged Elbow straight into Buff Boss's gut.

EPIC MOVE!

She timed her attacks to perfection and evaded incoming blows with practiced ease. Behind her, the crowd grew anxious, all eyes trained on her rising score.

"She's going to do it!"

POWER UP!

This is it! thought Tamiko. Buff Boss began to blink, which meant two things. First, that a few more well-timed hits would finish him off. But second—and more important—that he had transformed into a "super" version of himself, one that could end the match in just one move.

Before she could react, Buff Boss crossed the ring and grabbed Miss Creant.

"No, no, no!" she whispered.

It was too late. He lifted Miss Creant high above his head. Tamiko watched, helpless, as Buff Boss slammed her character onto the mat and pinned her. She tapped the buttons as quickly as she could to try to break free, but the in-game ref called the pinfall.

GAME OVER

She looked at her score: 95,052.

"I was so close!" said Tamiko. She dug into her pockets and found them empty. "Oh great. And now I'm out of quarters! Show's over, everyone."

Her gaggle of newly acquired fans dispersed. Fame was fickle and fleeting, but it didn't bother her. She'd try again next weekend. For now, all that gaming had worked up an appetite.

She made her way out of the arcade, eager to find her best friend and gather as many snacks as her arms could carry.

CHAPTER 2

OLLIE

"HEY! That's not fair. I've been waiting in line for ten minutes!"

Ollie Evander *really* needed to pee. But as he danced back and forth in the long line for the bathroom, it became painfully clear that, one, he would need to hold it; and two, that eighth graders were just as annoying at the arena as they were at school.

"What are you going to do about it, sixth grader?" demanded the eighth grader who had pushed his way past Ollie toward the front of the line. "Cry to your mommy?"

"I'm *not* a crybaby," said Ollie.

The eighth grader ignored him. "Actually, when you do, get her to sign this." He shoved an autograph book into Ollie's hands. "The Referee is my favorite wrestler. Now outta my way!"

Ollie instinctively reached for the magic gum in his back pocket. The second he tossed it into his mouth and chewed, he'd transform into Big Chew, the giant wrestler with arms the size of dump trucks. Then he'd give that eighth grader something to cry to his mommy about.

Only, there wasn't a wad of sticky gum in his pocket. A bit of lint, yes, and a hardened, been-through-the-wash piece of paper that he'd been doodling on—but no gum.

Right, he remembered. *I gave it up.*

The sound of a flushing toilet brought him back to reality. He bounced up and down, trying to see over the heads in front of him and think of anything other than having to pee.

"Gotta pee!" said another eighth grader as he cut in line.

"Grrr," said Ollie.

He opened the autograph book and thumbed past pages of hastily scratched wrestler signatures. On the first blank page he saw, he scribbled a drawing of Big Chew wrestling a group of scrawny eighth graders. Then, as dramatically as he could, he signed:

OLLIE

The arena *had* been theirs. He, his best friend Tamiko, and his older brother Hollis used to practically have Slamdown Town to themselves. But everything changed after he'd been gifted the piece of already-been-chewed gum for his eleventh birthday.

Ollie, as Big Chew, had wrestled all the way to a championship match against Werewrestler, the most despicable wrestler at Slamdown Town. Years prior, Werewrestler defeated Ollie's mother, then called Brash Banshee, now called The Referee, by using an illegal move. The outcome was an unfunny injury to her funny bone and she was forced to stop wrestling. But instead of leaving the ring entirely, she signed up to be the Slamdown Town referee, vowing to stop all cheaters and ensuring that each and every rule would be followed. It had become Ollie's lifelong goal to avenge his mother and, finally, he'd had his chance.

But then Linton Krackle, the CEO of Slamdown Town, announced he was closing the arena, and Tamiko, the only person in the whole world who knew Big Chew's secret identity, announced that she didn't want to be Ollie's friend anymore if he kept on being a jerk.

Ollie *had* been a jerk. And thinking back on it now, it still made his stomach hurt. He'd let the fame of being a wrestler get to his head and, in the process, he'd forgotten about Tamiko.

In the end, he'd been able to save their friendship and, together, along with his brother, they saved the arena from closing by making wrestling popular again at Slamdown Town.

"Whoops," said an eighth grader as he dropped his tray of gooey, cheesy nachos at Ollie's feet. "Looks like I'm making another trip to the snack counter."

Ollie shook his head and, carefully avoiding the spill, took another step forward in line.

He was glad that other people finally understood how amazing wrestling was, considering he'd been saying that for as long as he could speak. But, unlike the cheesy arena nachos, popularity came at a high price. He and Tamiko had to deal with jostling crowds, snaking lines for the bathroom, and, worst of all, sharing the arena with annoying eighth graders.

But it wasn't all bad.

His mom, who shockingly returned to wrestling not as Brash Banshee but as the law-abiding, rule-enforcing wrestler The Referee, had become the new singles champion, and he'd hung up his gum—or rather, stuck it on the back of an old belt in the Slamdown Town trophy room—in favor of watching wrestling each weekend alongside his best friend.

Ollie chewed on the tip of his pencil before erasing his signature. After all, this was an autograph book, and technically he was still a wrestler. So, in giant letters, he signed:

BIG CHEW

The deafening voice of Screech Holler, Slamdown Town's resident announcer, blasted out over the crackling audio system. "Folks, tonight is going to be a battle of epic propor—" he began, before being cut off by static feedback. The newcomers around Ollie winced. A few seconds later the announcement popped back in. "Epic proportions! Your reigning singles champion, The Referee, is taking on Tricia Rex, the prehistoric wonder!"

After business was *finally* taken care of, Ollie made his way through the crowded lobby.

"Excuse me," he said as he bumped into the throng of onrushing guests. "Pardon me. Lifelong fan coming through!"

But no one excused or pardoned him. Instead, he collided into the biggest, baddest eighth grader in school, sending Ollie onto the soda-coated, booger-strewn floor.

"Watch it, bro," said his older brother, Hollis. His acne-spotted face was only slightly less dirty than the sneakers he wore. "You almost made me drop my hot dogs." Hollis turned to the girl standing beside him. "Are you okay, Breonna-kins?"

Ollie still didn't understand how his brother, the resident town bully, had convinced Breonna Jemison, the nicest girl in school, to date him. Tamiko speculated that he had some sort of blackmail on her. While Ollie was pretty certain that wasn't the case, it was still baffling.

"You'll catch a cold if you stay on that dirty floor," said Breonna. "Gimme your hand."

Breonna pulled Ollie to his feet. She wore, like she did every day, her hand-knit Lil' Old Granny sweater, which wasn't surprising since Breonna was the wrestler's granddaughter.

In fact, the two spent so much time together that people joked Breonna was a mini Lil' Old Granny. She looked like Granny (minus the wrinkles) with her dark curly hair pulled up in a scrunchie and freckles dotting her face. She spoke like Granny, saying things like "You'll catch a cold" or "Back in my day . . ." And she was tough like Granny, never backing down from a fight, while at the same time being accepting, patient, and kind.

Basically: everything Hollis wasn't.

"Thanks, Breonna," said Ollie. He wiped some popcorn kernels off his butt. "But I'm pretty used to hanging out on the arena floor. Hollis likes to wrestle me every chance he gets. Even though my mom says he's not supposed to."

"Only because I beat you all the time," said Hollis. He looked at his watch. "In fact, it's wrestle-your-little-brother o'clock. Wouldn't want to be late to that."

Breonna giggled. "You never told me you were both wrestlers."

His brother jammed a hot dog into each of his nostrils. "You mean you haven't heard of The Walrus?" he asked. "I'm the greatest wrestler of all time!"

Breonna laughed so hard she snorted.

Ollie couldn't believe it. Somehow, someway, Breonna found Hollis's repelling behavior *appealing*. If Ollie had known that all you had to do to get a girlfriend was stick a pair of hot dogs up your nose and pretend to be a walrus, then he would've done it a long time ago.

"Well, actually, second greatest," said Hollis, pointing to his T-shirt. It read:

BIG CHEW'S #1 FAN

"He's not coming back," said Ollie. "Trust me."

But Hollis shook his head. "He'll be back. And when he is, I'm gonna be first in line for an autograph. After all," he said, "I'm his number one fan."

Ollie could attest to that. His brother used to hound Big Chew after every match, asking for autographs and even going so far as to dress up like him and call himself Lil' Chew.

Hollis had been his first and most vocal fan and, despite their differences, Ollie would always appreciate that. Even though his brother would never know it.

"Hey, Ollie," said Hollis. "Guess what kind of soda I was drinking?" He took a deep breath and belched in his face. "Spoiler alert. All of them."

Ollie gagged.

"Eww, Hollis. That's disgusting," said Breonna. She turned to Ollie. "Well, The Walrus and I had better get going. And you too. Don't want to miss your mom's match."

"Mom's going to send Tricia Rex back to the Cretaceous Period," said Hollis.

Breonna giggled. "You're so funny." She pulled a hard candy out of her backpack. "Here, for your breath."

Hollis popped the candy into his mouth and took her hand into his. "Happy two-and-a-half-week anniversary, babe."

"Aww, Hollie-poo, you remembered," said Breonna, blushing.

Ollie gagged again. "Hollie-who?"

But "Hollie-poo" wasn't listening. He only had eyes (and ears) for Breonna as the two scurried off, hand in hand, into the crowd.

Screech's voice cracked out of the arena speakers. "This is your final warning, folks. The matches are about to begin. So grab your snacks, grab a friend, and grab your seats!"

Suddenly, Ollie felt someone grab him from behind. He turned and saw Tamiko. She had that wild look in her eye when she went more than thirty minutes without a snack.

"He said grab a friend," said Tamiko, beaming. "Come on, let's hurry!"

CHAPTER 3

TAMIKO

TAMIKO led Ollie through the predictably packed hallway toward the snack counter. She zigged away from running kids squealing with joy, zagged around parents shouting for them to slow down, and completely avoided teenagers leaning against the wall hoping to look cool.

As they entered the snack line, she spotted her dad working behind the counter.

"Hey there, bug," he said with a smile when they finally made it to the front. He leaned over the counter, sending a cascade of messy, hastily brushed hair into his eyes that he swatted away, only for it to immediately fall back down.

"Hey, Dad. I'm gonna need—"

But he waved her off. "The usual fare. For you, a few bags of super-sour gummies, an extra-fluffy cotton candy, nachos with a triple serving of cheese, and a mystery-meat hot dog with mustard and ketchup kept, as always, at least twenty feet away from any relish during the preparation process. And for Ollie, the Double Patty Tag Team Burger with special sauce on the side, a licorice lace so long you can jump rope with it, and one butterscotch ice cream in a cup that's been microwaved for exactly four seconds."

Tamiko grinned. At least not all the newbies were a pain.

Her dad had been hired shortly after they'd saved the arena. The influx of customers required more staff to attend to them, a fact Linton and his wallet were reluctant to admit. So her dad traded in cosplaying for serving up sugar- and salt-induced happiness.

"You're the best, Dad," said Tamiko as her stomach growled with anticipation.

At home, he always knew when a bad day called for an emergency bowl of ice cream or a trip for some sweet treats from the market. Turns out his ability to read a stomach's desire translated outside the family. Her dad quickly developed a reputation for remembering everyone's orders, no matter how strange or particular a customer was.

"How do you do that?" asked Ollie, grabbing his snacks.

"Guess I just have a freakishly good memory," he said. "Speaking of which, Ollie, I hear your mom is taking on an 'ankle' today. Sounds pretty dangerous."

Tamiko groaned. "Dad, no. We talked about this. Tricia Rex is a 'heel,' not an 'ankle.' There are no 'ankles' in wrestling."

He looked puzzled. "But I thought you said 'cheeks' and 'ankles' hated each other."

"It's 'faces' and 'heels.' Faces are the heroes and heels are the villains. Remember?"

Her dad's impressive memory for snack orders was dwarfed only by his impressive lack of wrestling knowledge. Ollie thought it was hilarious, but Tamiko found it a little embarrassing.

"But if wrestlers don't have ankles, how do they climb in and out of the court?"

Ollie snorted with laughter so hard that his hand shook, and a wave of nacho cheese splashed from the paper container onto the sticky floor below. "I think you're thinking of basketball, Mr. Tanaka."

"It's the ring, Dad! The ring!"

"Oh, right! Well, good thing I have you around to help me remember."

Tamiko slammed her snack money onto the counter. "Thanks, Dad," she said in a hurry. "I'll meet up with you later."

"Bye, bug! Bye, Ollie!" he shouted after them. "I hope your mom gets to keep her gold medal! I mean belt! Right, it's belts? Anyway, who's next?"

Having successfully avoided further embarrassment, they made their way toward the arena in order to take their seats.

They passed a number of floor-to-ceiling posters that depicted fan-favorite wrestlers like The Referee, Werewrestler, Gorgeous Gordon Gussett, Silvertongue, Barbell Bill, Lil' Old Granny, and Dentures Dan. There was an empty slot where Big Chew's poster had hung, which had been removed after it was determined he would not be coming back. But dwarfing them all was a poster of Linton Krackle. It was adorned with green-and-yellow graffiti that read LINTON SOCKS, which they had always assumed was supposed to say LINTON SUCKS.

The typo had spawned an arena tradition.

"Linton socks!" they shouted as they snapped their socks in unison.

Ollie took off toward their seats, but Tamiko lingered in front of the empty spot on the wall. Lately she'd caught herself imagining her own larger-than-life wrestling poster hanging there, looking down at fans as they entered the arena. She even knew what her costume would look like: an all-black outfit covered in as many spikes as she was legally allowed to wear.

Too bad I don't have a magic way to turn into a wrestler, thought Tamiko.

She followed Ollie up the uneven stairs, past swaying guardrails and broken windows, elbowing their way through the crowd until they reached their dilapidated seats.

Seats that currently had unwelcome occupants.

Two scrawny fourth graders had settled in for an evening of wrestling and showed no sign of leaving. They took one look at Ollie and Tamiko and told them to get lost.

"No way, seat stealers!" yelled Tamiko. "Beat it."

"We can sit where we want to," insisted the girl in Tamiko's seat.

"Yeah. I don't see your names written on them," declared the boy in Ollie's. He crossed his arms and looked away, as if putting an end to the conversation.

Oh, he walked right into that one, thought Tamiko.

"Read 'em and weep," she said triumphantly. She pointed to her and Ollie's names written on the back of the chairs in permanent marker. "We claimed these seats years ago. Probably before you two were even born. Chop, chop. There's wrestling afoot."

Facts were facts and, after seeing the names, the boy and girl got up, grumbling.

"The nerve of some people," said Tamiko, plunking her butt in *her* seat.

Ollie did the same. "Seriously. But at least we made it in time."

"Ladies and gentlemen, boys and girls!" yelled Screech Holler into his microphone.

A hush fell. Tamiko's head snapped forward to gawk at the man now standing in the center of the ring. From his slicked-back electric-blue hair to his blinding-orange suit, Screech Holler commanded attention. And he had it.

"Welcome to Slamdown Town! Now, who's ready for some wrestling?"

CHAPTER 4

OLLIE

AS always, the day's opening matches did not disappoint.

Ollie and Tamiko cheered as The Bolt shocked the arena— and her opponent—when she emerged the winner of her no-holds-barred showdown. In a later match, Cheyenne Cutpurse told the audience that she was a changed wrestler after her stint in reform school. But Ollie knew it was a lie even before she robbed Emerald Emma of both the win *and* her jewels. And when Mop and Bucket joined forces to clean up the arena and their competition, another of Ollie's fan fiction pairings had finally come true.

With each match, Ollie remembered his own time in the ring. The weight of the top rope. The smell of his opponents' armpits. The sound of the crowd chanting his name. Wrestling as Big Chew had been undeniably awesome. There were times when he missed it. But being able to cheer on his favorite wrestlers every Saturday next to Tamiko, his best friend, felt right.

The crowd roared and booed, cheered and jeered with more ferocity than ever, but no one screamed harder than Ollie. He *loved* wrestling, and his favorite wrestler was up next.

Sudden entry music blasted out of the aging Slamdown Town sound system. But even over the eardrum-shattering feedback, Ollie knew the song "Rules Are Cool (And Meant to Be Followed)" by heart because his mom played it during her workout sessions at home.

Screech cleared his throat. "Keep your sugar intake within daily recommended standards and stop running in the halls because The Referee, your champion, the ultimate face, is here!"

She emerged from backstage, bulging muscles and all.

"'Face'?" asked an eighth grade boy with spiky hair in the seat next to Ollie. "Of course she has a face. Why would he say that?"

"No, a *wrestling* face. Faces are the best," explained Ollie. "They're the good guys. The ones who follow the rules. Everybody loves them."

"Well, if everyone loves faces, then I love faces, too," declared the boy. "Go faces!"

Tamiko shook her head. "No way. Faces are lame."

"Then who do you like?" asked an eighth-grade girl seated across from Tamiko.

A deafening roar echoed throughout the arena.

"That roar means only one thing, folks!" shouted Screech. "I spilled my coffee all over my pants and the prehistoric phenom has arrived. Give a hearty boo for tonight's heel: Tricia Rex!"

Scales ran all the way down Tricia Rex's arms and legs, reinforcing the rumors that she was part reptile. She wore a necklace of dino bones around her neck that belonged to her ancestors, famed dinosaur hunters. And if she couldn't hunt dinosaurs, then wrestlers would do just fine.

"*That's* who. Heels!" yelled Tamiko. "Heels are the baddest of the baddies. The ones who don't care about lame rules. The crowd loves to hate a heel."

"Wow, that does sound cool," said the girl. "Okay, I'm going with heels."

Ollie turned his attention to the ring, where The Referee and Tricia Rex stood with microphones held to their lips.

"Let's make sure we have a good, clean fight," said The Referee. "That will make your impending defeat far less humiliating."

Tricia Rex laughed. "Thousands of years from now," she roared, "a team of skilled paleontologists will put your bones in a wrestling museum next to a sign saying 'Loser.'"

Ding! Ding! Ding! The bell echoed through the arena, drowned out only by the thunderous applause of the audience. As always, the debate would be settled in the ring.

Tricia Rex surged forward. She locked The Referee in the Jurassic Jaws and quickly followed with a Triassic Throw. The Referee was sent hurtling toward the ropes. Looking to gain a cheap advantage, Tricia Rex caught The Referee with a furious (and illegal) Raptor Rake.

"Those little arms might be tiny, but they pack a punch," said Tamiko.

"Come on, Mom! You can do it!" said Ollie.

She broke out of Tricia Rex's Brontosaurus Barrage and

unleashed her patented Long Arm of the Law, which was wedged under both Tricia's armpits, holding her firmly in place.

"No one punishes rule-breakers like The Referee can!" shouted Screech.

The battle continued with neither wrestler wanting to lose. But despite going blow for blow, Tricia Rex was starting to waver. His mom, sensing victory, pulled out the massive rule book she kept safe and secure in her back pocket.

"She's pulled out the rule book," observed Ollie. "You know what that means . . ."

"Regulation Approved Slamdown!" shouted Tamiko along with the rest of the arena.

"I assure you this move meets all necessary arena standards and bylaws," said The Referee, closing the rule book before chucking Tricia Rex straight over the top rope.

"The Referee just finished the job that the asteroid started," declared Screech.

And he was right. Tricia Rex was out cold, her chances of winning extinct.

But The Referee didn't pin her opponent. The *actual* referee didn't count out the pinfall. And Screech—a man who never missed an opportunity to speak—didn't announce the victory.

That was because the arena lights cut out. Suddenly, a spotlight shone on the wrestler's entrance. Ollie turned and saw two kids appear and make their way toward the ring.

"Who are they?" asked Ollie.

"My goodness," announced Screech. "It's Leon and Luna Krackle!"

CHAPTER 5

TAMIKO

"DID Screech say Krackle?" asked Tamiko as the arena lights flickered back on. She knew only one person by that last name. "Those must be Linton's kids."

"Give it up, everybody, for Linton's kids!" shouted Screech Holler.

The twin boy and girl walking down the entrance ramp looked so alike that Tamiko thought she was seeing double. Not only did they look identical with their shiny, metal braces and freckled faces, but they sauntered in near perfect—and slightly creepy—unison toward the ring like they owned the place.

"Oh, yeah," said Ollie. "I've heard rumors about them. Apparently, they threw a massive fit when Linton surprised them with only two ponies for their birthday."

Tamiko laughed. "And then Linton had to pony up for a full circus and they still complained. They get what they want, no matter what. Or so I've heard."

Leon and Luna wore posh matching jackets and sleek ripped jeans that Tamiko guessed cost more than all the clothes she owned combined. Their stylish sneakers lit up with each step as they walked down the ramp, climbed over the ropes, and entered the ring.

Behind them, a man with white gloves and a black suit wheeled the biggest, fanciest-looking luggage she'd ever seen. Everything about him screamed prim and proper.

"Wow, they have a butler," said Tamiko. "The closest I've ever had to a butler was my parents' robotic vacuum. Wasn't very good at preparing lunch, though."

"He must've come with them. I think they live with their mom on the other side of the country," said Ollie. "So why are they here?"

"I bet you're wondering why we're here," said the twins into a set of microphones.

"You're right," said a squat, balding man in a cheap suit who appeared at the top of the ramp. "I *am* wondering that." Linton Krackle made his way toward the ring.

"It's a Krackle family reunion, folks," said Screech.

Tamiko and Ollie booed with the rest of the crowd. It was tradition to boo Linton—who had built a reputation for being cheap, greedy, and sweaty—anytime he appeared. He'd more than earned their heckling after nearly closing Slamdown Town a few months back.

"Daddy," said the twins. "You're here!"

"I am. But why are you here?" he asked as he climbed over the ropes and into the ring. "I didn't know you and the butler were coming. Where's your mother?"

Luna flipped her hair. "Mommy's on her way to an island-hopping shopping spree."

"And judging by the amount of credit cards and luggage she took with her," said Leon, "I think she's going to be hopping and shopping for a while."

"She said we could either go back to reform school or we could come stay with you."

"But you never want to stay with me," said Linton. His hand reached for his pants pocket, where Tamiko guessed his wallet was safely hidden away. For now, at least. "I need to know what it is you two want and I need to know now. But more important, how expensive it is."

Leon and Luna put their hands on their hips. "Do we always have to want something?"

"Well," said Linton, "that's the only time I ever hear from you two since the divorce." He sighed. "You know, you could call to chat once in a while and ask me how I'm doing."

"Now, this is some good, old-fashioned family drama," said Screech.

Tamiko loved every minute of it. Melodrama was a staple of the sport. Having it come straight from the first family of wrestling made the revelations all the juicier.

Linton tapped his foot. "So come on, out with it. A triple-decker yacht? A bouncy house made of jelly? Another mountain named after you?"

"That all sounds great," said Leon.

"Yeah," said Luna, "we'll take those, too! Thanks, Daddy."

"Too?" asked Linton. "I don't know how many more mountains I can afford. Maybe we could get you a nice pet rock instead."

"We don't want a pet rock," they said together. "We want to be wrestlers."

"Wrestlers?" asked Linton. "I didn't know you liked wrestling."

"Shows what you know," said Leon. "We're here to prove that we can be wrestlers."

"And not just any wrestlers . . ." said Luna.

". . . The Slamdown Town tag team champions," finished Leon.

"Why?" asked Linton.

"Because we said so."

A murmur rippled through the crowd. The thought of Leon and Luna wrestling—let alone becoming the champs—made Tamiko laugh so hard she blew snot bubbles out of her nose.

"That is the most unbelievable thing I've ever heard in my life," said Screech.

"Believe it," said Luna.

"Because it's happening," said Leon. "You believe in us. Right, Daddy?"

"As your father and a highly successful businessman with decades of experience," said Linton, "I must admit, I'm not sure about this."

"Not sure?" asked Screech. "What's there to figure out? Twelve-year-olds can't wrestle."

"Screech is right!" Ollie's mom yelled from the corner of the ring. "According to the approved Slamdown Town rule book, a wrestler must be at minimum eighteen years of age."

Leon and Luna laid their microphones down on the mat. Then they threw themselves down onto the mat, flailing their arms and legs.

CHAPTER 6

TAMIKO

HAD Linton gone mad? The idea of two kids fighting grown wrestlers was downright ridiculous. The newbies around Tamiko cheered the decision. But she knew better.

"They don't stand a chance," said Ollie.

"Took the words right out of my mouth," said Tamiko through a mouthful of sour gummies.

Down in the ring, the newest, scrawniest wrestlers leapt with glee. "Thank you, Daddy! We can't wait to wrestle!"

Linton beamed. "I'll schedule you a match for next week."

"Next week?" said Luna.

"No, no, no. We want to wrestle tonight," said Leon.

"Tonight? You can't wrestle tonight," stammered Linton. "Besides, I think the crowd has seen enough action for one evening. Isn't that right, everybody?"

"Give us more wrestling!" shouted Tamiko.

They sobbed. They whimpered. They blubbered and howled.

"It's a full-blown meltdown, folks!" shouted Screech. "You hate to see that. Let's watch!"

"I've thrown some decent tantrums," said Ollie, "but this is next level."

"Take notes," said Tamiko. "We're watching pros here."

"Calm down," said Linton. "There's got to be something else you want." He shoved his hands into his pockets, dug around inside, and pulled out a paper clip, an old receipt, and a penny. "How about a paper clip and an old receipt? The penny's mine, though."

Leon and Luna answered by flailing harder and sobbing louder.

Tamiko watched Linton wipe his glistening forehead with his sleeve. He was booed every time he entered the arena and was screamed at by wrestlers more times than she could count. However, nothing that didn't involve him losing money had ever seemed to affect him. But now, as his kids flailed about in front of him, Linton looked, for the first time, as if he were stirred.

"The rule book does say that wrestlers need to be eighteen. But," he said over his kids' cries, "can you tell me what the rule book says about the powers of the CEO and owner of Slamdown Town?"

"Of course," said Ollie's mom. "The rule book makes it clear that they're in charge of preserving, modifying, and updating any and all of the rules."

"Which is fancy talk for 'What I say goes.' And I say my kids get to wrestle."

The crowd roared in agreement.

"Sounds like they want to see more wrestling," said Leon.

Linton palmed his forehead. "But you don't even have your costumes."

"About that," said Luna.

They ripped off their posh jackets, revealing a matching set of sparkling singlets underneath. The words KRACKLE KIDDOS shone in diamond letters across each of their chests. Over the singlets, they wore suit jackets cut off at the elbow. Golden dollar signs were stitched into the fabric, rhinestones lined the lapels, and their cuff links had their faces on them.

Tamiko found it impossible to look away, the dazzling light of their costumes drawing her eyes toward them. "Now I know what moths feel like," she said.

"Those look fancy," said Ollie. "I bet they didn't raid anyone's attic for them."

The Krackle Kiddos stomped their feet. "We want to wrestle right now."

"Right now?" asked Linton.

"And we want to wrestle the best."

"The best?" asked Linton.

"Why, that'd be the tag team Nursing Home," said Screech. "Are we about to witness an impromptu title fight?"

"No," replied Linton with a sigh of relief. "But only because Lil' Old Granny and Dentures Dan aren't here. It's bingo night at the senior center, and they never miss it."

Leon and Luna put their hands on their hips. "Then we'll take the second best. *Today*."

Linton cleared his throat. "Let me see what I can do." He whipped out his cell phone and made a hushed call. He paced back and forth, arguing with *someone* on the other end.

"The second-best team?" said Tamiko.

"He can't mean . . ." started Ollie.

Finally, Linton hung up.

"So tell us, Daddy," said the Krackle Kiddos. "Who are we going to beat tonight?"

"Arooooooooo!"

Tamiko's jaw fell. She knew that bone-chilling howl.

Two burly men emerged through a plume of smoke at the top of the entrance ramp.

Werewrestler's blood-red eyes surveyed the crowd menacingly. His silver wolf pendant hung over his ripped shirt. Sasquat, his partner, stood next to him, his hands already formed into fists. He was a full head shorter than Werewrestler, but twice as buff, and five times as hairy.

"I hope you all brought an extra pair of underwear, because the Terrible Twosome are here to scare us silly," said Screech. "Those that didn't may purchase an additional pair at the gift shop, should yours become soiled during the match. In fact, I may need some right now!"

Werewrestler and Sasquat climbed into the ring. Next to them, the Krackle Kiddos looked like two tiny middle schoolers who had gotten lost on their way to the bathroom.

"For the newbies in the crowd," said Screech, "we're about to witness a tag team match. It's team-versus-team action, but only two wrestlers can be in the ring at a time. Teammates have to tag each other in to swap out. As always, winner declared by pinfall.

The rules may be straightforward, but let me tell you, a tag team match is anything but!"

"The only butts here are the two we're about to kick," said Luna as she and Werewrestler made their way to opposite corners of the ring and took their places outside the ropes.

Ding! Ding! Ding! The bell sounded, and the match began.

Sasquat charged at Leon with a Hairy Knuckles Knuckle Sandwich. But the strike was immediately stopped by the middle schooler, who held Sasquat's giant fist with his tiny hands.

Tamiko couldn't believe her eyes.

"That's one strong kid, folks," said Screech.

Leon tossed aside Sasquat's meaty hand and performed an I'm Number One Leg Sweep.

His opponent buckled under the noodle-y leg and fell onto his back, allowing Leon the opportunity to deliver a Trending Takedown Stomp with his kid-size sneakers.

"They're actually . . . good?" asked Tamiko in shock.

"I'm speechless," said Ollie.

Sasquat crawled over to his corner and tagged in Werewrestler. In the opposite corner, Leon strutted over to Luna. The two high-fived as she hopped into the ring.

"No one told me these kids were freaks of nature," said Sasquat.

"I'll handle these brats," growled Werewrestler.

He wound up to deliver a Howling Haymaker, but Luna was too quick. She slid her small frame in between Werewrestler's legs before the move landed. He stumbled forward, off balance, as Luna jabbed him in the back with a pointy I'm Better Than You Elbow.

Werewrestler rolled forward into the ropes, spun around, and charged at her with a Savage Beast Facebuster. Luna dodged out of the way again, sending him back into the ropes.

They might actually win this, thought Tamiko.

"Krackle Kiddos Knockdown!" shouted Leon and Luna together.

From outside the ropes, Leon snagged Werewrestler and held him in place with his scrawny arms. Despite all his strength, the legendary heel couldn't break free.

"Do it, sis!" said Leon.

Luna ran in place, gathering as much speed as she could muster, before launching herself forward with a Spoiled Rotten Spear. Her bony shoulder slammed into Werewrestler's chest.

"Yowza!" yelled Screech. "He's gonna feel that one in the morning."

The largest man legally allowed in the tristate area collapsed onto the mat.

Luna flopped on top of Werewrestler, pinning him.

"I cannot believe what I'm seeing, folks," cried Screech. "The match is over!"

Tamiko booed. Not because she didn't like what she saw. She loved what had happened. Booing was the greatest compliment she could pay to a heel. And against all odds, the Krackle Kiddos had proven that they were a heel duo that was not to be messed with.

Leon joined Luna in the ring and the siblings did a victory lap.

"Krackle Kiddos! Krackle Kiddos!" chanted Tamiko with the crowd.

Linton Krackle climbed back into the ring. "That's right, Slamdown Town. Give it up for my kids. Or should I say, kiddos!"

"What a crazy match," said Tamiko.

Ollie paused. "Werewrestler was the toughest opponent I ever faced. But they destroyed him and Sasquat like it was nothing. And they're only, like, twelve. I'm not saying it's impossible, but it just doesn't make a whole lot of sense."

"Maybe the Terrible Twosome had an off night?" She shrugged.

For Tamiko, it didn't matter how they won. What mattered was that they did. And seeing two kids her own age in the ring only made her think of her own wrestling ambitions.

Ollie was able to wrestle because he'd been gifted a piece of magic gum. The Krackle Kiddos were allowed to wrestle because their dad was the CEO of Slamdown Town.

And all Tamiko ever got to do was sit in the stands and watch.

CHAPTER 7

OLLIE

"COME on, Tamiko. You have to admit it's a little weird."

Ollie and Tamiko stepped off the school bus. Leon and Luna Krackle's shocking win had been a constant subject of conversation between him and Tamiko over the weekend, one that continued into Monday morning as they walked past chattering students toward their lockers.

"The only thing that's being a little weird is you," said Tamiko. She tapped away on her phone. "You've got to face facts. The Krackle Kiddos are awesome wrestlers who just happen to be middle schoolers that we get to meet today." She let out a cheer. "I can't believe we're going to be in the same class as them! And that I finally beat *Lawnmower Mania* using only the trimmer."

"But that's just it," said Ollie. "They're kids like us who beat two of the strongest wrestlers on the Slamdown Town roster. Something doesn't add up."

Tamiko laughed. "Did Hollis give you an atomic super-wedgie or something? Because I'd think you of all people could relate to twelve-year-olds wrestling for a belt."

"What?" asked Ollie. "No, I am nothing like the Krackle Kiddos." He raised a finger. "First of all, I wasn't held back a year." He raised another. "And second, when I was Big Chew, I had giant muscles. Have you seen their tiny little arms?"

"So they figured out how to win without magic biceps," said Tamiko as they reached their lockers. "Those are exactly the kind of friends I want to hang out with."

He had seen the Krackle Kiddos win with his own eyes. So why did he doubt it? For some reason, he couldn't shake the fact that Werewrestler had been the fiercest opponent he'd wrestled as Big Chew; and yet Leon and Luna, who looked like they couldn't lift ten pounds between them, threw him around the ring with ease.

Ollie grabbed a textbook from his locker and spotted Hollis and Breonna holding hands.

"You know the early-hall-monitor bird gets the rule-breaking worm," said Breonna. She wore her hall monitor sash over her knitted sweater and had her notebook full of demerit slips tucked under her arm. "I won't be gone long. I'll see you after my shift, Hollie-poo."

Hollis sighed. "I already miss you. My stomach hurts when you aren't around." He turned and belched into an unfortunate sixth grader's face. "See?"

"I know," said Breonna. "Your stomach, like your soul, is sensitive. Here, take these antacids." She placed a roll in his hand. "And think of me."

"I will," he said, pouring the entire roll into his mouth and chewing. He didn't take his eyes off her until she had turned the corner toward her classroom.

"Those two lovebirds are going to make me vomit!"

"Speaking of vomit . . ." said Hollis as he ran toward the nearest trash can. He stuck his head in and, foaming at the mouth, spit up the antacid tabs he'd just swallowed.

Tamiko patted his back. "Love hurts, huh, buddy?"

Ollie's eyes fixed on his brother's back pocket. Stuffed inside was a book entitled:

742 STEPS TO BEING THE PERFECT BOYFRIEND

"What's with the book?" he asked.

Hollis lifted his head out of the trash can. "Oh, just picked it up. Haven't gotten around to perusing it yet. Now, if you'll excuse me, I have some reading to do." He opened the book and flipped to the first page. "'Step one. Be nice.' Huh. I got a lot to learn. 'Step two. Comb your hair.' I'm learning so much!"

Breonna certainly had a strange and strong effect on his brother.

They left Hollis to his book and made their way toward Ms. Middleton's class.

"Ah, man, they aren't here yet," said Tamiko when they arrived. "I wanted to ask them to sit by us." She walked to their usual desks in the back and pointed a finger at the kids seated behind them. "Both of you, move!" She pulled out two signs from her backpack and slammed them on the desks. "Can't you read?" she asked, pointing to the papers. "Wrestlers only!"

As the two kids got up grumbling, Ollie knew that he'd soon be able to see who Leon and Luna Krackle *really* were. They appeared to be spoiled, bratty, selfish siblings who got to wrestle because they threw a temper tantrum. But he knew, better than any other middle schooler, that who you were as a wrestler wasn't necessarily who you were in real life. And considering they were now classmates, he had the perfect opportunity to get to know the real Kiddos.

At least, he could if they ever showed up.

The start-of-class bell rang and the Krackle Kiddos still hadn't appeared.

"What gives?" asked Tamiko. "I was promised wrestlers."

"And that's exactly what you're going to get," said a pair of voices.

Ollie turned and spotted the Krackle Kiddos wearing trendy jackets, stylish jeans, and—slung over their shoulders—the fanciest, most expensive backpacks he'd ever seen.

"Ah, you must be Leon and Luna Krackle," said Ms. Middleton. She smiled. "Welcome to our classroom. If there's anything you need from me to get acclimated, let me know."

"Oh good," said Leon. "I was getting famished." He turned to Ms. Middleton. "I'll take a double mocha frappe with two shots of espresso and extra whipped cream."

Ms. Middleton stopped smiling. "You must be confused," she said. "This is a school."

"Three shots of espresso, then," said Luna.

"I'm your teacher, not a barista! Please take your seats."

The Krackle Kiddos spotted the WRESTLERS ONLY signs placed on the desks behind Ollie and Tamiko. "Ah, a VIP section," they said. "It's not exactly red-carpet worthy but it'll do. Speaking of which . . ." They pulled out a roll of red fabric from their chic backpacks and rolled it down the aisle before walking to their desks.

I guess their spoiled act wasn't an act at all, thought Ollie.

Ollie was used to seeing his brother stand up to any and all authority figures, but nothing could prepare him for the way that the Krackle Kiddos treated Ms. Middleton.

"This is unacceptable," she said when Leon and Luna refused to take the pop quiz she handed out later. "You are required to do this assignment like everyone else."

"You know what we do to tests?" asked Leon. He leapt out of his seat, grabbed the papers, and tore them in half. "We pulverize them! Just like we do in the ring!"

Ollie's jaw fell. "This can't get any crazier."

But things *did* get crazier when the Krackle Kiddos threw their torn-up quizzes on the floor in front of them, leaned back in their chairs, and put their feet up on the desks.

Ms. Middleton looked appalled. "You two, clean that up right now."

"*You* clean it up right now," said Luna.

"Me?" said Ms. Middleton, a vein pulsing in her temple. "I'm your teacher, not your maid. It's not my job to clean up after you. It's my job to educate you."

"Oh, sorry," said Leon. "Should we use smaller words so you understand?" He cleared his throat. "Take trash," he said in a stilted caveman voice. "Throw away."

Ms. Middleton's eyes bulged. "I will not have you speak to me in that manner."

Ollie couldn't believe what he was seeing (again). Being an unbearable, whiny, and demanding heel duo in the ring was one thing. That was wrestling, and wrestling was home to larger-than-life personalities. But bringing those personas into school spelled disaster.

"Class isn't over yet," said Ms. Middleton as the Krackle Kiddos got up from their seats and walked toward the door. "And I haven't dismissed you."

"We dismissed ourselves," they said as they left.

Ms. Middleton snapped the piece of chalk she was holding.

"That was like being part of a real match," whispered Tamiko. "The smack talk. The drama!" She shuddered. "Exhilarating! We should see if they want to hang with us. Maybe we could show them around school and then they could show us some wrestling pointers?"

"All right," he said, a little annoyed that Tamiko kept forgetting that he *had* been a wrestler only a few months ago. But he could tell she really wanted to meet the two of them. "I'm in."

The Krackle Kiddos had proven to Ollie that who they were in the ring was who they were in real life. So did that mean that they were also two naturally talented twelve-year-old wrestlers? Maybe, but if they weren't, he figured hanging out with them might yield some answers.

After class, they made their way through the bustling hallway until they spotted the Krackle Kiddos filling their expensive water bottles at the water fountain.

"This isn't sparkling water," said Leon, spitting it out.

Luna gagged. "Plain water? I've never tasted something so disgusting in my life."

As Ollie and Tamiko approached, Leon and Luna held out their hands.

"Autographs are ten bucks," they said. "Selfies are fifteen. Pay up or get lost."

"Tempting," said Tamiko. "But no. We were wondering if you two wanted your own personal tour guides to show you the ropes."

"Those are in the gym," said Ollie. "But we can also let you know which stalls are the best to use in the bathrooms, which tables in the lunchroom are off-limits to any student who isn't an eighth grader, and most important, how to avoid Hollis's many body odors."

"So, you're the people Daddy hired to be friends with us," said Leon. He sounded disappointed, but whether in the hiring part or the selection of friends, Ollie couldn't tell.

Tamiko shook her head. "What? No."

"Oh," said Luna. "He must have forgotten. Can't count on him for anything."

"But he's the one who let you both wrestle," said Ollie. "Right?"

"Wrong," said Leon. "We got ourselves in on pure talent. And we won."

"Well," said Tamiko, "would you two winners want some people who haven't been paid to hang out with you to, you know, hang out with you?"

The Krackle Kiddos shrugged. "It's kinda weird. But sure."

"Cool," said Ollie. "We can all go over to my house."

But Luna waved him off. "Why would we go there when Krackle Manor has a state-of-the-art gaming room, a brick oven for gourmet pizzas, and an indoor pool big enough for our inflatable yacht? And that's just what we had him install when we visited last year."

"Yup," said Leon, nodding. "We have even bigger plans this time."

"What else you got?" asked Tamiko.

"We have a cat," said Luna. "Daddy kept saying something about being allergic, but we had the Krackle kitten flown in anyway."

"You had me at cat," said Tamiko. "I'm in!"

Ollie nodded. "Me too. We'll check with our parents and let you know."

"Wait, you speak with your parents?" asked Leon.

"Um, yes," said Tamiko. "Every day."

"Weird," said Leon and Luna.

CHAPTER 8

TAMIKO

THE Tanaka family car backed out of the driveway as the sun set below the tree line.

Tamiko's parents had insisted on taking her and Ollie over to Krackle Manor themselves, despite Leon and Luna's repeated offers to have their butler pick them up.

"Middle schoolers? Wrestling?" Tamiko's dad asked from the driver's seat. "I mean, can you even imagine such a thing?"

Of course Tamiko could. But that was a secret between her and Ollie. So instead she said, "It's definitely crazy. But hey, you can't argue with a win."

Her mom leaned toward the backseat and whipped out her phone. "Winning is exactly what we *aren't* going to do if we don't coordinate defending this base!"

The base in need of defense was from *Lunar Migration*, one of a dozen different mobile games Tamiko and her mom played together. The game pitted the first human lunar colony against an invading alien geese population that flew to the moon for the winter. The evil flock had just arrived in their Mother Goose Ship and were launching an all-out assault.

"I'm on it!" shouted Tamiko as her fingers furiously tapped her screen.

Tamiko's mom, like herself, was always juggling two things at once. For Tamiko, one of those things was gaming. For her mom, that thing was grading school papers. Tamiko could always tell from the angle of her mom's glasses and how many pens were sticking out of her hair (currently five) just how long she'd been at it. Even now, she graded a stack of tests while gaming and telling Tamiko's dad he'd missed the turn.

"You missed the turn, honey."

Tamiko wanted to be just like her when she grew up.

"So the Krackle Kiddos are a tug team," said her dad as he turned the car around. "That's 'tug,' like 'tugboat'?"

"Tag team, Dad," said Tamiko. "Like when you tag someone in and out of the ring. Right, Mom?"

"You got it," she said, tapping on her screen. "Also, watch out for that goose poop!"

"Are you sure?" he asked them, confused. "I'm, like, ninety-nine percent certain I read it was called a tug team. Or maybe that's what all the *cool* people call it."

"Yeah, we're pretty sure," Tamiko said, laughing. "Whoops, I stepped in it."

"I said, watch out for the goose poop."

"Either way," said her dad, "I just love watching all the action in the round box."

This time, her mom had to stifle a laugh. "I think you mean the squared circle."

"Squared circle? But if they fight in a square, why call it a ring?" he asked.

"You've got a point," said Tamiko. "But you're wrong."

"Right," said her mom just as her dad took a left.

"Whoops! Tamiko, why don't you text Ollie and let him know we'll be outside in one, two, three seconds! *Ding! Ding! Ding!* Pinfall, match over!"

"Pinfall's ten seconds, Dad," said Tamiko.

"Ten?!" he exclaimed. "I could have sworn it was three."

"Everywhere else it is," said her mom.

"But," said Tamiko, "at Slamdown Town it's ten. Linton realized the longer the matches lasted, the more snacks he could sell, and the more money he could make."

Her dad laughed. "I guess he really does make all the rules!"

They pulled into Ollie's driveway. He was already waiting on the front porch.

"Thanks for picking me up, Mr. and Mrs. Tanaka," he said as he climbed in.

"Anytime, Ollie," said her dad. "We just had to see Krackle Manor for ourselves. I hear it's quite impressive."

"What's in the bag?" whispered Tamiko.

Ollie patted his backpack. "Brought along my detective tool kit that I got for my birthday. Check it out." He unzipped the bag and revealed an evidence notebook, colored pens, a magnifying lens, fingerprint powder, barrier tape, stickers, and a deerstalker hat.

Tamiko snorted. "The only question I have, detective," she said as she took one of the question mark–shaped stickers and stuck it on his forehead, "is why you can't accept the fact that the Krackle Kiddos won fair and square?"

Ollie peeled the sticker off and placed it back in the bag. "I've just got a feeling."

"Well, I got a feeling that you've been watching too much *Smacktective*," she whispered.

Ollie nodded. "He's a wrestler who solves mysteries in his spare time. What's not to like? Just keep your eyes peeled. It's like *Smacktective* always says: Two heads are better than one."

"And I always say, six hands are better than four," shouted Tamiko's mom from the front seat. "Ollie, lend us your fingers to destroy their goose eggs!"

"Here, I'll lend a hand, too!" said her dad.

"Eyes on the road!" said everyone else.

The combined forces of Ollie, Tamiko, and her mom managed to bring down the Mother Goose Ship once and for all. Victory music played from their phones.

"These geese's gooses have been cooked," said Tamiko triumphantly.

"Woo!" screamed her dad.

"Excited much?" asked Tamiko.

"You bet," he said as he brought the car to a stop. "We're finally here!"

Subtle. Refined. Sophisticated.

Krackle Manor was none of those things.

The car idled in front of aging golden gates. Beyond them, Tamiko saw decaying marble statues, palm trees with sagging

fronds, and a fountain that barely managed to shoot water into the air. And, beyond that, the biggest, tackiest-looking house she'd ever seen. Perhaps at one point Krackle Manor had been impressive. But Linton had clearly let the place go.

"It's bigger and better than I could have imagined," said Tamiko's dad.

Tamiko shook her head. "Bigger? Maybe. But better? I don't think so. If he doesn't use his money on his house or the arena, what *does* that cheapskate spend it on?"

"Certainly not giving you a raise," said Tamiko's mom to her dad.

Just then, the gates screeched and slowly swung open. They drove down the lengthy driveway and pulled up to the front door, which was double the size of the car.

The massive door opened and a clean-shaven man wearing white gloves and a striking three-piece suit emerged. As he approached the car, Tamiko realized that he was the same man who had been wheeling Leon's and Luna's luggage at the arena this past weekend.

"You must be Master Ollie and Mistress Tamiko," said the man. He opened Tamiko's door and gestured for them to step out of the car. "My name is Billingsley Brightling III, but you may call me whatever you want."

"Can we call you Billingsley?" asked Tamiko.

"If that is what you want," said Billingsley.

"You're the Krackle Kiddos' butler?" asked Ollie.

"That is correct. I came with them from their mother's. The Kiddos are eagerly anticipating your arrival. Please follow me. I will lead you the rest of the way."

Tamiko turned to her parents and waved.

"Try not to break anything," joked her mom. "I don't think we can afford to replace it."

Billingsley pulled a comically large key out of his pocket and inserted it into a gaudy and slightly rusting keyhole. "Welcome to Krackle Manor."

CHAPTER 9

TAMIKO

"TALK about fancy," said Tamiko as they entered the foyer.

"And filthy," said Ollie.

Above them hung a massive chandelier that had its own mini chandelier underneath. Squinting, Tamiko could make out cobwebs woven between each bulb. Looking down, she saw that the marble floors they stood on were scuffed and unpolished and, in the corner of the room, a baby grand piano was missing most of its keys. But dominating the space in the middle of it all was a pile—no, a mountain—of shopping packages stacked nearly as high as the chandelier.

"Yeah, what gives?" asked Tamiko. "Aren't butlers supposed to, like, butler?"

Billingsley bristled. "I am in the employ of the children. Their mother was quite clear. I clean up their messes, not Linton's."

"What's this all about?" asked Ollie, looking at the boxes.

"Linton stated that he wanted the children to feel more at home. So he offered to buy them whatever would make that possible. Toys, clothes, gold-plated sporks."

"There you are, Billingsley!" The Krackle Kiddos rolled into the foyer on matching electric scooters. By the tone of their voices, they were not pleased.

"We've been calling for you forever," said Leon.

Luna huffed. "And you've been ignoring us!"

"I received all fifty of your calls and messages during my two-minute absence," said Billingsley. "Given that I was escorting Master Ollie and Mistress Tamiko, I was unable to field them. However, I have already anticipated your needs."

He led them into a nearby dining room. Displayed at each end of the lengthy table were two of the biggest, steamiest plates of food Tamiko had ever seen.

"Your seven-o'clock pheasant," said Billingsley.

Leon and Luna rushed forward and gobbled down their dinner.

"Want some?" asked Leon with his mouth full.

"What's in it?" asked Ollie.

Luna shoved a piece into her mouth. "Pheasant."

"That's a hard pass," said Tamiko.

When they had finished, Billingsley cleared away the empty plates. "Now that your seven-o'clock pheasant has been tended to, I must prepare your seven-thirty pheasant."

With a bow, Billingsley sprang out of the room.

"You two," said Leon, snapping his fingers. "Follow us."

Luna smiled. "We have something to show you."

The Krackle Kiddos hopped onto their electric scooters and

sped away. Tamiko and Ollie, unsure of what to do, quickly sprinted after them.

The manor seemed impossibly spacious. Each room was more outlandish and showier than the last. They passed a portrait room with portraits that appeared to look at Tamiko as she walked by. They passed a candy room filled with every size, color, and flavor of candy she could imagine. And they passed a solid-pink room devoted entirely to pink things like tutus, lemonade, and plastic flamingos. Yet, each room was as run-down and unused as it was impressive.

After passing what seemed to be the hundredth *spare* bedroom, all of which the Krackle Kiddos claimed were theirs, they mercifully came to a stop outside a large door.

"What's behind this door," said Leon, "may shock and awe you."

Luna nodded. "But in order to see it you have to shout your favorite wrestler."

"Silvertongue!" yelled Tamiko.

"Wrong," said Leon.

"The Referee!" shouted Ollie.

"Incorrect," said Luna.

"But those *are* our favorite wrestlers," said Tamiko, confused.

"Not anymore," said Luna. "Now, do you want to see what's behind this door or not?"

Suddenly, the answer dawned on Tamiko. "The Krackle Kiddos?"

"Aww, gee, thanks, you guys," said Leon, pushing open the door.

Tamiko nearly fainted. "Ollie," she whispered. "Are you

seeing what I'm seeing, or am I hallucinating after all that running?"

Before them was a full-size regulation wrestling ring. There was nothing old or outdated about it. The ropes were taut and the mat glistened. Racks of sparring gloves and helmets lined the walls. Metal steps leading up to the ring sat at opposite corners.

The Krackle Kiddos smirked at each other. "Why don't you climb in?"

It wasn't every day that Tamiko had the opportunity to enter an actual wrestling ring and she was *not* about to pass this up. She shot forward, squeezed herself between the ropes, and landed with a soft *thud* on the mat.

"Look out, Krackle Manor!" she shouted to the room. "The fiercest wrestler of all time, Tamiko Tanaka, is here to knock some heads around."

"But she won't be wrestling alone!" yelled Ollie as he struggled to slide under the ropes. "The sixth-grade wonder, Ollie Evander, will be right by her side."

Standing next to Ollie in the ring sent a rush of adrenaline through her body. She felt like she could take on the world. And while the world didn't enter the ring, the Krackle Kiddos did.

"The fiercest wrestler of all time and the sixth-grade wonder?" asked Luna. She turned to her brother. "That's certainly an impressive tag team, wouldn't you agree?"

A smile spread over Leon's face. "They sound like worthy opponents to me. What do you say? You two want to throw down with some real wrestlers?"

"Yes!" shouted Tamiko. She couldn't believe it.

She was going to wrestle *real* wrestlers.

"Don't worry," said Luna. "We'll take it easy on you."

Tamiko charged at Leon with a Middle Schooler Knuckle Sandwich. She expected the strike to be stopped by Leon, just as she had witnessed him do against Sasquat in the ring. But instead of Leon grabbing her tiny fist, Tamiko easily overpowered him, striking him in the chest.

She couldn't believe her eyes.

"Ouch," said Leon. "That really hurt!"

Leon tossed aside Tamiko's tiny hand and attempted to perform an I'm Number One Leg Sweep. But where Sasquat had buckled under his noodle-y leg, Tamiko stood her ground.

"Hmm, what's going on?" asked Leon.

"You don't have to hold back *that* much," said Tamiko.

"Hold back? I'm giving it my all."

Luna tapped him on the shoulder. "Tag me in, bro."

Tamiko turned and tagged in Ollie. "Go show them what's up," she said.

"I'll try," said Ollie.

He wound up to deliver a Study Hall Haymaker. Tamiko expected Luna to dodge it as she had with Werewrestler. But the punch hit its mark, sending Luna tumbling to the mat.

"Hey," she whined. "Not so rough."

"Sorry," said Ollie, confused. "I wasn't trying to hurt you."

What is going on here? thought Tamiko. She'd dismissed Ollie's concerns earlier on the grounds that she had watched the Kiddos beat the Terrible Twosome with her own eyes. But now those eyes stared in disbelief as Ollie, the tiniest kid in class, went toe-to-toe with Luna.

"Krackle Kiddos Knockdown!" shouted Leon and Luna together.

Leon snagged Ollie and held him in place with his scrawny arms. But, unlike Werewrestler, who couldn't break free, Ollie easily slipped through his grasp.

Luna, who had launched herself forward with a Spoiled Rotten Spear, completely missed Ollie and slammed her bony shoulder into her brother's gut.

"Yowza!" yelled Tamiko. "He's gonna feel *that* one in the morning."

The Krackle Kiddos, the newest, greatest wrestlers at Slamdown Town, collapsed onto the mat. They rolled around in pain and massaged their shoulders and chests.

"Are you two okay?" asked Tamiko.

Luna stood up and laughed. "Everybody has off days."

"Even future champs like us," said Leon.

But Tamiko knew something wasn't right. The Krackle Kiddos had beaten two of the biggest wrestlers on the Slamdown Town roster as if they were nothing. And "nothing" was approximately what she and Ollie had when it came to muscles.

"Well, that's enough wrestling for now," said Luna as she squirmed under the ropes.

"Last one to the ball-pit room has to use the silver-plated toilet," said Leon.

The Krackle Kiddos mounted their electric scooters and sped away.

"Hey," shouted Ollie. "Wait up!"

"Some of us aren't on scooters," said Tamiko.

They chased the Kiddos all the way back to the foyer where

they had first entered, until they had to stop, wheezing, hands on their knees. By then the Kiddos were long gone.

Tamiko righted herself as her breath steadied. But what came next floored her.

Across the foyer, in the frame of the largest doorway she'd ever seen, stood the Terrible Twosome themselves, Werewrestler and Sasquat. Facing them, with his back to her, was Billingsley. At first, she didn't think there was anything suspicious about a butler answering the front door. But then she heard what he said to them and saw what he handed them.

"It's time for you to leave," said Billingsley in a tone that brokered no argument. He pulled two envelopes out of his pocket, both sealed with a wax letter *K* stamp.

"Yeah, yeah. We got what we came for," replied Werewrestler.

"Pleasure doing business," said Sasquat.

But before Tamiko could make out anything else, Billingsley slammed the door shut and made his way down the long hallway in the opposite direction of where she stood.

"Okay, hold up," Tamiko said to Ollie. "What is happening here?"

"Something weird," Ollie replied. "It looked like Billingsley handed them two envelopes." He took his evidence notebook out of his backpack.

Tamiko looked over his shoulder as he penciled in a crude drawing of Billingsley handing the Terrible Twosome their envelopes.

"Why would they be getting anything from Billingsley?" she asked. "He's not part of Slamdown Town. Remember? He said it himself. He works for Leon and Luna."

"I don't know," said Ollie, closing the notebook. "But what I do know and is just as confusing is that we somehow kicked the Krackle Kiddos' butts tonight."

"Great job, by the way," said Tamiko.

Ollie frowned. "Thanks, but it felt wrong."

"Right," she said. "We shouldn't have been able to beat them. But we did. Easily. And they *said* they were trying their hardest. If that's true . . ."

Ollie nodded. "Then there's no way they could've beaten *actual* wrestlers." He stroked his chin and began to pace back and forth. "There was definitely something fishy going on in their match against the Terrible Twosome. The Krackle Kiddos looked unstoppable. Almost like there was nothing that Werewrestler and Sasquat could do to win."

Tamiko gasped, a horrible possibility dawning on her. "Maybe that's just what they wanted us to think. The Terrible Twosome should have been able to defeat them no problem. Instead, they lost. And if the Krackle Kiddos couldn't beat them on their own . . ."

". . . Maybe the Terrible Twosome threw the match," finished Ollie.

"But why would they do that?" asked Tamiko.

"I bet if we saw what was in those envelopes we'd have a better idea," said Ollie. "But there's no way a couple of kids like us could ever get our hands on them."

Tamiko scratched the back of her head. "Hey, didn't you tell me once that Werewrestler basically lived out of his locker at Slamdown Town?"

"Yeah, he keeps everything in there. His illegal contraband, his silver wolf pendants, and even his most prized possession: his fourth-grade Fairy Good Reading Award."

"Wow, he really changed," said Tamiko. "I bet he'd keep the envelope in there."

"Probably, but how are we going to get into the locker room?"

"Not we," said Tamiko. "You."

"But only wrestlers are allowed in there," said Ollie.

"Exactly," said Tamiko. "Which is why we need Big Chew's help."

CHAPTER 10

OLLIE

"WHAT in the wide world of wrestling is that stench?" asked Ollie, pinching his nose.

As he entered the dining room with a bowl of cereal on Saturday morning, a pungent odor invaded his nostrils. The smell came from a well-dressed stranger seated at the table. Upon closer inspection, Ollie discovered the stranger was in fact his brother.

"That would be Garçon Malodorant," announced Hollis from the table. "The fanciest cologne two dollars can buy."

Ollie tried not to gag. "It smells like the inside of a butt factory. I hope you kept the receipt. And why are you wearing the clothes Grandma and Grandpa got you for Christmas?"

Hollis pulled out his perfect boyfriend book. "'Step four hundred and ninety-six,'" read Hollis. "'Invest in some quality cologne.'" He flipped through some pages. "'Step two hundred and thirty-five. Always look presentable.'"

"You've read that whole book?" asked Ollie.

"Only twice," he said. "I never knew there were so many things I didn't know about being a good boyfriend."

"Well, I think you look and smell like a dapper young man," said their mom as she walked into the room. "But maybe next time use a little less cologne."

Hollis leapt up and pulled out a chair at the table for her to sit in.

"Oh, how kind of you!"

"'Step one hundred and eighty-three. Remember your table manners.' But, boy, I gotta say. There's a lot of them! Did you know you weren't supposed to talk with your mouth full?" he asked with his mouth full. "Whoops! Still got a lot to learn!"

Ollie cleared his throat. "Are you excited about wrestling today?" he asked, steering the conversation away from boyfriends and girlfriends. "You should go get ready."

He knew that Big Chew's imminent return would blow his brother's mind.

"I am ready," said Hollis.

"But you're not wearing your 'Big Chew's #1 Fan' shirt," said Ollie. "You always wear your 'Big Chew's #1 Fan' shirt to wrestling. It's practically, like, your uniform."

"Don't need it anymore," said Hollis. "This is my new uniform."

"And you look adorable in it, sweetie," said their mom. "Now hurry up, you two, so we can get a move on." She stood and collected their dirty dishes.

But Hollis waved his hand. "Don't worry, Mom. I got these," he said, taking the plates from her and bringing them to the sink. "'Step one hundred and eight. Always do your chores.'"

Ollie wondered if today could possibly get any weirder.

✳✳✳

The day got weirder.

Ollie and Tamiko stared at the wall of floor-to-ceiling wrestling posters lining the arena entrance. Or rather, the wall where the floor-to-ceiling wrestling posters used to be.

In their place was a huge, no, *massive* poster of the Krackle Kiddos that hung from one end of the entryway to the other. Their bony knees poked out of their gaudy singlets, their braces sparkled over gritted teeth, and their identical eyes stared down at onlookers below. They looked like baby giants, colossal but not intimidating in the slightest.

"I have many questions," said Ollie.

"I only have one," said Tamiko. "Why is this here?"

"Well, first," said Leon as he walked up to them, "because we're the best wrestlers ever."

"And second," said Luna, behind him, "because you guys said that we were your favorite wrestlers."

"You had this put up because you think you're our favorite wrestlers?" asked Ollie.

"Not think," said Luna. "Know. You said it yourselves, remember? So we told Daddy we wanted the biggest, most expensive poster money could buy. Which apparently is pretty big!"

"But you can't see the other posters," said Tamiko.

62

"Exactly," said the Krackle Kiddos.

Ollie couldn't believe his eyes. There'd be no more snapping their socks at LINTON SOCKS as they entered the arena. A lifelong tradition, gone.

"Well, we're off to get our second victory," said Leon.

"Wave to us from the stands," said Luna.

"Break a leg," said Tamiko. "Seriously."

The Krackle Kiddos ran off, leaving Ollie and Tamiko standing under their giant gaze.

"Being stuck-up is one thing," said Tamiko. "And I know there's something weird going on with them beating the Terrible Twosome. But messing with a piece of Slamdown Town history? They've crossed the line."

"Come on," said Ollie, waving Tamiko forward. "Let's get my gum back, and then we'll get some answers. Or, I guess, Big Chew will."

They strode through the crowded lobby, past chattering fans pouring in for the day's wrestling matches, and headed toward the trophy room. With each step down the hallway, the hustle and bustle of the arena became softer until, finally, as they reached their destination, Ollie and Tamiko were the only two people around.

Ollie approached a dusty case in the back of the room. There, under a flickering light, was the retired championship belt. He reached his hand around the backside, feeling the aging leather before finally touching something sticky, hard, and—his stomach lurched—a little hairy.

His gum.

"Well?" asked Tamiko, tapping her foot. "The suspense is killing me."

He plucked it off the backside of the belt and held it in the air for her to see. It looked just as it had the day he'd received it: colorless, crusty, and filled with bits of hair, dust, and other items he tried not to think about.

He tossed the gum between his lips and felt it float between his tongue and the roof of his mouth. "See you on the other side," he said.

And then he chewed.

At first the gum was flavorless. Then the familiar icy-hot sensation washed over his taste buds. A surge of power coursed through his body. And, as he'd experienced many times before, the wrestler within twisted himself free.

"Big Chew's back!" shouted Tamiko.

Ollie opened his eyes and found he had to look down to see her. He pushed his long, flowing (and somehow always perfectly conditioned) hair out of his face and spotted numerous reflections of himself in the dusty trophy cases. His arms were once again the size of dump trucks, his neck as wide as a beach ball. Splotches of a golden, muddy spray tan dotted his skin.

"Not yet," he said in a deep, gravelly voice. "Not without my costume."

He grabbed his costume out of his backpack and ducked behind a trophy case. He wriggled into the purple wet suit, pulled up his grandpa's golden pair of underwear, yanked on his gloves, shoved his feet into his colossal boots, and draped the red cape over his shoulders.

He was ready.

"How do I look?" asked Big Chew as he stepped out.

"Like a wrestler," said Tamiko.

He noticed that she didn't seem too excited. Or maybe that was his own nerves talking.

"Everything okay?" asked Big Chew.

"Yeah, why wouldn't it be?" said Tamiko. "Just another weekend of wrestling where you get to be a wrestler and I get to hang out in the arena by myself. Well, more snacks for me!"

She laughed it off, but he wondered if maybe there was something more going on.

"Smile!" she yelled, holding her phone up and snapping a picture of him.

✳✳✳

Big Chew marched through the lobby and watched as fans' jaws dropped and their eyes went wide. After being little again for so long, it felt good to tower above a crowd.

An eighth grader shoved an autograph book at him. "You're my favorite, Big Chew," she said. "I can't wait to see the look on Hollis's face when he sees that I got your autograph first."

Big Chew signed his autograph, quickly left the excited fans, and headed toward the WRESTLERS ONLY area. He didn't want to attract any attention, so he pushed open the locker room door as quietly as he could. But he was immediately confronted by his old pal, The Bolt.

"Hey, everyone," she yelled when he entered the locker room, "I guess lightning *can* strike twice. Big Chew's here!"

So much for not attracting attention, thought Big Chew.

Gorgeous Gordon Gussett, the crown prince of fashion, sauntered over wearing his sparkling costume. "I see you're still wearing last year's fashion."

"Can't compete with you," he said.

"I think you two look like garbage," said Silvertongue, the vipress, from her locker as she practiced her smack talk in a mirror. "Because you both belong in the trash."

"Good to see, and be insulted by you too, Silvertongue," said Big Chew.

A massive hand slapped Big Chew's back. It took all his strength to not fall over.

"You back?" asked Barbell Bill, the master of muscle. "I surprise."

"I mean, I'm not necessarily *back* back," said Big Chew, wincing.

"What did I tell you whippersnappers?" There was no mistaking Lil' Old Granny's voice. She shuffled over to the mob. "Each one of you said he'd gone on to work some other wrestling promotion, but Granny knew better. Pay up!"

The wrestlers grumbled as they handed Granny her money.

"Thanks for believing in me, Granny," said Big Chew.

"You young'uns love your grand entrances," said Granny. "But I knew you'd come crawling back to Slamdown Town one day. Just couldn't resist throwing down with Granny, could you?" She hunched over, her joints cracking. "In fact, I'll wrestle you right now. Don't think Granny's lost her touch while you've been hiding under a rock!"

"Actually, everyone," said Big Chew, "I think I forgot

my, um"—he struggled to think of a good excuse—"keys in my locker. Can't drive my car without them, you know?"

He escaped the mob of wrestlers and snuck toward Werewrestler's locker. It wasn't hard to find, considering the door was nearly bent off the hinges. Werewrestler had a habit of smashing heads against it. And even better, the wrestler himself was nowhere to be seen.

Big Chew pulled open the locker door and felt his heart skip a beat. Underneath a pile of baseball bats, crowbars, barbed wire, and other illegal contraband was the envelope with the splotchy letter *K* stamp. He reached out, looked inside, and made a curious discovery.

Money.

"I heard a rumor you were back," said a gruff voice behind him.

He knew that voice. Big Chew quickly tossed the envelope back into the locker and turned to find Werewrestler leering at him from across the room.

"Actually, I was just leaving," said Big Chew.

He moved toward the doorway, but Werewrestler stepped in front of him.

"So soon?" asked Werewrestler. "That any way to treat your old pal? You and me, we went through a lot together. Or more like, I sent you through a lot. Like the ropes and into an early retirement." He smiled, exposing his fangs. "But even I know a worthy competitor when I see one. The Referee might have stolen the win, and my belt, but you did all the work. Should we let bygones be bygones?"

To Big Chew's surprise, Werewrestler extended his hand.

He wasn't sure what was going on. But he was too confused by what he'd just discovered to think clearly. So he cautiously accepted Werewrestler's grasp.

"Gotcha." Before he could blink, Werewrestler tugged him forward, lifted Big Chew into the air, and tossed him across the room and onto the locker room floor.

"Still dumb as ever, I see," snarled Werewrestler. He howled with laughter. "The only thing you're worthy of is getting your butt kicked by me. Now get outta here!"

As Big Chew lay flat on his back staring up at the locker room ceiling, he knew two things: one, that he should never trust a heel like Werewrestler, and two, that he needed to get back to Tamiko as quickly as possible to tell her what he'd found.

CHAPTER 11

TAMIKO

QUARTERS rattled in Tamiko's pocket as she made her way toward the arcade to give *Brawlmania Supreme* another try. But before she did, she took a detour to the snack counter.

Can't get the high score on an empty stomach, she thought.

Tamiko got in the back of the snack line, only to discover that she was standing behind Hollis and Breonna. She wanted to slip away, but her stomach rooted her to the spot.

"I don't understand why you don't want to say hi to him," said Breonna.

"Hi to who?" asked Tamiko.

"Big Chew," said Breonna. "Didn't you hear? There's a rumor he's back!"

Tamiko sighed. "Oh, I heard. I also heard," she said, turning to Hollis, "that you were wearing something straight out of Dentures Dan's closet. You know, if you hurry down to the senior center you might still make it in time for afternoon bingo."

Breonna laughed.

"So why *don't* you want to see Big Chew?" asked Tamiko. "I figured you'd be first in line to get his autograph and ask him if your alien abduction theory was correct."

Hollis shook his head. "'Step seventy-three. You can only have room for one number one in your life.'" He took Breonna's hand. "And my number one is right here."

"Ah, Hollis," said Tamiko's dad as they reached the front of the line, "I almost didn't recognize you. Loving the new look, big guy."

"Thanks, Mr. Tanaka. I'll have a—"

"—Jumbo-size chocolate-dipped cotton candy with sprinkles, and two hot dogs, one for each nostril, with extra ketchup," finished her dad. "And for Breonna, a cup of tapioca pudding, a bag of prunes, and one club soda to wash it all down, just like your granny."

"Right as usual, Mr. Tanaka," said Breonna.

"Only," said Hollis, "the hot dogs aren't for the nostrils. Not anymore. 'Step two-hundred and forty-three. Don't play with your food.'"

"Well, I lost my appetite," said Tamiko as she headed toward the arcade.

✳✳✳

96,722 points.

Tamiko had had a good start, easily making her way through her pixelated opponents. But she needed 100,001 points to beat D-E-V, the diabolical game developers that had rigged the game and had occupied the first-place slot forever.

Her virtual character, Miss Creant, stood in one corner of the ring. In the other, the infamous and unbeatable CEO of *Brawlmania Supreme*, Buff Boss. Tamiko planted her feet on the mildew-riddled carpet, blew her hair out of her face, and prepared to wrestle.

PREPARE FOR FINAL MATCH!

The cutscene ended and Tamiko was given control of her character again for the hopefully *final* final fight.

She pulled the joystick toward her, dodging a Nine-to-Five Powerbomb from Buff Boss. She rapidly tapped in a combo that sent Miss Creant slamming into her opponent with a Scandalous Suplex. And the screen lit up when she dodged Buff Boss's I'll See You In My Office Piledriver and countered with a Lawless Leg Drop.

POWER UP!

Buff Boss began to blink in the center of the ring. If Tamiko could beat him, it would send her score skyrocketing well beyond the first-place slot.

But before Miss Creant could roll away, Buff Boss grappled her and lifted her high above his head. Like countless times before, Tamiko watched as he slammed her character onto the mat and pinned her. She smashed the buttons, trying to break free, but it was no use.

The in-game ref called out the pinfall and the dreaded words flashed on-screen.

"That had to have been a glitch!" yelled Tamiko as she slapped the control panel. How was it that, no matter how far away Buff Boss was, he *always* caught her once he'd powered up? It wasn't fair. Her final score was revealed to be nearly a thousand points short of her goal.

Screech's voice blared out over the arena speakers.

"Slamdown Town!" shouted Screech. "It's time for—" The speakers crackled and whined loudly. "Goodness me, that even made my ears ring. Well, as we all try to recover from that audio blast, why don't you make your way into the arena, because it's wrestling time!"

I won't even have an audience when I beat the high score, thought Tamiko.

It wasn't *just* the empty arcade that was making her feel alone. It was the Krackle Kiddos showing up, it was all the newbies infesting Slamdown Town and the fact that she couldn't even beat one stupid high score. But mostly, it was because despite really wanting to help, there were some things only a wrestler could do. And she wasn't one. Ollie was.

But that wasn't his fault. In fact, Ollie turning into a wrestler was one of the coolest things to ever happen to her. But that was the problem. It hadn't happened to her.

It had happened to him.

She eyed the *Brawlmania Supreme* arcade machine. It stared right back at her, as if mocking her inferior skills. She gritted her teeth, jammed her hand into her pocket, and shoved her last quarter in the slot. She couldn't control whether she was a wrestler or not, but she could grab a joystick and control the game. At least until she inevitably lost again.

I wish I could power up and become an awesome wrestler, too, she thought as she guided Miss Creant through her matches.

Tamiko arrived at Buff Boss with even fewer points than her last playthrough. The match kicked off after the cutscene and her fingers danced across the buttons.

Her attention drifted away from the boss fight. She wondered what Ollie and Tamiko might name their tag team. The Middle-School Dropouts? The Lunchtime Heroes?

POWER UP!

"Who cares," muttered Tamiko. She flicked the joystick toward her, knowing full well that the blinking Buff Boss would—

No way, she thought. Goose bumps spread up her arms as Tamiko watched Miss Creant dodge out of the way before Buff Boss could grapple her. Somehow, someway, Tamiko had avoided Buff Boss's foolproof attack.

Heart racing, she slammed forward on the joystick, sending Miss Creant running toward the ropes. She'd waited years for this chance, and Tamiko was not about to let it slip away. With a nudge of the controls, Miss Creant climbed up on the top rope.

"Sorry, Buff Boss," said Tamiko, licking her lips. "But I'm afraid you're fired."

Tamiko swung the joystick counterclockwise while bashing the punch and kick buttons together. Miss Creant leapt off the top rope and slammed Buff Boss into the mat with a Fearsome Flying Body Press.

The referee counted out the pinfall.

Her score shot up to 101,322, well over her goal. Fireworks splashed across the screen and eight-bit crowd cheers echoed out of the speakers.

YOU ARE A CHAMPION!

Tamiko couldn't believe it. She had beaten the unbeatable boss, and she had the sweaty palms to prove it.

"I did it!" she shrieked. "Ollie! Look, I—" But when she turned around, Tamiko remembered she was alone. There was no one there to celebrate her tremendous victory.

No matter. Years of hard work, late-night strategy sessions, and rolls and rolls of quarters had *finally* paid off. Victory had been so close so many times before only to slip away. It almost didn't feel real, but this was no dream. She'd enter her name on the top of the score list and that way there would be proof, forever, that she was the champion.

T-A-M!

It felt good to see her name at the top, above all the others. Time to let *everyone* in the arena know who was number one.

Another screen popped up that prevented her from leaving.

SHOUT POWER UP! TO UNLOCK SECRET FIGHTER

Beneath that, a timer started counting down from twenty-five seconds.

Shout power up? thought Tamiko. She scanned the machine. There were buttons for punch and kick, of course. But there was nothing anywhere labeled SHOUT.

It felt weird to be saying, let alone shouting, anything to a rickety old arcade machine. But as the countdown dwindled, her curiosity grew. In all of her research on the game, shouting had never come up.

Intrigued, she said, "Umm. Power up?"

The screen flashed white and a stream of red, black, and purple pixels shot out of it toward her. She instinctively blocked her face, but they didn't hit her. Instead, they swirled around her entire body and began to swirl faster and faster, like water going down a drain.

"This is the craziest video game effect ever!" yelled Tamiko as the pixels circled. The room appeared to be getting smaller. Or maybe she was getting taller? Either way, the muscles in her arms and legs felt all tingly like she'd fallen asleep on them. Suddenly, the pixels exploded and evaporated around her, as the *Brawlmania Supreme* screen returned to the home menu.

Tamiko was left barely able to stand. She tottered back and forth, needing to reach out and clutch the machine to stop herself from falling. The game unexpectedly slid back as she made contact. That's when she noticed her hands. They were much, *much* bigger than they were a few moments ago. Come to think of it, Tamiko didn't remember her feet being that big, either.

Tamiko glanced into the shiny screen of *Brawlmania Supreme* and stared at her reflection. Only, it wasn't the one she'd grown accustomed to over the past eleven years.

The woman who looked back at her was big—no, huge. Her hair was dyed a stunning purple and hung down to her shoulders. Two red streaks ran down each of her eyes. She was ripped. She was tall. She was *awesome.*

Not only that, she wore a killer outfit. She sported a sleek leather jacket with metal studs on the shoulders over a solid jet-black singlet. A retro controller necklace around her neck jingled with each massive step her knee-high combat boots took. When she turned around, she discovered a pixelated avatar of herself emblazoned on the back of her jacket.

"No way," she said in a gruff, biting voice that had never come out of her mouth before. "I'm a wrestler now, too!"

Then she remembered the strange screen had told her that shouting the phrase "Power up!" was supposed to unlock a secret fighter. Was the secret fighter . . . herself? She knew there was only one way to find out.

"Power down!" she said, and, in an instant, transformed back into her eleven-year-old self. But she didn't want to be herself. She wanted to be a wrestler. "Power up!" she shouted.

And in a flash of pixels she changed back into the hulking wrestler.

"Tamiko?"

She whipped around to find Ollie, mouth agape, standing in the entryway of the arcade. She took two lumbering steps forward, planted her hands on her hips, and grinned.

"Hey, dude. So, what's new with you?"

CHAPTER 12

OLLIE

"I can't believe it," said Ollie in shock, falling backward onto the floor.

"I know," said Tamiko in a deep, gravelly voice. She leaned down and examined the high-score list on the screen. "I feel like I could've gotten a much higher score than that."

"No, Tamiko! I can't believe you turned into a wrestler! But how?"

"For starters, I beat the Buff Boss, then I unlocked a secret fighter, and then all these pixels shot out of the screen and swirled around me and the next thing I knew I was muscly and the secret fighter was *me*!" she said, flexing her muscles. "Pretty cool, right?"

"Tamiko, Snowman Steve is cool. This is amazing!"

Ollie shook his head. First, a piece of already-been-chewed gum previously chomped by a Slamdown Town champion had turned *him* into a wrestler. Now the janky old arcade game had turned his best friend into one. What else might the giant aging arena be hiding? For all he knew there could be a secret lurking in every nook and cranny.

"But wait, I have to tell you something," said Ollie, remembering what had happened.

"I almost forgot," said Tamiko. "What did you find?"

"There was money inside the envelope. Lots of it."

"Money?" asked Tamiko. "Why would Billingsley be giving them money?"

"Why do you think?" asked Ollie. "This is what I was trying to tell you. Two middle schoolers can't wrestle. Billingsley must have paid the Terrible Twosome off to throw the match."

Tamiko gasped. "Wow, my gasps in this body are really deep." Then she gasped again. "I can't believe it. Wrestling, fixed? It's outlandish. It's preposterous. It's downright wrong and I won't stand for it happening in our arena. And for once, I can do something about it."

"What are you going to do about it?" asked Ollie.

"I'm going to march down to Linton's office and give him a piece of my mind!" She flexed her muscles and tossed her hair back. "Sure, he's the CEO, but he's also their dad. Now, make with the chewing already so we can get this tag team started!"

"Tag team?" asked Ollie.

"Yeah," said Tamiko. "You seriously think now that I'm a wrestler I'm not going to get into the ring and kick some butts? And that my butt-kicking best bud won't be standing right beside me? 'Cause if so," she said, turning and running toward the doorway, "think again."

He popped the gum into his mouth, transformed into Big Chew, and chased after her.

They ran through the lobby, where fans gawked and pointed as they passed. They ran by the locker room, where wrestlers were getting ready for the night's matchups. And they ran down the hallway toward Linton's office, where Linton was probably counting his money.

Big Chew raised his hand to knock, but Tamiko stopped him.

"Allow me," she said as she kicked the door open.

"Take me, not the money!" shouted Linton, leaping up from his desk chair and throwing his entire body on top of his metallic safe.

His office was a dimly lit space with tacky leather furniture. A single photo frame sat on a cluttered desk of papers, coin wrappers, and stacks of bills. Behind his desk was a bulky computer and monitor with a peeling SECURITY COMMAND CENTER sticker slapped on it.

"We're not here for the money," said Tamiko.

"Or for you," said Big Chew.

Tamiko stepped forward. "We're here to wrestle."

"Big Chew? Is that you?" Linton rubbed his eyes.

"Good to see you again, Mr. Krackle," lied Big Chew.

Linton leapt up, did a little dance, and shook Big Chew's hand.

"I thought I'd never see you again! Where have you been? Don't you dare tell me you've been wrestling for another league. I promise you they won't pay you what I do."

"But you don't pay me," said Big Chew.

"That's one of my favorite things about you. Oh, I'm so glad you're back. I had all sorts of cheap Big Chew merch made

before you left." He gestured to several boxes full of shirts, mugs, and magnets with Big Chew's face on them. "Now I can finally sell it. And who knows? If you're as big a draw now as you were then, maybe we'll go big-time and invest in bumper stickers. So, Big Chew," he said, taking a seat behind his desk. He glanced over at Tamiko. "And really buff lady I don't know. What can I do for you?"

"Your kids—" started Tamiko.

But Big Chew cut her off. "Well, Mr. Krackle. I found a partner."

"A partner?" Linton narrowed his eyes. "And who are you, anyway?"

That's right, thought Ollie. *Who is Tamiko?*

"I'm Game Over," she declared. "The combo-savvy wrestler with a flair for turning her opponents into pixels. And yes, I did just make that up on the spot."

She was good.

"I'm going to nod and pretend like I know what those words mean," said Linton. "I'm also going to pretend like I know how to use the internet to look up your credentials." He pretended to type away on the keyboard in front of him. "My kids were supposed to help me learn to use this newfangled machine." He mock-typed some more. "Yep, just as I thought. A nobody. There's the door," he said, pointing to the doorway they walked in through.

"But she's my partner," said Big Chew.

"Not unless I approve it, she's not." Linton massaged his mustache. "I'm sure you know this already, but I just signed two new, fresh-faced wrestlers. My kids."

"Oh, we know," said Game Over. "Speaking of them . . ."

"So why should I sign another?" interrupted Linton.

"I'll wrestle for free," she said.

Linton considered her offer. "Hmm . . . What else have you got?"

Game Over checked her pockets and pulled out a string of video game prize tickets from the arcade. She offered them to Linton, who quickly swiped them out of her hands.

"You've got yourself a deal!" he said. "See? That's how you play hardball. I like you, Game Over. You better be careful, Big Chew, or your new partner will upstage you! Now, speaking of partners, I'm not really seeing much coordination between the two of you."

"Coordination?" asked Big Chew.

"Yeah," said Linton, "you know. Your gimmick. I don't get it." He pointed to the framed photographs on the wall behind him of various tag teams. "Take The Super Nice Guys, for example. They're your stereotypical faces. They wear bright colors and are all about being friendly with the crowd and playing by the book. Audience loves them. Then you have someone like the Terrible Twosome. They're obviously heels. They wear all black, boo their fans, and have a knack for breaking the rules. Crowd hates them. Well, loves to hate them. It's confusing. So what's your gimmick?"

Big Chew went to speak, but Game Over beat him to it. "Hold on to your seat cushions because you're about to get blown off your feet," she said. "Our team is going to be the loudest, the meanest, and the most punishing-est team there ever was.

I'm talking all-black outfits with skulls and flames and spikes. Nobody is going to mess with us because we'll mess with them first. And you know what we're going to be called?"

"What?" asked Linton, on the edge of his seat.

"The Devastating Destroyers of Doom!"

Linton leapt out of his chair. "I love it! I can see it on the marquee now. Classic heel."

But Big Chew didn't feel the same way. "Hmm . . ."

"I can see you're speechless by how awesome my idea is," said Game Over with pride.

"Actually, Game Over," he finally managed to say, "I was thinking something else."

"What, like chain gloves? Yeah, I considered that, too. But is it too much?"

"No," said Big Chew. "I meant another tag team gimmick. Drumroll please! We should be . . . the Goody Goody Two-Shoes. Get it? Because there's two of us?"

"Hmm," said Game Over, the smile on her face fading.

Big Chew pressed on. "The Goody Goody Two-Shoes will be the shining defenders of the arena. We'll dish out ringside justice with a smile."

"I think we have a winner. Classic face."

"No offense, Big Chew," said Game Over, "but Devastating Destroyers of Doom is way cooler."

"What?" said Big Chew in shock. "No way! The Goody Goody Two-Shoes are clearly the better choice."

"Quit your bellyaching," said Linton. "They're both good, but you have to pick one. Tag teams need to work as, well, a *team*."

But they couldn't decide. Try as they might, every argument Big Chew gave, Game Over didn't like, and every argument Game Over gave, Big Chew didn't like.

After a few minutes Linton stepped in. "Did you not listen to anything I said? The crowd wants a straightforward, simple-to-identify team. You either have to be faces or heels, or I'm not signing you. So, even better than you deciding, I'll decide. You can be, *err*, the Ragtag Team!"

"What? That's not anything close to what we suggested," said Big Chew.

"Plus, doesn't 'ragtag' mean disorganized? Which is, like, the opposite of a team?"

"You two sound like my kids. Expecting me to do everything for you. I already gave you your name free of charge. You'll have to figure out the rest of the stuff yourselves."

"Speaking of your kids—" began Game Over.

Big Chew cleared his throat, cutting her off. "We want to wrestle them."

Linton nervously chuckled. "Look, Big Chew. I like you a lot, but I can't pit you against my newest, most popular wrestlers, especially in your first tag team match."

"But we know that they're up to—" started Game Over.

"Something amazing," Big Chew interrupted.

"They're going all the way to the top," said Linton. "In time, maybe you can get there, too. But you're trying to fly before you can crawl. Speaking of which, you'll be facing Birds of a Feather next weekend, so work on both your crawling *and* your flying."

Big Chew gulped. Birds of a Feather were a high-flying tag team that starred Paulette Parrot, the resident copycat who turned her opponent's own strengths and words against them, and Bald Eagle, the prideful wrestler who wore a wig that he was *very* sensitive about due to early-onset balding. They wouldn't be easy to beat.

Linton smacked his lips. "I can already taste the money. Or maybe that's the new, money-flavored toothpaste I just started using. Either way, I should probably rinse better!"

Linton shuffled them both out of his office and closed the door.

"Dude, why'd you stop me from telling him about the cheating?" asked Game Over.

"Because we don't have enough proof yet," said Big Chew.

"You said you saw a wad of cash in the envelope. What more proof do we need?"

"A lot more. Besides, you said it yourself. He's their dad. If we tell him now without definitive proof, he's never going to believe us. Or worse, we might make him angry, and he won't let us wrestle at all. Remember, the Krackle Kiddos have him wrapped around their fingers."

"Good point," said Game Over. "So what do we do?"

"I'll tell you what we're going to do. We're going to wrestle and win so much that they'll have to face us. And when they do, we'll prove in the ring with everyone watching that they can't actually wrestle. In the meantime, we'll keep our eyes open"—he held up the evidence notebook—"for any other weird stuff going on."

"Sounds good to me, partner," said Game Over. "Now we just need our gimmick."

"Right," said Big Chew. "Faces or heels? I'd go faces."

"Of course you would," said Game Over. "And I'd obviously choose heels. Which means we settle this in the most ancient form of combat known to kid-kind."

"Rock, paper, scissors," they said in unison.

"Best two out of three?" she asked.

Big Chew nodded. "And whoever wins gets to pick the gimmick for our team."

His first choice was easy. He held out paper like he always did. But it was quickly cut in half by her scissors.

"How did you know?" asked Big Chew, exasperated.

"You always start with paper." She grinned. "And team heels thanks you for it."

As he pounded his fist into his palm, he decided to go scissors on the logic that Game Over might think to cover his rock with paper. And he was right.

"Scissors? You were supposed to go rock!" she shouted.

"Sorry to disappoint you," he said. "But when we're both faces, you'll understand."

It all came down to this. A final choice of three basic hand shapes that would determine the fate of their entire wrestling career. He'd never been more nervous in his entire life.

But he knew what he had to do. She flashed rock and he lowered his paper over it.

"This can't be happening!" she shrieked. "How could I lose? Faces it is."

"Don't worry. This is going to be awesome," he assured her. "It's going to be a challenge for both of us. But by next weekend, I *know* that we'll be the greatest face team ever!"

CHAPTER 13

TAMIKO

"I don't want to watch wrestling," said Tamiko as she plopped down in her seat to watch wrestling. "I want to wrestle!"

Her stomach groaned, a combination of nerves at getting signed to the Slamdown Town roster moments earlier and the two oversized boxes of sour gummies she had just swallowed.

Ollie smiled through a mouthful of fries. "I know the feeling."

Tamiko wanted to charge into the ring and take on the whole world. After years of waiting her turn, her dream of being a wrestler had finally come true. But when the lights dimmed, the familiar rush of an approaching match commanded her attention.

"Ladies and gentlemen, boys and girls." Screech could barely contain the excitement in his voice. "It is my pleasure to welcome back the middle-school phenoms, the kids with the fighting spirit of ten grown wrestlers. Give it up for the Krackle Kiddos!"

The arena erupted in a chorus of boos appropriate for a heel tag team.

"I doubt that they had enough gold coins to pay off the Scallywags," said Tamiko as the Krackle Kiddos made their way down the entrance ramp and into the ring.

Ollie nodded. "Those two pirates take what they want. And what they want more than buried treasure is to bury their opponents. And they *really* want buried treasure."

Boom!

"The sound of cannons can mean only one thing," said Screech. "The Scallywags have weighed anchor in the arena!"

Hornswaggle and Landlubber, the fearsome pirate duo, marched to the top of the entrance ramp, each waving a black flag. They had tattooed skulls, swords, and ships on their arms and legs for each victory. And they were running out of space for new ones.

The Scallywags strode down the entrance ramp and into the ring. The referee began his pre-match inspections. Only, something was different about the way he looked.

"Hold up," said Tamiko. "That's not the normal ref."

Linton had hired a new referee after Ollie's mom had become the singles champion and hung up her stripes. While they didn't know him all that well, they knew him well enough to know that that wasn't him in the ring. Unlike the normal referee, who was short and clean-shaven, the new ref towered over the wrestlers and sported a big bushy mustache.

Most fans probably wouldn't even register that there had been a ref swap. But she and Ollie weren't normal fans. Nothing about the arena escaped their eyes.

"I've never seen that guy before," said Ollie.

"Same. Although, there is something oddly familiar about him."

"Maybe this one's cheaper." Ollie bit into his burger, sending a splash of ketchup toward her. "Whoops! All hands on deck!"

"Hey," said Tamiko as she leaned out of the way. "Watch the new shoes!"

Ding! Ding! Ding!

Hornswaggle took one step toward Leon as the starting bell rang, prepared to unleash a devastating Shiver Me Timbers Clothesline—

Fweet!

But the sound of the ref's whistle stopped Hornswaggle mid-charge.

"Illegal use of counterweight shift," declared the ref.

Tamiko looked over at Ollie. "Is that some weird rule I don't know about?"

"I've never heard of it," said Ollie.

Hornswaggle shook her head. "Ye can't be serious, mate. I took nary a step!"

"Rules are rules," said Leon, grinning.

The referee wiggled his mustache aggressively. "And if you don't follow my commands, you will receive a disqualification."

Hornswaggle turned around and threw her meaty, tattooed arms into a Salty Seadog Body Lock around Leon's petite frame.

Fweet!

"Illegal use of hands by Hornswaggle!" yelled the ref. "You better watch yourself."

"Me?" asked Hornswaggle. "Me hands may be unwashed, but they ain't dirty!"

Leon stuck his tongue out. "You better watch it!"

"I don't know what's happening here," said Screech. "But if Hornswaggle isn't careful, she'll be tossed out of the match."

Both tag teams went to their corners and swapped in their partners. Landlubber hit the mat, ran forward, and lifted Luna's scrawny body high above his head.

Fweet!

The ref blew his whistle before Landlubber could execute a Barnacle Backbreaker.

"What now?" asked Tamiko.

"Improper use of elevation," said the ref.

"Wait just one scurvy moment," said Landlubber.

But before he could say another word, Luna smacked him with a Need It Now Knee to the back of his head. Landlubber toppled forward, releasing his hold on her. She pounced and hit Landlubber with a Daddy's Precious Princess Back Rake that sent him squirming to the mat.

"You should've stuck to swabbing poop decks," said Luna.

"Now, that is dirty," said Screech.

But the ref's whistle remained silent.

"Whoever this new ref is," said Tamiko, "he really has it out for the Scallywags."

"Next thing you know he'll say they're breathing too much," said Ollie.

Fweet!

"Excessive inhalation by Landlubber," shouted the ref.

"Told you," said Ollie. "Wow, he's really protecting the Krackle Kiddos here."

Tamiko stroked her chin. Something suspicious was happening in the ring.

"Out of breath?" asked Luna.

"Yes! Me mean, no! Me was just catching it," said Landlubber. He turned to face the ref. "Methinks ye have a dislike for the way me be doing me business."

Fweet!

"Threatening an official," called out the ref. "That is completely unacceptable. Due to extreme repeated violations, I am *ending* this match. The Scallywags have been disqualified."

"Well, my oh my, folks," yelled Screech. "I haven't seen a disqualification in years. But it is up to the referee's discretion and he did issue a lot of warnings to the Scallywags. That means that the Krackle Kiddos are victorious once again!"

"What? That ref was not fair," said Ollie.

"I agree," said Tamiko. "Some random guest ref shows up and calls the match in favor of the Krackle Kiddos? *That's* weird. I want to know who he is and what his deal is."

She spotted him leaving the ring and scurrying up the ramp.

"Good point," said Ollie. "If we hurry, we can catch him."

They leapt out of their seats and sprinted down the stairs, through the lobby, and down the hallway toward the WRESTLERS ONLY entrance. But as Tamiko turned the corner, she found herself face-to-face—literally—with Billingsley as they collided and fell to the sticky floor.

"Oh, dude, I'm so sorry," she said as she pulled herself off the ground. "Didn't see you."

Billingsley reached down and picked up a duffel bag he had dropped. "Oh, Mistress Tamiko. The fault was entirely my own," he said. "Please accept my apology."

"Where are you off to?" asked Ollie.

"I'm on my way to the limo to grab the foot ointment," he said.

"Foot ointment?" asked Tamiko.

Billingsley nodded. "The Kiddos will want their post-match foot massage."

"Gross," said Tamiko.

"Indeed," he said. "Good evening, children." With a bow, he hurried off.

Just then, Tamiko spotted something on the floor where the butler had fallen. She bent down to pick it up. "Hey, Billingsley," she said, "you dropped your . . ." Tamiko gasped when she realized what she was holding. "Mustache?"

Ollie grabbed it from her. "And not just any mustache. A *fake* mustache."

Tamiko's mind began to race. "Quick! Ollie! Draw Billingsley in the evidence notebook."

He pulled it from his back pocket and drew a crude sketch.

"Now draw him with a mustache!"

Ollie quickly sketched facial hair on his lip. Tamiko's heart was racing.

"Now draw him in referee stripes!"

He did, and as he did they both gasped. There was no denying it.

"Billingsley was the guest referee," said Tamiko. "That's why he looked vaguely familiar. But with the mustache, I didn't recognize him."

"This is big," said Ollie. "Paying off the Terrible Twosome was one thing. But hiring a referee to call the match in the Krackle Kiddos' favor? That's low."

"But don't you see? It's the perfect crime. That way they wouldn't have to wrestle and everyone continues to think that they're amazing, unstoppable wrestlers. If only we'd caught him in the referee stripes. That way we'd have definitive proof."

Ollie considered this for a moment. "He *did* have that duffel bag with him."

"That's it," said Tamiko, snapping her fingers. "I bet if we get our hands on that bag, we'll find the referee outfit inside."

CHAPTER 14

TAMIKO

WHY didn't I choose scissors? thought Tamiko as she sat in Tuesday afternoon study hall.

In the days since the match, her decision had haunted her, playing over and over in her head. But facts were facts. Game Over, or rather Tamiko, would need to turn face.

As a natural heel, a tiny fear that she would fail had lodged itself in her heart.

"What did you think about our victory this weekend?" asked Leon, leaning forward.

"Pretty one-sided match," said Luna.

"I'd say," said Tamiko, turning to face them. "The ref called everything in your favor."

"Well, that's because the Scallywags are dirty, rotten cheaters," said Luna.

Ollie coughed.

"Are you feeling okay, Ollie?" asked Leon, handing him a cough drop.

"Oh, yeah," he said, "my throat is just tickly from, umm . . ."

"Cheering for you both so hard," finished Tamiko.

"Aww," said Luna. "We'd expect nothing less from our number one fans."

"Number one what?" asked Ollie.

"All right, everyone," said Mrs. Martino from the front of the room. "This is study hall, not chatty hall. I need you all to work quietly and stay diligent."

"What's the point of study hall if Billingsley does all our homework, anyway?" asked Leon.

"Well, not everyone has butlers," said Tamiko.

Luna crossed her arms. "That's everyone else's problem. Why should we suffer for it?"

Mrs. Martino cleared her throat. "Need I remind you all what *quiet* means?"

The Krackle Kiddos busied themselves with scratching their names into their desks. "Ready to begin our face training?" asked Ollie, careful to keep his voice low.

Tamiko really wasn't, but she needed to learn. "Ready as I'll ever be," she whispered.

He reached into his backpack and pulled out a heavy-looking binder. "Here. I was able to ask my mom for one of her copies. Thankfully she has plenty."

When she looked inside, Tamiko discovered she had been given the official Slamdown Town rules and regulations. All four hundred and ninety-two pages of them.

"Oh, this looks riveting," she said, unable to keep the sarcasm out of her voice.

"Let's begin with a simple review of faces," said Ollie. "We're the good guys. Which means we win matches by sticking to the rules and winning the crowd's love. If they aren't cheering, then we did something wrong."

"Dude, I know what faces are," she said, annoyed. "I've been going to the arena as long as you."

"Check it out," said Ollie as he reached into his backpack. "I already got us started. Take a look at some of these pieces I got from my attic."

Ollie pulled out several items—old wrestling singlets, decorative bath towels, scuffed cowboy boots, flashy magician gloves, gold knee pads—that all had one thing in common: They were bright, they were sparkly, and they were the stereotypical face costume. Tamiko had a hard time mustering any enthusiasm. Even less so when Ollie revealed an arts and crafts box filled with plastic diamonds, metallic wrapping paper, and rainbow confetti.

"What do you think?" asked Ollie.

She tried to sound impressed. "They're certainly shiny. Like, *really* shiny."

"You think? I snagged a giant bottle of glitter from my mom's craft supplies just in case they weren't glittery enough for you. I can start putting the outfits together tonight."

Tamiko had wanted to be a wrestler for, well, forever. But the fact that her big debut would be in *that* sparkling getup made her stomach drop.

"What've you got there?" asked the Krackle Kiddos.

"Nothing!" said Tamiko, zipping up Ollie's backpack before they could see.

"Quiet," said Mrs. Martino, her voice rising, "means making little or no noise. That's the definition. You can *quietly* look it up in the dictionary if you want to."

Tamiko needed to step out and take a breather, but she saw that the bathroom pass was already taken. That wasn't a big deal. She was a seasoned pro when it came to roaming the halls during study hall and pillaging the vending machines for snacks. First, she'd pretend like she was sharpening her pencil.

Since the pencil sharpener was next to the door, she would wait until Mrs. Martino wasn't looking, then quickly step out into the hallway undetected.

"Where are you going?" asked Ollie as she stood up.

"To sharpen my pencil."

Unfortunately, she knew that Ollie knew that was the code phrase for "Sneak out of study hall."

"Tamiko, that's not very face of you," he whispered.

"I'm still learning," she said as she approached the pencil sharpener, sharpened her pencil, then quickly backed out of the doorway and into the hallway without anyone noticing.

She walked past the lunchroom and arrived at the vending machines.

"Halt right there, Tamiko," said Breonna.

Breonna was a hall monitor, a role she took very seriously. She had ultimate authority over the school halls and handed out justice in the form of a pink warning slip. Which was unfortunate because Tamiko didn't take the rules of the hallway seriously at all.

"You know you're not allowed to roam the halls without a hall pass," said Breonna.

"That's true," said Tamiko. "Which is why I have one right here."

She produced a makeshift hall pass she'd assembled after her last one was confiscated. Tamiko was sure it would fool even the most observant eye.

"This is illegal contraband," said Breonna.

Except for Breonna, apparently.

"It's only illegal if you get caught," said Tamiko.

"You *did* get caught," said Breonna. "By me. Just now."

Tamiko shrugged as she punched the code for gummy worms into the snack machine and triumphantly retrieved her gooey, bagged specimens.

"If munching down on snacks during class is wrong," said Tamiko through a mouthful of gummy worms, "then I don't want to be right."

Breonna shoved a pink slip in Tamiko's hand and marched her back through the hallways toward study hall. Suddenly, she heard footsteps rapidly approaching from behind.

"There you are," said Hollis. "I wanted to see you. So I chugged a buttload of water. That way, I didn't have to lie when I said I had to go to the bathroom. And look, I have a hall pass."

He whipped out his hall pass and waved it in their faces.

"But, dude," said Tamiko, "you hate hall passes. Almost as much as I hate the fourth level of *Laundry Legends: Spin Cycle*. You have a stack of pink slips in your room that proves it."

"'Step six hundred and eighty-five. Follow the rules.' If my girlfriend is a nice, rule-abiding hall monitor, well, then I want to be a nice, rule-abiding hall monitor. Minus the hall monitor."

Tamiko saw that Breonna had a prepared pink slip in her hand. She squinted and thought she could make out a little heart drawn on it. Inside the heart were the initials *B + H*.

"So, yup, no pink slip for me," said Hollis, grinning. "I'm a changed man."

Tamiko watched Breonna pocket the slip. She almost looked disappointed.

"If you'll excuse me"—Breonna motioned to Tamiko—"I have official hall monitor business to attend to. I need to transport this whippersnapper back to class."

Breonna waited until Tamiko had taken her seat in study hall before leaving.

"I told you you'd get caught," said Ollie as she took her seat.

"There's nothing I won't do for snacks," said Tamiko.

"Yeah," said Luna, leaning forward. "We've seen you eat what passes for 'snacks' at the arena. I wouldn't feed that junk to my worst enemy."

"Oh, it's not that bad," said Tamiko, "once your stomach gets used to it. Besides, it's not like your dad would spend a penny to make them better."

"Speaking of better," said Ollie, "you better be careful about sneaking out of class or you'll get in trouble." He leaned in and whispered, "It's not very face."

Tamiko shrugged. "She confiscated my hall pass, but I have four more in my backpack, anyway. Even worse, I ran into Hollis, who smelled and looked wonderful."

"And that's a bad thing?" asked Leon.

"If you knew him you'd know anytime his name came up, a bad thing was close behind. Well, emphasis on the 'was.' Now he spends all his time gawking over Breonna. I'm sure underwear everywhere appreciates the sudden drop in wedgies."

"I know mine does," said Ollie. "Still, sometimes I just wanna lock him in the shark cage and throw away the key."

The Krackle Kiddos leaned forward.

"A shark cage?" asked Leon. "For ..."

"Sharks?" finished Luna.

"I want one of those!" said Leon.

"You have one," said Tamiko.

Luna looked puzzled. "We do? We did get a lot of presents for our birthday last year."

"So many that we didn't open them all," said Leon. "Must be one of the big packages."

"No, you didn't get a shark cage for your birthday," said Ollie. "There's a shark cage in the utility room at Slamdown Town."

"For sharks?" asked Leon.

"No, for wrestlers," said Ollie.

Luna still looked puzzled. "You can lock a wrestler in a shark cage?"

"For shark cage matches you can," said Tamiko. "Don't you two know about shark cage matches?"

"Well, who doesn't?" said Leon unconvincingly.

She was beginning to think that they didn't.

"Either way, no one's getting locked in the shark cage, because it's broken."

"Yeah, has been for years."

"Well," said Luna, "maybe we'll just have to ask for a new one."

"And a shark, too!" said Leon.

Tamiko and Ollie slapped their foreheads in unison.

Mrs. Martino appeared at their desks. "Consider this your final warning. I need you working quietly or you'll have plenty of time to do so in detention."

"If only there was a class about wrestling," said Luna when Mrs. Martino walked away.

"We could probably even teach it," said Leon.

That gave Tamiko an idea. She and Ollie needed to get back to Krackle Manor and locate the referee outfit. They just needed the Krackle Kiddos to invite them over.

"There might not be a class about wrestling, but we do know someone who can train you to be the best wrestlers ever. And she happens to live in Ollie's house."

"That's right," said Ollie, catching on. "My mom is a personal trainer."

"Why would *we* need training?" asked the Krackle Kiddos. "We're already the best."

"Think about it," said Tamiko. "You could have the singles champ sharing everything she knows with you. With your combined knowledge of wrestling and her insane workout routine, you'd be even *more* unstoppable than you already are."

"Will you both come and cheer us on?" asked Luna.

"Of course," said Tamiko. "After all, we're your number one fans, remember?"

Playing to the Krackle Kiddos' vanity was always a good route to go. She just wished that she felt a little better about it. After all, it was decidedly un-face.

"We like the sound of that," said Leon. "You may make the arrangements."

CHAPTER 15

OLLIE

"RIGHT this way, everyone," said Billingsley.

The cordial butler—and probable referee impersonator—led Tamiko, Ollie, and his mom through the winding corridors of Krackle Manor. Tonight was the Krackle Kiddos' first workout session, and Ollie hoped it would provide the perfect cover to search for the referee uniform.

Billingsley bowed, and in one swift motion opened the door to the home arena.

"This is where I leave you," he said. "More packages arrived today and I need to sort the playthings by color, size, and most fun."

"How do you know which are the most fun?" asked Tamiko.

"Whichever ones give me childlike wonder." Billingsley bowed again and walked away.

"Who's ready for a workout?" asked Ollie's mom as they entered the home arena.

The Krackle Kiddos ran up to Ollie and Tamiko. "We are!"

"I hope you brought sunglasses," said Luna, "because if you stare directly at this workout, you might go blind. If you didn't, we can have Billingsley grab you a designer pair."

"We're good," said Ollie. "I know how intense the workout is, right, Mom?"

She nodded. "Most trainees don't live to tell the tale. Or, at the very least, they don't sign up for a second session."

Leon gulped. "Is that true?"

"We'll find out!" said Tamiko.

Ollie watched as Leon, Luna, and his mom climbed into the ring. They had no idea what they were getting themselves into. To be fair, no one could be properly prepared for one of his mom's workouts. She exercised on an entirely different (and slightly deranged) level.

"A limber body is a happy body." His mom dropped to the mat and began doing push-ups. "And a happy body can be molded into a champion. Join me, future champs!"

The Krackle Kiddos followed suit. For every twenty push-ups his mom did, they barely completed one. At the arena, they were unstoppable tag team partners who had defeated some of the most formidable wrestlers ever to step foot inside Slam-down Town. Here, they were two twelve-year-olds who could barely complete a push-up.

"Okay, enough of the warm-up," said his mom. "Let's get this workout started."

The Krackle Kiddos looked horrified. "You're telling us that *wasn't* the workout?"

"This is our chance," Ollie whispered to Tamiko.

Tamiko nodded. "I got this." She turned to the ring. "We need to use the bathroom. In fact, I may be a while. My dad cooked his famous three-bean chili yesterday. It tastes great going down, but the next day I always feel it was one bean too many."

"Yeah, okay," said Leon, panting from his workout.

"You know where the bathroom is," said Luna. "And also how to overshare."

Ollie and Tamiko left the room and made their way down the hallway.

"We need to find Billingsley's room," said Ollie. "I bet the duffel bag is there."

"Time to bring down that no-good, super-polite butler," said Tamiko. "Who knows what other diabolical secrets we'll find in there."

But Krackle Manor was even bigger than they could have imagined. And Ollie prided himself on having an extremely active imagination. They found a library full of dusty books. There was a gift-wrapping room and a room filled with porcelain pigs.

"Must touch piggies," said Tamiko.

They discovered a drawing room full of family portraits, a ballroom, and three temperature-controlled rooms containing stacks of smelly cheese wheels, which they couldn't help but sample. But Billingsley's room was nowhere to be found.

"Just how big is this house?" asked Tamiko.

"Big enough to house the greatest thing to ever happen to this town."

Ollie knew that voice. He turned to see Linton Krackle

walking toward them wearing a swanky bathrobe and fuzzy pink rabbit slippers.

Ollie couldn't help but boo. It was automatic, from all his years at Slamdown Town.

"Boo!" he yelled along with Tamiko.

"I know, I know," said Linton. "I see you're wrestling fans. Boo all you want. Are you two friends with my kids, or did you wander in off the street?"

Tamiko nodded. "Yeah, we're their friends."

"We got lost on our way back from the bathroom," said Ollie.

"It happens to a lot of guests. And to me last week. I'll show you the way back."

"Actually," said Ollie, "it would be pretty cool to get a tour of Krackle Manor from the man in charge of it." He turned to Tamiko. "Might be quite *revealing*."

"I bet you know everything there is to know about this place," said Tamiko.

Linton beamed with pride. "Of course I do. I paid someone with *these* two hands to lay every brick in this house with *their* two hands. You two stick close to me. I'll give you the grand tour."

"For starters, what's that?" asked Tamiko.

"That," said Linton as he walked toward a door bearing a sign that read DAD—KEEP OUT, "is Leon and Luna's wing. All the rooms past this point belong to them."

"They get a whole wing to themselves?" asked Ollie.

Linton shrugged. "I was surprised they only asked for one this time. Besides, my kids only visit when they're kicked out of boarding school or when their mother is off on her fancy trips. I don't even use these rooms when they aren't here. Now, on with the tour!"

He showed them the money-counting room, where he counted his money. He showed them the cheap-suits room, where he kept all his cheap suits (and bragged that they had all been bought at a discount). And he showed them the throne room, where he went to the bathroom.

"Nothing like a silver-plated toilet to make a man feel like he's king of his castle," said Linton. "I used to be king of the gold-plated toilet, but the kiddos conquered that one."

"Gross," said Tamiko.

As they continued the tour, Linton motioned to a trophy of a fish hanging above the main living room's mantlepiece. "This is my famed krackle fish. Biggest one ever caught!"

"What's a krackle fish?" asked Ollie.

"It's a type of fish. The greediest, most selfish fish in the sea," said Linton. "It lies, it cheats, it steals, and it spends all day in its tiny cave counting its tiny pebbles, which is like the fish equivalent of money."

That sounded familiar. But Ollie kept his mouth (and his nose) shut. Despite being long dead, the krackle fish trophy still retained its fishy scent.

"We owe everything to the krackle. My great-great-grandpa Krackle was a krackle fish fisherman. It's how our family made its fortune. He would lie, cheat, and steal the fish straight from their salty caves and sell them to fisheries up and down the coast. Then spend all day in his office counting his money." Linton wiped a tear from his eye. "I respect him so much."

Tamiko yanked on Ollie's sleeve to get his attention.

"Dude, we need to ditch this old man," she whispered. "If I have to listen to him talk any longer, I can't promise I can keep pretending this isn't the most boring tour I've ever been on."

Ollie nodded. "I don't suppose you know where Billingsley's room is?"

Linton looked stunned. "I offered him a pantry room next to the north-wing kitchen. Not for free, of course. I don't run a charity. Can you believe that those places actually *give* money away?"

"That is pretty crazy," lied Ollie. They needed to get to the north-wing pantry, and fast. But first they needed to get rid of Linton. And he had a good idea how to do that. "Almost as crazy as spotting that *penny* on the ground while we were passing the cheap-suit room."

"Penny?" asked Tamiko, winking at Ollie. "Pretty sure that was a *nickel*, dude. I told you we should have picked it up."

Linton's eyes bulged. "A nickel? Back by the cheap-suit room? Out of my way!" he cried before barreling off down the hallway.

"Well, that was easy," said Ollie.

With Linton gone, Ollie and Tamiko made their way north (using the compass on Tamiko's phone) through the hallway and toward the north-wing kitchen.

"This must be it," said Ollie as they stood in front of a lop-sided pantry door.

Billingsley's room was the smallest room Ollie had been in that day. In fact, it was the smallest room he'd been in any day. But unlike the rest of Krackle Manor, the space was clean and organized. Since the room used to be a pantry, cans of beans and tomatoes still lined the walls. But, like Billingsley himself, there wasn't a can, sock, or blanket out of place.

Except for the duffel bag poking out from underneath the bed.

"Look," said Ollie, "we've got those cheaters now."

But when he opened the bag, he found the most disappointing thing of all.

"What's in it?" asked Tamiko.

"Nothing."

The bag was empty.

"Um, dude," said Tamiko from across the room. "You might want to take a look at this."

Ollie took out his magnifying glass and joined Tamiko, who was staring into a closet at the other end of the room. Inside was a referee uniform. But that wasn't all. There was a cowboy outfit, a space suit, a police officer's uniform, a chef's coat, and a pirate's hat.

"I mean," started Ollie, "we caught him with the referee uniform."

"And, like, a hundred other outfits," said Tamiko. "What is this dude's deal?"

"I don't know," he said, swapping out his magnifying glass for the evidence notebook.

"So he had the fake mustache and the referee uniform," said Tamiko. "It's not crazy to think that they ordered him to pose as the referee and call the match in their favor."

"No, it's not. We're building a solid case," he said. "But, apart from catching Billingsley red-handed, we'll need more evidence if we're going to convince Linton. We stick to the plan. We focus on beating Birds of a Feather to get our shot at the Krackle Kiddos in the ring."

"And to beat Birds of a Feather," said Tamiko in a serious tone, "we need the Ragtag Team to be total faces."

"Speaking of Birds of a Feather," said Ollie. He pulled a full-body chicken suit out of Billingsley's closet. "What's up with this?"

CHAPTER 16

TAMIKO

TAMIKO walked into study hall.

"My oh my," said Mrs. Martino, "what a lovely dress!"

"Thanks," said Tamiko. She'd been hearing that *all* day. That morning, she'd woken up and resolved to put her best foot forward. Or rather, her best "face" forward.

If Hollis can make a face turn, then so can I, she thought.

So she got out of bed and put on the outfit she'd successfully hidden in the back of her closet for years: the disgustingly adorable, polka-dotted, floral-print dress her grandparents had given her when they visited from overseas.

And though it pained her, she even wore the matching polka-dotted bow on her head.

She hardly recognized herself. So it was no surprise to her that no one—not her parents, not her teachers, not even her best friend—had recognized her, either.

"I hardly recognized you!" said Mrs. Martino.

"Get in line," said Tamiko. She paused, remembering the task at hand. "I mean, thanks."

She crossed the room and took her seat.

Ollie leaned over. "I still can't get over this face turn, Tamiko. Also, I thought I remembered you saying you buried that outfit so it couldn't harm anyone."

Part of her wished she had, but that's not what faces did.

So she turned, smiled, and said, "Figured I should look the part."

"What part?" asked the Krackle Kiddos as they took their seats. "Judging from that outfit, Tamiko, you look like you're auditioning to be the teacher's pet."

She wanted to say that Leon and Luna could keep their spoiled opinions to themselves. But faces didn't say that, either.

So instead she said, "There's nothing wrong with looking presentable."

"Exactly right, Tamiko," said Ollie as he tucked in his shirt.

"But wait," said Luna, eyeing Tamiko, "I think something is missing."

"Missing?"

Ollie gasped as he realized. "Your phone! It's gone."

Tamiko raised both of her empty hands up. "Rules are rules. It's safe in my pocket. Besides, this might be a good time to get a little bit of reading in." She scooped out the rule book Ollie had given her from her backpack. "I read it cover to cover. Pretty interesting stuff."

She felt her stomach turn as the words came out of her mouth.

Luna squinted. "You're acting very weird today."

"Since when do you care so much about rules and dressing up?" demanded Leon.

She might have been a face, but faces fought back, too—albeit by the book.

"Rules are actually pretty interesting," she said. "Especially when you realize how many of them can be *broken*. Makes you think about how important it is to win fair and square."

"She makes a good point," said Ollie, in support.

"Duh," said Leon. "*We're* the wrestlers here."

"We know how the rules work," said Luna.

"That's funny," said Mrs. Martino from the front of the class. There was no hint of laughter in her voice. "Because for students who know as many rules as you four apparently do, you all seem to have forgotten that one of them is that study hall is meant to be silent."

The Krackle Kiddos ignored her and started watching a livestream video of a newborn baby panda at maximum volume. Tamiko *really* wanted to watch, but she wasn't done showing off her face turn yet. She stood and crossed the room.

"Where are you going?" asked Ollie.

"To sharpen my pencil," she said as she approached the pencil sharpener, sharpened her pencil, then grabbed the hall pass and held it up for all to see.

"Tamiko, that's *very* face of you," he whispered.

Tamiko hustled toward the vending machines. It felt good to have Ollie acknowledge her face turn and she didn't want to disappoint him by being away too long.

However, her path was predictably blocked by Breonna.

"First, that outfit is the best," said Breonna. "Please tell me where you got it. But second, and more important, I'm going to need to see a hall pass. A *real* one."

"Here you go." Tamiko dug her hall pass out of her backpack. "It's official."

"I'll be the judge of that."

Breonna examined every inch of the hall pass. She even chewed the laminated corner.

"Does it taste real?" asked Tamiko.

"I can't believe I'm saying this, but yes, this pass is official," she declared, handing the saliva-covered hall pass back. "I'm proud of you, Tamiko."

Another face test passed, she thought.

"Just be careful not to change too much," said Breonna.

Tamiko made her way back to study hall and quietly took her seat.

She felt Ollie's eyes on her the entire period. A few times her hand instinctively drifted down to her pocket, and the urge to play games nearly overcame her. But, by the time the bell rang, Tamiko hadn't pulled her phone out once.

"Wow," exclaimed Ollie. "That was the full study hall and you didn't crack."

"I know! It's not easy, but it kinda feels good to be good."

Emphasis on the kinda, she thought.

Tamiko carried her good vibes home, where there was more face work to be done.

Each night she would boot up *Slimey Soccer*, the highly

popular multiplayer sports game where you played soccer on a field covered in a green, gooey slime.

She launched her video game stream and made a stunning announcement to her followers, one that sent numerous shocked-face emojis into the chat log.

"We're going for sportsmanship here, people," she said into her gaming headset. "Got to play nice and set a good example."

Tamiko hopped into a match. Her squad had a strong start, but her teammates began to miss simple plays and, despite *her* incredible efforts, the team suffered a lopsided defeat.

Normally, she'd tell them to delete their games and sell their consoles.

But tonight was different.

That didn't mean she didn't *want* to say that. She wanted to, maybe more than ever, *because* she knew that she couldn't. However, she swallowed her heel and took a breath.

"We all make mistakes," she said in an encouraging tone. "Occasionally even twelve times in a row!" She stopped herself before finishing. "So don't worry about it."

No matter how bad the loss or how egregious the error, Tamiko kept her trash talk nonexistent. Her teammates were appreciative, her followers confused. They kept asking if someone had hijacked her stream. She'd laugh and say that she decided to turn over a new leaf.

A more gentle, caring, and understanding leaf.

The dozen or so subscribers she lost were unfortunate but necessary sacrifices. No cost was too high when it came to beating Birds of a Feather tomorrow.

"It's been good, streamer family," she said after a devastating overtime loss. "Great effort out there. We've all accidentally scored on our own team when it mattered most. Well, I haven't, but I can see how it could happen. But this gamer is officially done for the night. Remember to keep those chats clean and polite. See ya later."

She shut off her console. The night was far from over, however. One more read-through of the Slamdown Town rule book before lights-out was in order.

Just in case she'd forgotten any of the bylaws.

CHAPTER 17

TAMIKO

"LET'S do this," said Tamiko. "After you, of course."

Wrestling Saturday had arrived, and with it, the Ragtag Team's first match, against Birds of a Feather. After spending the school week working on becoming a face, Tamiko was ready to put her skills into action both in and out of the ring. So, in true face fashion, she and Ollie held open the front door of Slamdown Town for her dad.

"Well, aren't I getting the royal treatment," he said as he walked into the lobby. "You've both been so polite this morning."

"Being polite really sets the day off on the right foot," said Tamiko.

"Which is the foot people like to start off on the most," added Ollie.

Her dad laughed. "I'm a lefty myself, but I appreciate the sentiment."

They passed a trio of eighth graders wearing BIRDS OF A FEATHER FLOCK TOGETHER tees. She wanted to tell them that the Ragtag Team were about to ruffle their feathers, but that wouldn't be very face of her. So she kept her mouth shut.

"What is that smell?" asked Ollie.

Tamiko sniffed the air. "I don't know. And I don't like it."

"Speaking of things we don't know," said her dad. "Who is that?"

Behind the snack counter stood a squat man with a waxed goatee and a bulbous, protruding gut. He wore a droopy chef's hat and a long white chef's coat over solid-black pants.

"Who are you?" asked Tamiko.

"I am Jean-Pierre Le Papon," said the large man as he tossed spices into a skillet with one hand and chopped vegetables with the other. "World-renowned chef. Culinary extraordinaire. Master of fine cuisine. And now resident Slamdown Town snack counter worker."

"Oh, good," said her dad. "I guess we'll be cooking together."

Jean-Pierre laughed. "Jean-Pierre does not create masterpieces with another. He cooks alone. Which is exactly what the Krackle Kiddos hired me to do."

Tamiko looked at the menu, which was filled with foods she had never eaten before with prices that she definitely couldn't afford. Things like linguine with clams, lobster bisque, and something called "huitlacoche" that had the horrifying words *corn fungus* next to it.

"Is this some kind of joke?" asked Ollie.

"More like a nightmare," interjected Tamiko. She wanted to

scream, but her face training kept her anger in check. At least temporarily.

"Where are the nachos with cheese?" cried Ollie.

"And the candy and hot dogs?" asked Tamiko.

Jean-Pierre turned his nose up in disgust. "Who would ever serve such atrocities?"

"That would be me." Her dad smiled and held out his hand. "I'm in charge of the snacks 'round these parts. Or I guess I used to be."

But instead of shaking his hand, Jean-Pierre handed him a plate of food.

"Here. You try what *real* food is meant to be."

Her dad popped the tiny morsel into his mouth and crunched. "Hmm, tastes like . . ." He chewed, and chewed, and chewed some more. "Nothing?"

"Precisely," said Jean-Pierre.

"Who wants to eat nothing?" asked Ollie.

Jean-Pierre laughed. "Silly boy. You do not eat Jean-Pierre's food. You experience it."

"People don't come here to experience expensive food they can't pronounce," said Tamiko, shaking with anger. "They come to eat junk and watch sweaty people hurt each other."

"Specifically," said Leon and Luna as they entered the snack area, "they come here to watch us hurt everyone who stands in our way. What do you think of the new snacks?"

Tamiko would not let them get away with this. Her dad's livelihood was at stake.

And so were their snacks.

"Why did you do this?" asked Tamiko.

"You said how much you liked snacks, so we figured our friends deserved the best snacks that money can buy. That," said Leon, pointing to Jean-Pierre, "is one of the greatest chefs in the world. Daddy threw a fit when he saw how much Jean-Pierre's contract was . . ."

"But then we threw a bigger fit and he made the call," finished Luna.

"But this kind of food doesn't belong here," said Ollie.

"A little change never hurt anyone," said Luna.

"It did hurt someone. My dad. *He* was the guy you both fired."

"Hello," said her dad, waving.

Leon sighed. "We'll have Jean-Pierre whip him up something."

"To go," said Luna.

That did it. Tamiko was going to end this right here, right now. She took a step forward, prepared to transform into Game Over and knock some sense into the Krackle Kiddos.

"Ladies and gentlemen," boomed Screech Holler's voice. "Tonight's matches are about to begin. Please make your way to your seats to ensure you see every minute of the action!"

"Oh, wrestling calls," said Leon.

"We'll catch up with you two after we win again," said Luna. "Can't wait to hear how great you think we did and how much you like the new food."

And with that, the Krackle Kiddos ran out of the snack area.

"That is all for today," said Jean-Pierre to Tamiko's dad. "You will leave now."

Jean-Pierre clapped his hands and two burly security guards appeared. They both grunted and put a muscled arm on each of her dad's shoulders.

"I think those grunts mean it's time for *me* to go," said her dad.

"This isn't fair," shouted Tamiko. She was beyond angry; she was furious. Forget face training, her dad did *not* deserve to be treated like some nobody. "I demand justice. Or a boycott. Or at least some salty nachos, because I'm about to kick those Krackle Kiddos' spoiled butts!"

"Oh, bug," said her dad, leaning in and tousling her hair. "It's okay. Really. I'm fine. I know how much wrestling means to you. And you too, Ollie."

Ollie sighed. "I wish we could do something to help you."

"Don't even worry about it. You two enjoy your night. I'll pick you both up after."

Her dad gave Tamiko a kiss on the head before being led away by the guards.

Tamiko was stunned. Had that all really just happened? Her dad may not have known much about wrestling, but he knew what wrestling crowds wanted to eat. She watched as fan after fan approached the counter, read the menu, and walked away empty-handed and disappointed. Those that *wanted* to eat the advertised food were shocked to realize they couldn't afford it.

She took a deep breath. If she wasn't motivated to win before, she was now. The Krackle Kiddos cheating was one thing. But now they'd made it personal. Leon and Luna had to be stopped. Defeating Birds of a Feather was the first step toward doing so.

"Come on," said Tamiko, "I'm ready to kick some butt." Then she remembered her face training. "With a smile."

CHAPTER 18

OLLIE

BIG Chew stood next to Game Over at the top of the entrance ramp leading to the ring.

They were decked out from head to toe in the dazzling outfits that Ollie had assembled during the week. Their shimmering singlets, gleaming knee pads, sparkling boots, and flowing, tasseled capes were a symbol of the face gimmick they hoped to portray.

Emblazoned across their chests were the words:

RAGTAG TEAM

But there was nothing "ragtag" about them. Big Chew couldn't believe that, within a few days, they'd actually become a *team*: a united face duo prepared to win the crowd *and* the match.

"All right, everybody," shouted Screech Holler. "Put down

that expensive cuisine and give a hearty Slamdown Town welcome for our newest tag team partnership: the Ragtag Team. Featuring veteran wrestler and fan favorite Big Chew and the rookie Game Over!"

They made their way down the ramp and high-fived, fist-bumped, and elbowed every fan who stuck their hand or fist or elbow out. And that meant *every* fan.

The Ragtag Team needed to win the crowd's love, and there was no better way to do that than by directly interacting with the fans themselves. But, as he and Game Over made their way through the stands, Big Chew noticed that some people were beginning to get restless.

"I'm beginning to get restless," said one eighth grader. "Hurry up and wrestle!"

"We want wrestling," chanted the crowd, followed by a series of aggressive claps.

Screech seemed to agree. "I'm sorry, folks. I thought this was a wrestling match, not a meet and greet. We'll be here all day at this point, and I only get paid for the next two hours."

"Hey, Tamiko—er, Game Over," said Big Chew as he pulled her away from the crowd. "Maybe we should head to the ring now."

Game Over shook her head. "But I thought we were here to win the crowd?"

"We are, and that's why we have to get moving."

"Coming," she said as she signed one more autograph. "I think if I sign one more autograph my hand is going to cramp! Okay, just *one* more."

Big Chew and Game Over left the stands, wiped their feet on the mat outside the ring, and leapt over the ropes. They grabbed their microphones and, standing side by side, addressed the adoring crowd.

"It's great to see you again, Slamdown Town," said Big Chew. "And let me introduce you to my new partner, the faciest face you've ever seen. Give it up for Game Over!"

"Thank you," said Game Over, "that's me, a total face. And may I just say that wrestling in front of such an awesome crowd like this one is my dream come true."

Suddenly, a deafening *Cacaw* flew out of the speakers.

"That birdcall can mean only one thing," said Screech. "The tag team Birds of a Feather have landed. Throw some birdseed in the air for Paulette Parrot and Bald Eagle!"

Big Chew saw Birds of a Feather descend from the rafters with the help of a marginally safe pulley wire system. And as they soared over the ropes into the ring, he looked at Game Over and smiled. He was about to wrestle with his best friend in the whole world.

And while watching wrestling with her was great, this was way better.

With all the wrestlers gathered in the ring, the referee completed his pre-match inspection with no violations from either side. Not surprising, since both teams were faces. But while the referee may not have found anything odd, Big Chew certainly had.

"I noticed that the ropes were below the necessary tautness as I jumped in," said Big Chew to the referee. "The requirement is quite clear in the official rules and regulations."

Game Over agreed. "There are also multiple issues with mat cleanliness."

Big Chew walked to the turnbuckles and began to tighten the screws with his bare hands. Behind him, Game Over got down on her knees and wiped the mat down with a towel.

"When is the wrestling going to start?" asked Screech. "What do you say, folks? Are we here to watch a bunch of friendly janitors or are we here to watch some wrestling?"

"Wrestling!" shouted the crowd.

Big Chew left the ropes alone and rejoined Game Over, who tossed her towel aside. They had only been trying to help, but if the crowd wanted them to wrestle, then they'd do just that.

"Only one wrestler allowed in the ring at all times," said the referee. "Tag teams, choose your starting wrestler."

"Starting wrestler, starting wrestler," repeated Paulette Parrot, who, ironically, left the ring. That meant Bald Eagle and his oversize golden wig would be the first opponent.

"You know what, Game Over?" said Big Chew. He knew that what he said next would win the crowd *and* his partner. "Since this is your first match, you should wrestle first."

Game Over shook her head. "No. I couldn't. After all, you have all the experience."

"I insist," he said. "You should really go first."

Big Chew wouldn't budge. He needed to be a face, after all.

"You're clearly the right choice." Game Over waved to the crowd. "And I think everyone would agree."

"I think everyone would agree that we want the match to start!" yelled Screech. "What do *you* think, Slamdown Town? Would you rather see Big Chew or Game Over go first?"

"Game Over," answered the crowd.

Big Chew wasn't expecting that. After all, he was the

returning wrestler, the one who had practically saved Slamdown Town from closing. And now the crowd liked his new teammate better? He hated to admit it, like, *really* hated it. But there was no denying the arena's chants.

They had made their choice. And it wasn't him. A good face won the crowd's love, and in this moment, they seemed to love Game Over.

He leapt outside the ropes and readied himself to watch his best friend.

Ding! Ding! Ding!

The starting bell sent the two wrestlers colliding into each other. And from the moment the bell rang, one thing became immediately clear: Game Over could wrestle!

Game Over unleashed a blistering combo of strikes that sent Bald Eagle reeling. Bald Eagle regained his balance and landed a High-Flying Forearm into Game Over's gut. Game Over pounded her chest and countered with a Squeaky-Clean Toss that nearly toppled Bald Eagle out of the ring. But he recovered midair, launched himself off the top rope, and hit Game Over with a diving Spread Your Wings Spear.

"These moves just keep coming!" yelled Screech.

Being outside the ring was strange. Big Chew had watched many wrestling matches over the years, but none from the ropes. He was bewildered by Game Over's raw power and skill. It had taken him a few matches to get his footing, but not her. She was trading blows like she'd been doing it forever. It almost didn't seem right considering *he* had all the experience and she didn't. He wanted to be in there showing off what he knew he could do.

But Big Chew would need to wait for Game Over to tag him in, which, in the opposite corner of the ring, was exactly what Bald Eagle was doing to Paulette Parrot.

"Fly free, Paulette!" yelled Bald Eagle as he sailed over the ropes.

Paulette Parrot landed in the ring. "Fly free! Fly free!" she shouted.

"I'm guessing you could use a little break," shouted Big Chew, extending his hand over the ropes. "I'd be more than happy to take on Paulette."

But to his horror, Game Over shook her head. "No need. What kind of teammate would I be if I didn't do my part?"

She charged forward and attempted to grapple Paulette with a Hey How Are You Nice to Meet You Hold. That proved costly, as Paulette Parrot got her with a Tropical Trap Body Lock. She wrapped her feathery arms around Game Over and held her in place as if she were locked in a birdcage.

"If you could please let me go," shouted Game Over.

"Let you go! Let you go!" repeated Paulette Parrot as she slammed Game Over's sweat-covered face smack into the mat.

Game Over shook her head. "Well, I did ask you to let me go."

"She's given it all she's got, folks! But I do have to wonder when Big Chew's going to make his debut. After all, this is a team sport and I'm only seeing one teammate."

Screech was right. Thankfully, Game Over seemed to agree because she chose to sprint toward Big Chew rather than go another round with Paulette.

She slapped his hand and tagged him in.

"Sorry, buddy," said Game Over. "I was just trying to do what's best for the team. Now it's your time to shine."

He was finally going to get to wrestle.

"You've done an incredible job so far," said Big Chew. "Now I'll be sure to do my part for the team."

Big Chew turned to face Paulette.

Wham!

A blistering hit smacked him. He was fairly certain that it had not come from Paulette Parrot or Bald Eagle. That's because this blow came from behind. Which meant there could only be one culprit.

"Tamiko—err, Game Over," said Big Chew, rubbing the back of his head. "What gives?"

"The glitter, it burns!" yelled Game Over.

He turned around and saw Game Over thrashing around outside the ropes. Big Chew guessed that some glitter had gotten in her eyes. He didn't have time to ask because Game Over's muscly arm walloped him in the chest.

He stumbled, tripped on his cape, and toppled backward into the ropes.

"Looks like the Ragtag Team is having a fashion disaster, folks," said Screech.

He was suddenly grabbed by arms covered with brown and gold feathers.

"Here," said Bald Eagle as he scooped him up. "Let the soaring symbol of our proud nation show you how it's done!"

One moment, Big Chew was looking straight up at the cracked jumbotron. The next, Bald Eagle was slamming him into the mat with a Macaw Muscle Buster.

"That hurt my back, and I wasn't even in the ring," said Screech. "But that also might be my chiropractor's fault. I never should have gone in for that experimental treatment."

Big Chew had hoped for a better start for his big return. The match was not going his way. He looked up to see what Game Over was doing, but she wasn't in their corner.

He spotted her farther up the entrance ramp, dumping the contents of a water bottle into her eyes.

"Looks like you're on your own, Big Chew," said Bald Eagle. "As a solitary bird of prey, I understand. But as your opponent, I will totally take advantage of this."

The crowd began to chant, "Bald Eagle!"

Big Chew was hit with a Swooping Smash. And then a Wingspan Strike. *And then* a Birdbrain Body Press. It was hard to keep track of each and every move.

The barrage only stopped when Bald Eagle turned to the crowd and strutted back and forth as they cheered him on.

Big Chew crawled over to the ropes. He'd faced his fair share of bad situations in the ring. Going toe-to-toe with Gorgeous Gordon Gussett, Silvertongue, Barbell Bill, and Werewrestler had not been easy. Somehow, he'd always come through in the end.

But now it wasn't just on him. He wrestled with a partner. And even though they were both excellent faces, Big Chew and Game Over had somehow lost the crowd. And if they weren't careful, the Ragtag Team would lose the match, as well.

CHAPTER 19

TAMIKO

GAME Over felt cool relief as the water from the bottle splashed over her face. She wiped the moisture out of her eyes. Finally, she could see again.

And what she saw was Big Chew stretching his hand through the ropes.

"Pretty please with a cherry on top," said Big Chew from the ring.

Game Over sprinted toward him. "Don't worry. I'm ready to face them."

Wrestling had been everything she'd dreamed of, and more. And that was after having glitter fall into her eyes and nearly blinding her. But she didn't feel like herself.

Being a face made her feel like she was being held back. If that was what it took to win, however, then she'd do it.

Game Over slapped Big Chew's hand and pulled herself over the ropes.

She sprinted across the mat toward Bald Eagle.

"As a friendly warning," said Game Over, "you're about to get smacked."

Game Over swung her arm down on Bald Eagle's chest with a Can I Help You Chop. Then she hit him with another. And another. And as Bald Eagle staggered back and forth, Game Over wrapped her arms around him, locking him in a Have a Good Day Grapple.

The crowd began to chant.

"Game Over! Game Over! Game Over!"

She was pushing the pace now, and there was nothing that could slow her down. Well, except a face full of forehead.

Bald Eagle leaned forward and smashed Game Over with a Bashing Beak Headbutt. She fell face-first into the mat.

"That's using the old bird brain," shouted Screech.

Game Over got back up on her feet and saw Bald Eagle tag in Paulette.

"Hey, Game Over," said Big Chew from outside the ring. "I'm feeling so much better. If you need a rest, just let me know."

She got the feeling that Big Chew wanted to wrestle. And even though she wanted to keep going, it would not be very face if she refused.

She turned around to tag him in. "Of course. That's incredibly thoughtful of you. I'll take you up on that right—"

Big Chew's eyes went wide. "Look out behind you!"

Game Over felt Paulette's arms grapple her from behind.

This isn't going to end well, she thought. She didn't need Big Chew yelling that the Goose Step was coming to know that she was about to get a front-row seat to the signature Birds of a Feather tag team finishing move.

"It looks like the Ragtag Team's goose has officially been cooked," said Screech.

Paulette pulled Game Over to the center of the ring. She noticed Bald Eagle had hopped the ropes and was walking straight toward them.

"I hope you stowed any carry-on items you might have brought with you," said Bald Eagle. "Because you've been cleared for takeoff."

"Takeoff! Takeoff!" shrieked Paulette.

Bald Eagle hit Game Over with a devastating Goose Step High Kick that spun her around into Paulette's equally devastating Goose Step High Kick. Before she could regain her balance, both Bald Eagle and Paulette Parrot kicked Game Over once more at the same time.

She felt her legs give out as she tumbled to the mat. The Goose Step had lived up to its reputation.

Paulette Parrot lay on top of her, poking Game Over with her many feathers. And she was too dazed to wiggle free.

"I was always told not to count my chickens before they hatched," said Screech, "but I'd say that the Ragtag Team is cock-a-doodle-doomed!"

There was no escape. The referee pounded out his count on the mat.

"One! Two! Three . . ."

While the crowd counted out the pinfall, Game Over knew she was moments away from being defeated in her first match.

But she hated losing. Sure, she'd certainly lost her fair share of online video game matches. But being counted out in the ring and not being able to stop it was a whole other level of humiliation. She willed her body to break the pinfall.

"Seven! Eight! Nine . . ."

And at the last second she kicked out.

Thank goodness for Linton's greed, she thought. Otherwise, she'd have been pinned.

Game Over was lifted high into the air by Paulette. Her blue and green feathers brushed her skin as she was carried, flailing, toward the ropes.

"Look out below!" shouted Screech.

"Look out below! Look out below!" said Paulette, who for once meant what she said. And with that, she tossed Game Over over the ropes and out of the ring.

"Keep your fancy feathered hands away from my partner!" shouted Big Chew. "Please."

She looked into the ring, where Big Chew tackled Bald Eagle to the mat with a Let Me Carry Those Bags For You Takedown. Apparently Big Chew was too mad to bother tagging in.

But her attention was drawn to something glinting nearby.

An arm's length away, a folding chair jutted out from beneath the ring. One whack with that would send Birds of a Feather from soaring high to a crash-landing. While unbelievably tempting, that would not be a face thing to do.

But it was definitely something she would do. So she yanked the chair free.

"Did Game Over just grab an illegal chair?" asked Screech. "That's not very face-like!"

Inside the ring, Game Over watched Big Chew spear Bald Eagle into the mat. He was certainly seeing little birdies of his own circling around his head. And he was about to see more.

Game Over rolled under the ropes with the chair firmly in her hands.

It's time to end this, she thought.

"What are you doing?" asked Big Chew as she marched toward him.

"What I have to!"

She leveled the chair toward Bald Eagle's face and swung.

Bald Eagle (barely) remained standing. But his golden, luxurious wig flew off his head and sailed over the ropes, out of the ring, and into the crowd. The overhead lights bounced off of Bald Eagle's bald head and forced Game Over to squint.

"My goodness," yelled Screech. "It's like staring directly into the sun!"

"Don't look at me," cried Bald Eagle. He unsuccessfully attempted to shield his overwhelming baldness with his hands. "It's a genetic condition. And there's nothing the specialists can do about it!" He dissolved into a sobbing fit.

The heel turn had given her the in, and she was going to take it. She leapt on top of him and pinned him to the mat. The crowd chanted the pinfall.

"Eight! Nine! Ten!"

Ding! Ding! Ding!

"It wasn't pretty, folks," said Screech. "But thanks to that sudden and unexpected heel turn by Game Over, the Ragtag Team has won the match!"

Game Over stood up as the crowd booed her like they would a true heel.

"Game Over! Game Over! Game Over!"

This was what she had been waiting for. All those times watching Big Chew wrestle. All those nights dreaming about what it would finally be like to be in the ring.

She had won her first match in her own way. And the crowd loved her for it.

CHAPTER 20

OLLIE

BIG Chew and Game Over were surrounded by wrestlers the moment they entered the locker room. But despite winning as a team, he hadn't heard his name mentioned once.

"That was one good-looking debut performance out there, Game Over," said Gorgeous Gordon Gussett.

Barbell Bill gave Game Over a thumbs-up. "You strong. Me like."

"Using a chair to beat down old Baldy?" Silvertongue smirked. "That's a match with a little bite to it!"

A few months ago, it had been *him* that was surrounded by wrestlers the moment he completed a match. Now, Game Over was getting all the glory and she hadn't even stuck to the plan. He thought his first victory with his best friend would feel more like a . . . victory.

Game Over smiled. "That's right, everyone! Game Over is here, and despite the name, I ain't playing any games. I'm here to win! I mean, we're here to win. Isn't that right, Big Chew?"

"Oh, yeah," he said. "I'm here to win, too."

"Oh hey, Big Chew," said Silvertongue. "Nice job on getting such an awesome partner."

Barbell Bill nodded. "You smart. Pick good."

"I know I could never stand to share the runway," said Gorgeous Gordon Gussett.

After the last wrestler departed, Big Chew finally had a chance to chat with Game Over. He wanted to address the heel in the room.

"Dude, wasn't that amazing?" asked Game Over.

"Yeah, but it got pretty close there for a moment."

"Right? But we brought it back. My chair to Bald Eagle's face sealed the deal."

"It did," he started, "but despite involving a face, it really wasn't very face."

"You're right. I'm sorry for turning heel," she said.

He hadn't been expecting that.

She continued after a pause. "I know that wasn't part of the plan or what we had trained all week for, but I really thought we were going to lose if I didn't make the switch. And I've got to say, it was so much better than being a face. Once I had that chair in my hands I finally felt like myself. Does that make any sense?"

"For you," he said, "but I can't imagine Big Chew slamming anything into anyone's face, let alone an illegal chair. He can't do it. *I* can't do it."

He heard the words come out of his mouth. Sure, he'd won

rock, paper, scissors. Yes, they'd become faces. But Tamiko had *won* the match for them by turning heel. While he felt uncomfortable with the turn, they were a team, and that meant they needed to work together.

The sounds of wrestlers moving around the locker room filled the uncomfortable silence.

"Actually," said Big Chew, "you're right. If we want to win, we need to win together."

"And to do that . . ." started Game Over.

"We *both* need to get a heel-over," finished Big Chew.

"A heel-over? You'd do that?"

He smiled. "You did it for me."

"Well, if you're cool with it," said Game Over, "then I'm ready to officially turn heel. I just know that once we get on the same page we're going to be unstoppable."

Big Chew wished he shared Game Over's enthusiasm. But they had to try. After all, the Ragtag Team had turned face in a week. Kind of. They would figure it out, together.

"For now," said Big Chew, "how about we celebrate our win with a night of wrestling?"

Game Over smiled. "You know what, partner? That sounds like an excellent idea."

He heard Screech's voice over the crackling speakers. "If you aren't in your seats, you better get moving. Because the Krackle Kiddos are making their way toward the ring!"

So Big Chew and Game Over took his advice. They transformed back into their eleven-year-old selves and sprinted out of the backstage area and into the lobby. But as they made their way to the arena entrance, Ollie was distracted by Hollis and Breonna arguing.

"But Breonna-kins," he heard Hollis say, "all these changes are making me better."

"Did you even stop to consider what I want?" asked Breonna in an angry tone.

Whatever was going on between those two sounded intense. But love was for eighth graders and there were more important matters to attend to—like proving the Krackle Kiddos were cheaters and getting Mr. Tanaka his job back. Ollie and Tamiko didn't want to miss a second of their match and didn't stop running until their butts were firmly placed in their seats.

As he sat, he saw that the Krackle Kiddos were already hamming it up in the ring for the crowd, which happily rained boos down upon the middle-school duo.

"They don't deserve those boos," said Tamiko.

"Don't worry," said Ollie, noticing that the normal referee was standing in the ring. "They don't have a guest referee to save them this time."

Suddenly, the sound of ocean waves crashing flooded out of the arena speakers.

"Looks like there's choppy waters ahead, folks," announced Screech. "Because the tag team Tsunami is in the building! Let's hear it for Big Tuna and Cuttlefish."

Ollie watched as Tsunami made their way toward the ring. Big Tuna strutted down the entrance ramp, his massive belly leading the way. His hair was pulled back in a man bun and a necklace of fish bones hung around his neck. His partner, Cuttlefish, stood shoulder to shoulder with him. Cuttlefish wore shoulder pads that were fashioned to look like squid tentacles and he had pink face paint that streaked from beneath his eyes all the way down to his feet.

"There's no way the Krackle Kiddos beat them," said Ollie. "Right?"

Tamiko laughed. "I can't wait to see the looks on their spoiled faces when they get pinned."

"Are we supposed to be scared of a couple little fishies?" asked Leon as Tsunami climbed over the ropes and walked toward them as intimidating as possible.

"Come closer and see what real wrestlers look like," said Luna.

Tsunami brought their microphones up to their mouths.

"Ahh!" they both shouted, pointing above them.

"Ahh?" asked Screech. "What's ahh?"

It happened in the blink of an eye. Ollie watched as one moment Big Tuna and Cuttlefish were about to speak into their microphones. The next, the very large and very broken shark cage was plummeting down from the rafters, directly over the spot in the ring where they stood.

"Look out!" Ollie shouted.

But they didn't have time to move. Instead of diving out of the way, Big Tuna and Cuttlefish lifted their hands above their head and caught the cage upon impact.

They teetered, they tottered, and they gasped as the weight of the shark cage proved too great. The two behemoths collapsed and were pinned under the cage, caught like fish in a net.

"They're stuck," said Ollie in shock. "How are they going to fight if they can't move?"

Ding! Ding! Ding!

The starting bell sounded. Ollie watched as the Krackle Kiddos sprinted forward. The two middle schoolers each grabbed on to an opponent's leg—the only visible body parts sticking out from under the shark cage—and lifted it into the air.

The referee slid beside them and slapped out the count.

"Eight! Nine! Ten!"

"This is the most insane, the most ludicrous, and the most egregious use of a shark cage I have ever seen," shouted Screech. "The Krackle Kiddos have won this match in record time!"

No one clapped. Or booed. Ollie wasn't sure if anyone had even realized the match was over yet. But Leon and Luna were parading around the ring, pumping their arms in excitement.

Above them where the shark cage had fallen fell a giant victory banner that read:

KRACKLE KIDDOS FUTURE CHAMPS

"Those cheaters did it again," said Tamiko. "And what's more—we gave them the idea. They only knew about the broken shark cage because we told them about it."

Ollie considered for a moment. "But they would have needed someone to lower the cage for them while they were in the ring. And there's only one man they could order to do that."

"Billingsley!" shouted Tamiko. "We need to investigate this. And fast!"

They ran off toward the staging area in the attic above the arena. Ollie and Tamiko had discovered the room years ago during one of their unauthorized explorations of the arena.

Anything that needed to be lowered into the ring was controlled there, whether that was wrestlers descending from the ceiling on pulleys, the shark cage, or a victory banner.

When they arrived, Ollie and Tamiko found the door to the staging area wide open. Lights on the control board blinked between the many levers, buttons, and switches. Farther down, an assortment of pulleys hung above the ring.

But the room was completely empty.

"He got away!" yelled Tamiko. "But maybe he left some sort of evidence behind."

Ollie whipped out his magnifying glass. "Let's investigate."

But there wasn't a muddy footprint, an incriminating strand of hair, or a written confession to be found. In fact, there was no sign of any wrongdoing at all. Ollie tried dusting for prints, but either there were no fingerprints anywhere or the toy kit was too cheap to work.

Tamiko stomped her feet. "But it has to be him. We already saw him handing the Terrible Twosome the money. Then we caught him with the fake mustache and the referee uniform. He's a criminal mastermind. He probably knew to clean the place before he left."

Ollie was just about ready to give up when he spotted it. There, sitting in plain sight for anyone to see, was a lone camera hanging from the ceiling in the corner of the room.

"I bet that camera caught Billingsley in the act," said Ollie.

"Nice detective work," said Tamiko, examining the camera. "But there's a problem. That footage is only stored in one place, and I'm pretty sure you know where that is."

Ollie did know. He'd seen the SECURITY COMMAND CENTER sticker as Big Chew last Saturday when they had first confronted Linton in his office.

"So what are we going to do?" asked Ollie.

"I'll tell you what we're going to do."

Ollie had a feeling he wasn't going to like this.

"You're not going to like this, but we're going to have to break into his office."

His feeling was correct. He didn't like it. Not one bit. But he also knew they didn't really have a choice. If they wanted that footage, they would need to plan—and pull off—a heist.

CHAPTER 21

OLLIE

BZZ! Bzz!

Ollie's phone vibrated in his pocket. His eyes went wide when he checked who it was. "Why is Linton Krackle calling me at school on a Monday morning?" asked Ollie.

"I gave him your number for Game Over's manager, remember?" said Tamiko.

Ollie felt like he was going to faint. "Ugh! Why? I'm terrible at stuff like this."

"You'll be great. Come on, pick up," demanded Tamiko. "You totally owe me for all the times I had to talk to him as Ms. Manager. Pick up, pick up, pick up, pick up . . ."

Tamiko was right. She'd previously handled all of Big Chew's match arrangements by pretending to be a high-powered businesswoman with a super-important client.

And though he hated talking on the phone to anyone, much less a sleazy slimeball like Linton Krackle, he supposed he should return the favor.

"Fine, but here?"

The second bell had yet to ring and the hallways were flooded with traffic. Ollie was fine—enough, anyway—to talk to Linton, but he couldn't do it in front of an audience.

Bzz! Bzz!

"We need to go somewhere private." Tamiko grabbed him by the collar and dragged him down the hallway.

"Where are we going?"

"Somewhere private. How about"—they rounded another corner—"here?"

The sign on the open door read:

TEACHERS' LOUNGE

"Can't you read?" asked Ollie. "No students are allowed in there."

Tamiko ushered him into the empty lounge and closed the door behind them. Ollie felt calling the blank room a lounge was a stretch. Stained coffee mugs and stacks of forgotten papers littered the tables. There was a poster on the wall of a sandy beach with a taped note that read:

IS IT SUMMER YET?

"You're a heel now, Ollie." Tamiko grabbed a doughnut from an open box on the table and stuffed it in her mouth. "That means the rules are meant to be broken and you no longer care about what other people think. Everyone else can deal! Wow, this is stale. Want one?"

"I know what a heel does." The phone continued to buzz in his hand. "But this is crazy!"

"He's just going to keep calling until you answer. So pick up already!"

Ollie gulped, accepted the call, and put it on speaker.

"Is this Game Over's manager?" demanded Linton over the phone.

"Yep. This is he," said Ollie in his most serious voice. "And you're—"

"Linton Krackle. The one and only. Unless I accidentally dialed the IRS, then there are many Linton Krackles and I'm most certainly not the one you're looking for. Pleased to meet you, Mister . . ."

Ollie stood there, mouth open. He could be *anyone*, but no one was coming to mind.

"Say something," hissed Tamiko.

"Uh, Mr. Manager?" stammered Ollie.

Tamiko's jaw dropped.

Ollie covered the phone. "Sorry. I panicked," he admitted.

"Mr. Manager. Huh. Any relation to Ms. Manager?" asked Linton.

"What? No! Anyway, how can I make you money today?"

"Already thinking about what's profitable. I like that." Linton smacked his lips. "Exciting news about your client's first win, hey? Bit rocky on the team's, you know . . . teamwork, though."

"Don't worry." Ollie took a deep breath. "Faces are out. Heels are in."

"I'm glad to hear that! You know, the fans want somebody they can easily get behind. Cheer for the good guys, boo for the bad. But it sounds like they know what they're doing. I can already hear the sweet melody of dollar bills dancing their way into my wallet."

"I don't actually think that's a sound," said Mr. Manager.

"I stand by my statement. Mainly, my bank statement." The sound of shuffling papers drifted through the phone speaker. "Which is where I scribbled the name of Game Over's next opponent. Here it is! 'Overdue late payment fee'? Wait, no, that isn't it. Ah, here we go: Full Throttle."

Ollie took a sharp breath. Full Throttle was the fierce, high-octane duo of Mack Truck, the wrestler known for his unending fuel for revenge, and Road Rage, whose legendary temper earned her tickets inside and outside the arena. They wouldn't be easy to beat.

"The Ragtag Team will beat them easily," lied Mr. Manager.

"We'll see about that," said Linton. "I'll call Ms. Manager to confirm Big Chew."

Tamiko leaned into the speaker and added, "Make sure to have a tow truck ready because the Ragtag Team is going to turn Full Throttle into total wrecks!"

"Who said that?" asked Linton.

"Goodbye!" yelled Ollie, who promptly hung up.

"Hello," said Breonna, who was standing in the office doorway. "I thought I heard you whippersnappers in here. I gotta say you have an incredibly deep phone voice, Ollie."

"Um, thanks."

"You're welcome," she said with a smile. "But it is my duty as hall monitor to also say that the teachers' lounge is not for personal phone calls. Back in my day, we respected the rules and I expect the same from you two."

"Sorry, Breonna," said Ollie. "We were here to, umm . . ."

"Ask about extra credit," lied Tamiko.

"But there were no teachers here, so we decided to call them," added Ollie.

He was certain they were caught. But to his great surprise and relief, Breonna nodded.

"Understandable, given the circumstances," she said. "It warms my heart to see students so dedicated to their studies. I'll let you both off with a warning. Now move those keisters, bell's about to ring."

They beat a hasty retreat. Or tried to, until they ran directly into Hollis.

His brother had bags under his eyes and a vein in his forehead throbbed. Ollie knew that vein only throbbed when Hollis was super upset.

"I'm super upset," he said. "Breonna, can't we just talk about this?"

"Do you have a hall pass?" she asked flatly.

Hollis pulled one out of his pocket.

"I do," said Hollis. "And I also have a hall pass in my heart for you."

Breonna snatched the slip out of Hollis's hand.

"Still carrying hall passes?" she asked, her voice rising. She examined the paper. "Gosh golly, this isn't even one of your fakes. What's gotten into that head of yours, Hollis? I don't even know you anymore."

"Um, what's going on here?" asked Ollie.

Breonna sighed. "Hollis and I are taking some much-needed time apart."

"It's been an hour. Isn't that long enough?" Hollis asked.

"No. I'd give you a warning for being in the hall without a hall pass, but since you already have one, let me give you a warning to respect my decision to no longer date you."

And with that she headed off down the hallway.

"What did you do, Hollis?" asked Ollie. Even though he didn't know what had happened, he knew his brother well enough to know that it was probably his fault.

"According to her friends, Breonna likes . . ." He gulped. "Bad boys. And I'm too good now, apparently. Whoever thought that being nice would make you feel so bad?" He held the guide to being a perfect boyfriend up and smacked it against his forehead.

Ollie tried to think of words to console his brother, but before he could, he felt himself being yanked backward by Tamiko's strong grip.

"Well, good luck with that, Hollis," she said. "We've got things to attend to."

They left Hollis sitting on the floor alone, sniffling to himself.

Whatever was going on, Ollie wanted no part of it. While he felt a tiny bit guilty leaving his brother alone and upset, he had enough on his plate already.

"We gotta stay focused. This is heel week, so any future apologizing stops now," said Tamiko as they walked to English class. "Not only do we have to figure out a way to get into Linton's office and access the security footage, but we've only got a few days to train in the ancient heel ways. It's gonna be great!"

For the first time, Ollie dreaded the fact that he was going to wrestle. Despite their victory, the weight of this weekend's match still burdened him. He'd been certain that having the Ragtag Team fight as faces would lead them to victory. They'd won, but only when Tamiko had gone rogue and turned heel. Now it was Ollie's turn to, well, turn.

He gulped. "I don't think I'm built for this."

"You aren't," confirmed Tamiko. "But that's why you got me, okay? We got this. By the way," she continued, "I was thinking about the costumes, and we can't salvage them. I've got glitter everywhere and glitter is *definitely* not heel. But I spent all day yesterday rummaging through my dad's old cosplay outfits for the nastiest, darkest, most intense pieces I could find. I really had to dig deep." Ollie followed Tamiko to her locker, where she pulled out a trash bag. "Take a peek inside. They're a work in progress, but what do you think?"

He felt his stomach drop. Dark didn't even begin to describe the items inside. He spotted a set of crumpled black pants and T-shirts that looked (and smelled) filthy, along with two pairs of ebony leather gloves. There was a tube of neon purple face paint, a pile of tangled silver chains, and, for some reason, a handful of ketchup packets. Whatever Tamiko had in mind, their costumes would be downright sinister. And while that design may work great for Game Over, Ollie doubted Big Chew could ever pull off that look.

"Whoa. That's a lot of black," said Ollie.

"Huh? Really? I thought we could go a little darker. And by a little I mean a lot."

"And the ketchup packets?" asked Ollie.

"How else are we going to write our names in blood-splattered letters?"

Ollie stepped toward the classroom, but walked straight into Tamiko's outstretched arm.

"What are you doing?" he asked.

"Rules are there for heels to break, piledrive, and hit over the head with an illegal chair. So today you're going to break one by being late to English class."

"But I've never been late to class. And I've got the perfect attendance award to prove it!"

Tamiko shrugged. "Well pre-congrats then, because today is your first day of tardiness."

A bead of sweat dripped down his back as the clock ticked. Was this really necessary? Yes, a heel wouldn't worry about being late to class. But his perfect on-time record was the one his mom was most proud of. She framed each award and hung them prominently on the walls at home.

"I can't do this!" screamed Ollie. He lurched forward and dove into his seat a second before the bell rang. Tamiko accepted her late marking from Mr. Fitzgerald before sitting down next to Ollie with a clear look of disappointment on her face.

"A heel would have no regard for tardiness," she whispered while taking out her phone. "We show up when we want to and don't let anyone tell us otherwise."

"But it's against the rules. Plus, my mom would be super disappointed in me."

Tamiko looked frustrated, either at the game she was playing on her phone or him. Or both. "The only rule for a heel is that there are no rules! Also, disappointed moms are probably a badge of honor for heels, don't you think?"

If this was what it took to be a heel, then Ollie *definitely* knew he wasn't cut out for it. That fact didn't excuse him from trying, though. The Ragtag Team needed to be united or they wouldn't stand any shot of beating Full Throttle or the Krackle Kiddos.

As if summoned by his thoughts, Leon and Luna Krackle walked into the room. And not in a hurry, either. Each sipped on large drinks that Ollie bet were imported from somewhere very expensive and far away but only cost them a temper tantrum.

"Late as usual, I see," said Mr. Fitzgerald as the Krackle Kiddos strutted past him.

"You say that like it's a bad thing," said Leon.

"It is a bad thing!" said Mr. Fitzgerald. "Now, take your seats so we can begin."

They crossed the room and sat in the chair behind his desk. Yes, the big leathery one with the extra-cushiony butt cushion that Mr. Fitzgerald had proudly showed off when it arrived. Every kid in class knew that he never let *anyone* sit in it.

And now Leon and Luna were splayed out, leaning back, and spinning around in it.

"What do you think you're doing? I said take *your* seats."

"We did! We claim this one. It's got really nice butt support."

Everyone in class laughed, Ollie included.

"Heh, 'butt,'" said Tamiko.

But Ollie could see that Mr. Fitzgerald's patience, like his hairline, was running thin. "Quiet down, everyone! There's nothing funny about butt pain."

Everyone howled with laughter.

"I said quiet down! And you two," he said, rounding on Leon and Luna, "you may be king and queen of the ring, but in this arena *I* am in charge. Now take your seats this instant!"

Ollie waited with bated breath for their reaction. Was an epic Krackle Kiddos tantrum coming? To his surprise, they stood and crossed the room.

"If this is your arena," said Luna, "then it stinks."

Leon pinched his nose. "Just like your breath. And we want no part of either."

They took their seats in front of Ollie and, once seated, turned and winked at him.

He smiled back, but quickly remembered he was supposed to be a heel. So he furrowed his brow, gritted his teeth, and contorted his face to look as intimidating as possible.

"Feeling okay, Ollie?" asked Luna.

"Yeah," said Leon, "you look constipated or something."

"My goodness, folks," said Tamiko in her best Screech Holler impression. "I sure am glad I'm not seated behind Ollie because the only thing he's going to pass today is gas!"

"You sound like that arena guy," said Luna. "Squawk Shouty? Yelly McLoudface?"

Tamiko snorted with laughter. "Screech Holler, the iconic voice of Slamdown Town."

"Is he though?" asked Leon. "His one claim to fame is being loud."

"But Screech is a whole other level of loud," said Ollie. "A night of listening to him makes my ears ring the whole next day."

"Mine are still ringing right now!" yelled Tamiko.

Mr. Fitzgerald cleared his throat. "And mine are still ringing from everyone talking during class. So everyone, please take out your notebooks and get to work."

The students responded in the same rowdy manner the Krackle Kiddos had. Namely, they ignored him. Classmates openly chatted with one another. Tamiko blatantly played games on her phone without even trying to hide it. Ollie doodled wrestlers in his notebook, but at least he was being quiet about it. That's what he had been asked to do, so he made sure to do it.

"That is enough," cried Mr. Fitzgerald. "If you all do not settle down this instant, I will assign everyone here extra homework tonight. Oh, yes," he assured them when they scoffed, "I have that kind of power. Now, keep your heads down. Be quiet, and get to work."

His threat brought the classroom to order. Everyone has a line, and apparently extra homework crossed it. The room grew silent as the students focused on the work in front of them.

Ollie felt a sudden tap on his shoulder.

"This is your chance to go heel," whispered Tamiko. "Earn the crowd's hate!"

She had to be kidding.

"But we'll all get punished," he whispered back.

"You're not thinking like a heel, Ollie! Heels gotta act out, do stuff that makes the crowd hate them. And you know what the crowd would hate more than anything right now?"

Ollie knew the answer but didn't want to say it.

"You know the answer but don't want to say it," said Tamiko. "So I will. Extra credit." She reached under her desk and pulled out a straw and a spitball to go with it.

"I can't do that," he whispered.

"Come on." She shoved the straw toward him. "Give it a try. It'll feel good."

Ollie was frozen. Yes, he knew this was what heels did. But why did doing what heels did make him feel so wrong? He couldn't bring himself to accept the straw. Instead, he focused his full attention on his own desk. Tamiko was probably staring daggers at him from behind. He knew she was disappointed in him, but worse, he was disappointed in himself.

When the bell finally rang, Ollie wondered whether it signaled the end of class or the end of the Ragtag Team's chances of turning heel.

CHAPTER 22

TAMIKO

"DAD? Are you almost ready?"

Tamiko's heart thumped against her chest. Part of it was nerves, part adrenaline. Either way, she was anxious to get moving. It wasn't every day that she and Ollie planned on breaking into Linton's office. But that's exactly what they were going to do tonight.

That morning, Tamiko had asked her dad to drive her and Ollie over to Slamdown Town after school.

Obviously she couldn't tell her dad why, but he usually didn't ask too many questions.

"Going to the arena on a school night?" he'd asked. "That sounds fun. Can I come? What's the occasion? Should I dress business or casual?"

Ever since he'd been let go from his job he'd been obsessed about anything and everything Slamdown Town. And since

Tamiko was a huge wrestling fan (and a secret wrestler, to boot) it was mentioned a lot.

"Wrestling's only on Saturdays, Dad." She tried to think of a convincing lie. "I'm trying to get the high score on *Brawlmania Supreme*. Ollie's going to coach me through it. It's easier without so many other fans there."

Little did he know that she'd already claimed that spot.

"Oh, video games. Of course. Silly me. You don't need me for that."

He'd been really weird about video games, too. She figured it was because, despite the hours she'd spent training him, he still didn't know how to play them. Even the easy ones. Which was why gaming was something she did exclusively with her mom.

"Yeah! I'm super-duper close to beating it. Pretty please, Dad?"

"Well, okay! I'll drive you," he'd said before handing her a lunch bag and sending her out the door to the bus. Now it was after school and she was ready to go.

"Dad? Did you hear me?"

"Hey, bug," he yelled from the basement. "Can you come down here? There's something I want you to see. It's a surprise!"

She ran downstairs and discovered her dad's head poking out from behind a makeshift curtain. In front of the curtain, on her dad's workbench, were heaps of clothing (some of it intact, most of it in tatters), scissors, glue, and an industrial-grade sewing machine.

"Dad?"

"Take a seat and prepare to be wowed," he said, pulling the

curtain closed and hiding behind it. "Presenting the newest wrestler at Slamdown Town. The one, the only, Snack Guy!"

He pulled the curtain back and skated out into the open.

Tamiko's jaw dropped.

She was used to seeing her dad in costumes, but this was something else. To start, he was wearing his old Slamdown Town concession stand uniform. But over that, he'd built a giant serving tray with oversize, fake hot dogs, nachos, and soda cartons. He wore a cape of empty chip bags and, on his head, had placed a jumbo-size popcorn tub as a hat. He'd slipped on some roller skates and, across his chest, had written SNACK GUY in gold sparkly letters.

"Well, what do you think?" he said as he skated around her.

"I'm . . ."

"Speechless? I know, right? How cool is this! Now I'll be able to hang out with you again at Slamdown Town each weekend. Just like it was before!"

"Wait, you don't mean . . ."

"Yup, I'm going to try out for wrestling!"

Tamiko imagined her dad roller-skating down the entrance ramp, not being able to stop, and crashing into the "rounded box," as he called it. He'd probably think the turnbuckles were turnstiles and that whichever wrestler made all the bowling pins fall down first won the match.

"But, Dad, you don't know anything about wrestling."

"I know a little! And besides, you're a wrestling expert. You can show me the ropes! Like, the actual ropes that the wrestlers launch themselves off of."

Tamiko was conflicted. On the one hand, this was the

happiest she'd seen her dad since he'd been fired. But on the other hand, her dad *didn't* know anything about wrestling.

If—somehow—he managed to convince Linton to sign him (which she knew from experience wasn't very hard), he'd be absolutely destroyed.

"Look, I know, I know, it needs some work," he said as he crossed his roller skates and crashed into his workbench. "But I think I can do this! Don't you?"

"Are you sure this is what you want?" she asked, concerned.

She wanted to support her dad and, like he said, who knew more about wrestling than her? Perhaps she could help him, after all.

"It is! Look out world . . . Snack Guy, with help from his daughter, is going to be the new Slamdown Town champion!"

"You'd have to defeat Ollie's mom first."

"I'm glad you guys are best friends because that lady scares me!" He shivered. "Any advice on how to take her down?" He skated across the room and crashed again.

Tamiko laughed. "Maybe start by ditching the roller skates."

"I knew something was off! Good call! I'll change and then we'll pick up Ollie and head over to Slamdown Town. I have a good feeling you're going to beat that high score!"

Lying to her dad may have made him feel good, but it left Tamiko feeling uneasy. It certainly was a very heel thing to do. Her dad had about the same chance of becoming a wrestler as Hollis did. Basically, none bordering on impossible. But she'd worry about that later.

For now, she and Ollie needed to get their hands on that security footage.

CHAPTER 23

TAMIKO

BREAKING into Slamdown Town after hours was surprisingly easy. In fact, it was far less "breaking in" as it was she and Ollie walking straight through the unlocked front door.

"Good thing Linton never installed any kind of *real* security system," said Tamiko.

"Are we even sure those cameras are real? Maybe they're just for show."

"I hope not, or this whole operation will be a bust."

Tamiko had never been to Slamdown Town when it was closed. Most of the lights were off and their footsteps echoed down the hallway—at least the parts that weren't coated with nacho cheese. It was nice having the arena to themselves without hundreds of jostling fans. It almost felt like the good old days. Except now they were breaking and entering.

"If we get caught, my mom is going to ground me for life," said Ollie.

"So then we make sure not to get caught. If we want to prove that the Krackle Kiddos are cheating, this is how we do it. Besides, this is heel week."

"So?" asked Ollie.

"Start acting like one," she responded, slapping his back. "All the proof we need is in Linton's office. And I know exactly how to get in there."

She pulled out her phone and dialed Linton's number.

"Do you really think this will work?" asked Ollie.

"Of course," lied Tamiko.

Suddenly, Linton answered the phone. "Hello and how can you make me money?"

Tamiko pinched her nose to disguise her voice. "Congratulations, Mr. Krackle. You're the winner of our National Best Parking Lot sweepstakes."

"I am?"

"You are! We've searched far and wide for the best parking lots across this great nation and, what do you know, yours is the best. We've taken the liberty of dumping the prize money onto your truly remarkable parking lot. But you better get out there before it all blows away."

"Prize money? It is blustery out today!" he said, hanging up.

Suddenly, his office door flew open and he sprinted out toward the parking lot. The sound of his cheap shoes slapping against the floor grew quieter and quieter.

Tamiko gave Ollie a look that said *Told ya so* without her even needing to say it.

"Told ya so," she said anyway.

They scurried into the broom closet–size office and shut

the door. The cluttered space seemed a bit bigger now that she wasn't a massive wrestler but still smelled of stale coffee, mothballs, and leather. On his desk was an unorganized pile of messy financial papers.

"Let's get what we need and get out before we get caught." Ollie looked at the clock. "We don't know how long it will take Linton to find out there wasn't actually a sweepstakes."

"All right, all right. Keep your wrestling undies on."

Tamiko plopped down in Linton's big leather chair and wiggled the computer mouse.

A prompt displayed on-screen:

PASSWORD REQUIRED

Tamiko grinned. "This'll be easy."

MONEY. MOREMONEY. ILOVEMONEY.

None of them worked. Linton was smarter than he looked. So she decided to get more creative with her tries.

OFFSHOREACCOUNT. PILESOFGOLD. TENSANDTWENTIES.

"This isn't working," said Ollie, who kept staring at the door.

"I don't get it. I've entered everything about money that I can think of."

Ollie sighed. "Look, maybe we should leave and come back another day."

"No!" They were close. She wouldn't give up now. "There

must be something we're missing here. Ollie, put your detective cap on and look around the office for clues."

She and Ollie (with the help of his magnifying glass) searched for anything that might double as a password. And considering that Linton's office was the size of a broom closet, there wasn't much to look at. Scattered among the stacks of papers was a half-eaten beef sandwich, several fake gold chains, and the latest issue of *Sell Your Soul for Money* magazine.

"The only thing left on his desk was this." Ollie handed her a picture frame. Inside was a photo of twin toddlers who Tamiko guessed were Leon and Luna.

"Hmm, I wonder . . ." Tamiko typed in her worst password attempt yet.

LEONANDLUNA

It wasn't like it would work—

Her jaw dropped.

"It worked!" she said, hardly believing it.

"His password was his kids?" asked Ollie, shocked. "That doesn't make any sense."

"Maybe his heart isn't made of money after all. Now come on, let's get that proof."

The video files were arranged on the desktop by date. The mouse hovered over the file from last weekend. She wiped her sweaty hands on her pants and clicked.

Footage popped up on-screen from all over the arena. Or rather, anywhere Linton had a working camera. She saw guests picking their noses when they thought no one was looking, employees napping in the break room, and a janitor dancing with a mop down a hallway.

"Found it." Ollie tapped the screen. "That's the staging area."

Tamiko saw an attendant fastening the harnesses on Bald Eagle and Paulette Parrot for their entrance. Two others stood at the control board, hitting buttons and flipping switches.

"And there's Bald Eagle and Paulette Parrot," said Tamiko.

"Right," said Ollie, "we wrestled them before the Krackle Kiddos match."

"Let's catch us a butler," said Tamiko.

She dragged the progress marker with the mouse. Everyone looked like they were running super-fast as the footage zipped forward. All their questions were about to be answered.

Suddenly, the screen went black.

The staging area footage disappeared and was replaced by a message that read:

FILE MISSING/DELETED

"What?" she asked.

"Could be a glitch." Ollie leaned in. "Everything else seems fine."

Tamiko wiggled the mouse back and forth, moving through the timeline. One moment, the video showed no one by the control board. The next, the footage was gone.

Tamiko shook her head. "That's no glitch."

"How do you know?"

She pointed to the screen. A camera by the arena entrance ramp showed the Krackle Kiddos making their way down the ramp and toward the ring.

"Because this footage is exactly when Billingsley would have needed to have been in the staging area to lower the shark cage." She skipped forward. "And look! It comes back after Tsunami got trapped. Someone didn't want us to see what they were doing at the control board at that specific time. And like the screen says, if the file isn't missing . . ."

". . . it was deleted," finished Ollie. "Why didn't I dust for fingerprints?"

Back on the screen, someone was lowering a victory banner from the staging area.

"Wait," said Ollie, "is that . . ."

She leaned forward and saw the unmistakable figure of Billingsley.

"Billingsley!" shouted Tamiko. "Why didn't we think of that? Someone had to lower the banner. This puts him at the crime scene. He was smart enough to delete the footage of him actually dropping the shark cage, but *not* smart enough to get rid of the footage of the banner."

Tamiko watched Billingsley pull the banner back up and sprint out of the control room.

"We totally caught him leaving the scene of the crime."

"Which is exactly what *we* need to do," said Ollie, putting the picture frame back on the desk, "because I think I hear Linton coming back."

She heard it, too. Linton's footsteps echoed down the hallway and into his office.

Tamiko quickly shut down the computer. They sprinted out of the office and closed the door behind them. They safely rounded the corner and were out of sight just as Linton arrived.

"Two quarters and a nickel," said Linton excitedly as he rattled the coins in his hand. "They weren't kidding! I really struck it rich."

Tamiko and Ollie made their way back down the empty hallways toward the exit.

"Ollie Evander turning to a life of crime. Never thought I'd see the day."

"Shh! Not so loud. What if my mom hears?"

Tamiko laughed. But she stopped teasing Ollie. His mom *did* have a strange way of finding out about rule-breaking. It wasn't worth the risk.

"At least we saw Billingsley backstage," she said instead. "Shame we didn't have the footage of him actually sabotaging the shark cage, though."

It wasn't the definitive proof she had hoped for. Every time, they'd gotten *this* close to apprehending Billingsley, but had never actually been able to catch him in the act. But seeing him on camera was further evidence that the Krackle Kiddos were using him to cheat. He would do anything they told him to, even if that meant sabotaging shark cages *and* security footage.

"It doesn't matter," said Tamiko. "We know the truth. Add it to the evidence book. Once we have enough proof, we'll show Linton that his kids are dirty rotten cheaters. Then he'll either kick them out of Slamdown Town or we'll have to expose them in the ring."

"But first we have to beat Full Throttle," said Ollie. He took a deep breath. "And to do that, we have to make sure the Ragtag Team has our heel turn down pat."

CHAPTER 24

OLLIE

"WHAT are you looking at, pip-squeak?" shouted Hollis from across the dinner table.

Ollie made a mental note of that. He needed to step up his heel game. Especially since the match against Full Throttle was only a few days away. Lucky for him, his brother provided an unlikely source of inspiration.

When Hollis came home from school, he'd stomped straight into the garage. He'd returned with armfuls of his old ripped clothes, his fart machine, and his self-published memoir, *The Art of the Wedgie*.

"If Breonna likes bad boys, then I'll give her a bad boy!"

In the span of one afternoon, nice, polite Hollis was gone. His brother swore to go back to his bullying ways. Except, the new Hollis would be even meaner and nastier than the old one. He claimed his quota for wedgies was now double what they used to be.

Ollie knew this couldn't end well. But this was heel week, and, little did Hollis know, every insult, flare-up, and threat was being written down by his little brother.

"Are ya deaf?" shouted Hollis. "I said quit staring at me!"

"I will not have that kind of language in my house," said his mom. "Apologize to your brother. And don't think I can't see you're hiding your peas in your napkin, young man."

His mom would keep the peace—and the peas—but only while they were at the dinner table. Ollie averted his gaze so as not to incur more of his brother's wrath.

Later that night, Ollie snuck into Hollis's room while he watched television downstairs.

His brother's room was a treasure trove of adolescent belongings. A tube of punk putty hair gel was on his bed stand next to three bottles of pimple cream. Crushed soda cans and candy wrappers littered the carpet. On the computer screen, Ollie saw an article titled "How to Act Cool When You're Emotionally Devastated." He rolled his eyes. Eighth graders were so weird.

Ollie scooped up one of his brother's skull T-shirts, a set of studded armbands, and the sunglasses that Hollis had insisted made him look like a secret agent. (They didn't.)

He carried everything back to his room.

As soon as his alarm went off the next morning, Ollie gathered up everything he had pilfered. Everyone at school knew that his brother used to be the biggest, baddest bully in town. And while Ollie didn't feel that way, that was *exactly* who his reflection looked like in the mirror, wearing his brother's stuff.

A big, bad bully.

Wearing incredibly baggy clothes.

This is going to be some entrance, Ollie thought.

✲✲✲

The school bell rang loudly. And for the second time that morning, Ollie was not in class. He had skipped the entire first period. Was he feeling the rush of being bad or the fear of getting caught? Either way, he was ready for his grand entrance.

As he reached the door, he heard Mr. Fitzgerald's voice from inside the classroom.

"Ollie? Ollie Evander? You didn't tell me he was sick today, Tamiko."

"I didn't know he was, either," he heard her say.

That was his cue. His heel moment had come.

"Oh, I'm not sick," he said dramatically as he stepped inside. "I'm right here—late."

The shocked look on everyone's faces was priceless. But none more so than Tamiko's. Ollie was certain her jaw would fall right off.

Mr. Fitzgerald stared as if not believing his eyes.

"That is one intense outfit you got there. Why are you wearing sunglasses? We're inside."

Seeing with sunglasses on *was* proving a challenge. But Ollie wasn't about to admit that. Heels didn't care about what other people thought. Besides, the sunglasses made him feel cool.

"Because I don't want to look at a bunch of losers all day long," said Ollie.

The class began to laugh. It was working!

Mr. Fitzgerald looked unconvinced. "Ollie, this isn't like you. Did your brother put you up to this?"

"My brother? No. *I'm* the bad boy in the family."

"Well, apparently that's true, because as you said, you're late, Mr. Evander. And you know the rules. I'll have to give you a tardy slip."

Ollie gave what he hoped was a nonchalant shrug. "Yeah, well, I don't *follow* the rules."

Mr. Fitzgerald wrote him up. Ollie took the slip and scoffed. "Oh, good. I needed a tissue."

And without skipping a beat, Ollie blew his nose right into the tardy slip.

That *really* got the class rolling with laughter. But it also earned him a demerit slip. Ollie took his seat by Tamiko and the Krackle Kiddos, all of whom had stunned expressions.

"Dude, I don't know what's going on with you," said Tamiko. "But I *love* it."

Ollie gave a brusque nod. "Figured I should look the part."

"You hang around us for a few weeks and suddenly you're a bad boy?" asked Leon.

"Way to come out of your shell, Ollie," said Luna.

"I figured it was time for a change. Live life by the seat of my pants."

"Well, for now you might want to pull up the seat of your pants," said Leon. "Because your underwear is showing."

He'd made a great entrance. But Ollie had his own lesson plan for today. It called for disobedience, unruly behavior, and hopefully not getting grounded. Although that would be pretty heel of him.

Mr. Fitzgerald cleared his throat. "Now I need everyone to settle down."

Ollie stood up. "Nobody tells me what to do!"

"Wrong," said Mr. Fitzgerald. "I'm telling you that I want you to take a seat now."

"Well, I'm the type of kid who doesn't care. I'm doing what I want."

Mr. Fitzgerald was red in the face. "Need I remind you all that I can give out a book report anytime I choose to? I demand silence with *no* shenanigans at all. One more peep from anyone and I promise you, you'll all regret it. And that's final!"

Ollie took a seat. But he wasn't done. There was one more outburst needed. The perfect cherry heel on the heel cake. He reached into Tamiko's bag and pulled out her straw and spitball.

"Hey, Ollie," she whispered. "This would be a perfect opportunity to—"

But Ollie was already loading the spitball into the straw. "Way ahead of you."

"Wait, did you swipe that from my book bag?" He nodded. "Dude, stealing? Total heel move. I can't even with you right now."

He aimed the straw at Mr. Fitzgerald. But despite his massive dome, the spitball flopped lamely out of the straw and landed with a *splotch* on the ground.

"Ah, dude. You weren't even close!"

"Unless you were aiming for the floor," said Leon. "In which case, good job!"

Luna grabbed for the straw. "Maybe you should leave this to the professionals."

"I refuse to give up," he said through gritted teeth. "Not when I've come so far."

This time, he loaded up a much bigger, *much* wetter spitball into the straw.

"That's the biggest spitball I've ever seen," whispered Tamiko.

Ollie aimed and he unleashed the spitball terror. It flew high and true, and this time landed with a *splotch* directly on the back of Mr. Fitzgerald's balding head.

The class held their collective breath.

Mr. Fitzgerald turned around. "Okay, that does it. You all are out of control. Now, I want whoever did that to fess up right this instant. If you're so big and bad, then own it."

So Ollie stood up and raised his hand.

"Ollie Evander," shrieked Mr. Fitzgerald. "Of all the students! Why would you do this?"

A second spitball collided with Mr. Fitzgerald's forehead. Everyone turned to see Tamiko, straw still in mouth, her eyes wide with adrenaline.

"Because we don't care if other people hate us," she shouted.

"In fact, we want them to," said Ollie.

The Krackle Kiddos shot out of their chairs and began to yell. "Anarchy! Anarchy! Anarchy!"

All around Ollie, his classmates cheered. Students climbed

on desks, pulled out their phones, and screamed at the top of their lungs.

It took Mr. Fitzgerald the better part of ten minutes to calm everyone down.

"Rules are rules and I made it clear that if anyone acted out, I'd punish the entire class. So I really hope no one had any plans this weekend, because you are all going to write me a three-page paper on Virginia Borjenowitz's acclaimed follow-up short story to 'The Deadliest Pigeon,' 'An Ostrich Most Fowl'!"

Ollie received quite the talking-to from his mom when he got home that night.

"What is happening with you, Ollie?" she asked. "First you skip science class and then are late to English. Then I hear you're instigating classroom riots. This is unacceptable behavior."

The cost of Ollie being a great heel was his mom's disappointment. It nearly broke him. He hated making her upset. Once they'd proven the Krackle Kiddos were cheating, he resolved to put a stop to his heel antics. The arena would be as it always had been, Mr. Tanaka would have his job back, and Ollie could drop his act.

"I expect you to do your chores and then head right upstairs to your room."

Cleaning up after himself was definitely not heel. So instead of doing the dishes, he left them there, unwashed and dirty. Which was how Ollie felt for disobeying so many rules.

But he needed to keep trying. Refusing to do the dishes wasn't enough.

So when he got upstairs to his room, Ollie dug out his lam-inated Slamdown Town rule book and tore it into pieces. Well, he tried to as Ollie, but couldn't. So he popped the gum into his mouth, chewed, and then *Big Chew* tore the rule book into pieces.

He snapped a picture and sent it to Tamiko with the caption:

FULL THROTTLE DOESN'T STAND A CHANCE

CHAPTER 25

OLLIE

OLLIE was not messing around. Not today. The duties of being a heel required his complete focus. That meant getting up late that morning and *not* eating a balanced breakfast. He hadn't even brushed his teeth before being driven over to Slamdown Town.

"Because rules are for chumps and Ollie Evander is no chump," he declared with pride.

Tamiko nodded, impressed. "Not bad, though a little late to the game. I gave up basic hygiene days ago." She lifted her arms, and the smell trapped under her armpits wafted toward Ollie. It took all of his willpower not to vomit at the rancid odor. "*That,* my friend, is the smell of our impending victory."

As he and Tamiko made their way through the lobby of Slamdown Town, there was no doubt in his mind that the Ragtag Team's heel training would pay off. There'd be no repeat of the first match. This time, he and Tamiko would be one hundred percent in sync.

"Wedgies, one dollar. Fresh, painful wedgies!" said Hollis.

He stood by the snack counter, harassing all who dared pass by.

Ollie and Tamiko walked up to him. "Who would pay to get a wedgie?"

Hollis grinned and grabbed an unsuspecting fifth grader by the underwear.

"Hey, put me down," said the fifth grader as he dangled helplessly.

"That'll be one dollar," said Hollis.

The fifth grader reached into his pocket, produced a dollar, and eagerly paid.

"See?" said Hollis. "It pays to be bad."

But he didn't put the fifth grader down. With his free hand, Hollis grabbed a plate of leftover caviar and jammed the stinky, mushy bits up each of his nostrils.

"What are you doing?" asked Tamiko.

Hollis laughed. "Fish egg snot rockets incoming!"

"Take cover!" screamed Ollie as he dove out of the way.

He and Tamiko grabbed two lunch trays and held them up in defense. They blocked one snot rocket. They blocked another. But the barrage just kept coming.

That is, until Breonna heroically stepped in front of them.

"Breonna?" asked Hollis, his voice cracking and the snots ceasing. He cleared his throat. "I mean," he started again, leaning against the wall, trying to look cool. "S'up, babe?"

"Help me, kind girl!" pleaded the fifth grader, still dangling from his underwear.

"Drop the kid and stop shooting overpriced boogers at your brother and his friend."

"But, Breonna," he stammered, "I'm doing this for you!"

"For me?" she asked.

"Yes. I heard from your friends that you liked bad boys . . ."

She looked puzzled. Then said, "Well, I don't." She shook her head and walked off.

Hollis dropped the fifth grader and stormed off in the opposite direction, probably, Ollie assumed, to wreak even more havoc and resupply his snot artillery.

"Well, that's one way to start the day," said Tamiko.

They were on their way to the locker room when they heard Screech Holler's voice over the speakers.

"Welcome, Slamdown Town, to another evening of wrestling. Before we get the action started, let me share an important message that I was told would kick off the fun!" The sounds of Screech unfolding a piece of paper reverberated around the arena. "Says here that my services are no longer necessary, I've been canned, and that starting today my parking spot will no longer be validated. Well, isn't that—wait, what?"

Impossible. Had Ollie heard wrong? There was no way Slamdown Town could exist without the iconic voice of Screech Holler. It would be like having fries without ketchup or pizza without cheese. You just didn't do it.

"They can't fire Screech," said Ollie.

"He's Slamdown Town royalty," agreed Tamiko. "And besides, if he's gone, then who's going to announce the matches?"

"Hey, let go," shouted Screech. The sounds of a scuffle could be heard. "That's mine. Get your expertly manicured hands off of *my* microphone."

Ollie grabbed Tamiko's hand. "Come on. Let's go to the announcer's table."

She offered no resistance as Ollie dragged her through the lobby.

When they finally arrived ringside, they discovered Screech Holler had lost the fight for the microphone to a stylish woman in a chic dress. She tossed her expensively styled hair out of her perfectly done-up face with ease and brought the microphone up to her mouth.

"Hello . . . Slamdown Town," she said, glancing down at the cue card in front of her. "And welcome to another night of"—she peered at the notes—"wrestling. Are you excited? You should be. Because I'm here now. When Penelope Dunnelly is on the job, you know you're in for a good time. No matter how run-down and decrepit this place is, I'll shine through it all."

"Wait a minute," said Tamiko. "What is Penelope Dunnelly doing here at Slamdown Town? And why is she doing the pre-match announcements?"

That was where Ollie recognized her voice from. Penelope Dunnelly was a hotshot host of a zillion different talk shows, game shows, and travel shows. *Mornings with Penelope, Are You Smarter Than a Houseplant?*, and *Watch Me Travel to Places You Never Will* were some of the most popular shows on TV. Penelope's celebrity status made her current appearance at Slamdown Town more than a bit perplexing.

"Isn't this great?" asked the Krackle Kiddos as they approached.

Ollie turned to see Leon and Luna, all smiles in their matching, overpriced wrestling costumes, walking up to them. "What did you two do now?"

Leon pointed to Penelope. "We told Daddy that we simply *must* have her."

"And after a solid hour of us throwing a tantrum, he agreed," said Luna triumphantly. "Besides, this is what you asked for. Wasn't it?"

"When did we ever say we wanted Screech Holler fired?" asked Ollie, confused.

"You said he left your ears ringing the whole next day," said Leon.

Luna nodded. "Now you don't have to worry about that anymore. Penelope speaks at far more acceptable volume levels. Plus, she's actually iconic."

"Penelope may be the voice of *Skiing with Squirrels*, *The Wonderful World of Toilets*, and *Help, I Married a Cheesecake*," said Tamiko, "but Screech is *the* voice of Slamdown Town."

Ollie could feel anger growing within him. He'd been pretending to be an angry heel all week, but now, for the first time, he really felt it. "You can't get rid of him like that!"

"Oh yeah?" they asked.

They snapped their fingers and several Slamdown Town security guards poured into the arena, grabbed Screech by his suit, and led him away from the announcer's table.

"What crime have I committed?" he asked. "Loving wrestling too much?"

The security guards grunted in unison.

"I'll take that as a yes," said Screech.

Penelope's bubbly voice was channeled through the microphone and out into the arena. "I'll be the first to admit that I don't know or care about wrestling. But what I do know is that I am extremely famous and overqualified for this position, and two whiny children forced their father to pay me a *lot* of money to be here, so I'll have to get over it. So sit back, relax, and we'll see how many home runs these wrestlers can score before the night is up."

Ollie groaned. "She doesn't know diddly-squat about wrestling. She said it herself!"

The Krackle Kiddos shrugged. "Who cares?"

"She doesn't," said Tamiko. "She literally just said that!"

But the Krackle Kiddos didn't seem bothered by it. "She's super-famous and that's what matters. And if we're going to win the title match, we want *her* calling it."

"Maybe she'll learn quickly?" asked Ollie.

"This reminds me of the time when I hosted the National Canine Tap Dancing Competition," continued Penelope. "Which is *way* more famous than whatever this little sideshow is. So I'm going to talk about that instead. The thing about parading poodles is—"

"Okay, maybe not."

"Fame is like a virus," said Luna.

Leon nodded. "The closer we are to it, the better chance we have of catching it!"

And with that, they ran off toward the announcer's table.

Having no interest in listening to another moment of the announcing train wreck unfolding in the arena, Ollie and Tamiko headed backstage to prepare for their match.

"Okay, this is getting out of hand," said Ollie. "Now they're taking away Screech? What's next?"

Tamiko stamped her foot. "I don't know. Screech was one of my favorite things about Slamdown Town. I can't imagine a match without him calling it. We can't let this continue."

"You're right," he said. "But without concrete proof that they're cheating, the only way to show Linton that they're gaming *his* system . . ."

"Is to beat them in the ring," finished Tamiko. "And we can start that today!"

"We're going to take everything back," said Ollie. "By bashing our opponents in the face with an illegal chair."

CHAPTER 26

TAMIKO

THE strikingly unfamiliar voice of Penelope Dunnelly commanded the arena's attention. "Penelope Dunnelly here, everyone. I'm being told that we are about to see the Ragtag Team, featuring two wrestlers named Big Chew and Game Over. If memory serves me correctly, this is the part where the wrestlers will come out, and if they see their shadows, we are guaranteed another six months of winter. Fingers crossed for spring!"

"Gorgeous Gordon Gussett, that was painful to listen to." Game Over turned to Big Chew. "Remember, stick to being heels and we win."

"Way ahead of you," said Big Chew as they made their way toward the ring.

They emerged from the wrestler's entrance wearing the jet-black T-shirts and dark exercise pants cut off at the knee that Tamiko had gathered for them. Game Over shook her fists, which were covered in a set of studded fingerless gloves, and rattled the flashy silver chains around her neck. She roared, drawing attention to the neon skull painted on her face.

Only one costume element remained from their face turn, which was written on their chests in dripping, blood-red lettering:

RAGTAG TEAM

The crowd responded to their entrance by booing as loudly as their lungs would allow.

"That's right, Slamdown Town, boo all you want," shouted Game Over.

Game Over scowled at the crowd as she walked down the ramp toward the ring. It felt good to finally debut her heel persona. Before, she had come out feeling like she was playing a part. Now she felt ready to take on the world, and with her friend by her side, they couldn't lose.

"I haven't seen this much face paint since I hosted *So You Think You Can Mime*," said Penelope. "And I got to say, I think they would've been contenders on that show!"

Big Chew strutted alongside Game Over.

In place of his usual toothy smile was a grimace. He ignored requests to sign autographs and pose for pictures, and even ripped a sign out of a fan's hands that read:

I LOVE THE RAGTAG TEAM

"We don't need your stinking love," he said before tearing it up. He threw the pieces into the stands. "Now toss that in the garbage, where it belongs. And don't you dare recycle it."

Game Over smiled, then scowled. She was proud of Big Chew. Not wanting to be upstaged, she stole a bottle of Jean-Pierre's sparkling water from a fan, chugged it, and belched it in his face. She wondered how much money that burp cost.

It felt good to be bad. That is, until she noticed the fan whom Big Chew had stolen the sign from was crying. And feeling bad while trying to be *bad* felt, well, bad.

"I don't know much about wrestling," said Penelope. "Like, I *can't* stress that enough, but making fans cry? Somebody get that girl a tissue and an autographed picture of me."

Big Chew walked over. "This seems to be going well. I mean, bad. I mean . . ."

"Let's just get into the ring," said Game Over.

The deafening *vroom* of a car bellowed from the speakers as they hopped over the ropes.

The crowd booed as Mack Truck and Road Rage walked out from backstage. From the ring, Game Over could see their matching outfits made from real leather interior. Racing stripes ran down their sleeves. Their hair had been slicked with oil grease and their shoes lit up like signal blinkers.

"If you think that's exciting," said Penelope, "be sure to tune in tomorrow night at nine as I unveil the *World's Most Wanted Sloths*. You won't believe who is number one. Oh, and"—she shuffled her cards—"Full Throttle is apparently the name of a wrestling team and they're here."

Full Throttle headed down the entrance ramp and did a few doughnuts around the outside of the ring before climbing inside. Game Over knew this match would not be some weekend drive through the countryside.

After all, Mack Truck had a chassis powered by revenge after the tragic day he missed his exit and crashed his beloved eighteen-wheeler head-on into a wrestling arena. His partner, Road Rage, had outstanding tickets in all fifty states and was currently failing seven anger management courses.

Road Rage brought a microphone up to her face. "I'm revved up, gassed up, and ready to drive you both into the mat. Get ready to eat my dirt!"

"The only thing you're going to eat is my boot," said Big Chew.

Game Over raised her boots. "Polished them just for this occasion. Tied 'em, too."

Mack Truck rolled his eyes. "You think you're hard-core now? Some of us were factory-built that way. Isn't that right, Road Rage?"

"Actually, I was cobbled together from junkyard parts."

"Spare us the lame backstory," said Game Over. "And let's do this thing!"

"If it's thrilling stories you're looking for," said Penelope, "you won't believe what happened to me on the set of *Say I Do to the Kangaroo*."

"Someone arrest this woman for crimes against wrestling," shouted Game Over.

With all the wrestlers gathered, the referee completed his pre-match inspection. Full Throttle had shown restraint and had only one illegal brass knuckle between them. But the referee found the Ragtag Team's secret stash. He removed two boxes of thumbtacks from each of them, Game Over's hidden bat, and a rubber chicken from Big Chew.

"I just grabbed anything I could find," he whispered.

"I like the effort," said Game Over. "And besides, a rubber chicken in the right hands is the most dangerous weapon there is."

The referee sent each team to their corners. Road Rage exited the ring, leaving Mack Truck to wrestle first. Game Over knew she could take him on, no problem.

And a heel didn't ask for permission.

"Time to suspend your license!" yelled Game Over as she stepped forward. But a strong arm held her back.

"That's my line," said Big Chew as he shoved her toward the ropes. "If you think I'm not wrestling first, you're crazy!"

She had a mind to tell Big Chew to shut his face. But she reminded herself that he was simply staying in character. They were supposed to act tough. Besides, she had an ace up her sleeve.

"We can settle this like last time." She turned to the crowd. "Who do you numbskulls want to see wrestle first?"

"Game Over! Game Over! Game Over!" chanted the crowd.

Big Chew laughed dismissively. "You think I care what they want? I'm going first and no one is going to stop me."

That was the most heel response she'd ever heard. And since Big Chew was already sprinting toward Mack Truck, she begrudgingly exited the ring.

Ding! Ding! Ding!

Big Chew ran across the ring and immediately threw a cheap Whoops Didn't See You There Elbow. But Mack Truck countered with a Four-Way Merge Palm Strike that sent him stumbling backward. Big Chew recovered and launched himself off the ropes. He smacked into Mack Truck with a Rules Are for Chumps Facebuster that sent both wrestlers hurtling into the mat.

"Long story short," said Penelope, "never come between a kangaroo and true love. Oh, and it looks like the one called Big Chew is winning the match. But back to talking about me!"

Big Chew was undeniably impressive. But Tamiko was raring to go. After the last match, all she thought about was getting back into the ring. Now, like before, she was on the outside looking in.

"At the next turnbuckle, pay the Ragtag toll," shouted Big Chew as he hurled Mack Truck into their corner toward Game Over.

This was her time to dish out some pain. She leaned over the ropes and bashed Mack Truck from behind with a My Soul Is Darkness Punch.

"Toll paid. The destination is now directly below you," she said.

Mack Truck lurched forward and crashed into the mat. "I need a pit stop," he shouted. He rolled out of a pin attempt by Big Chew and sped over to Full Throttle's corner. "Road Rage. Get in here!"

Road Rage sprang into the ring. "You know I hate wrestling during rush hour. Why can't anyone just listen and do what they're supposed to?" It appeared that Road Rage was in quite the angry mood. But Game Over knew how to use that to her advantage.

"Hey, Big Chew," she shouted. "Tag me in."

But Big Chew waved her off. "You think I'm scared of her? Not a chance."

That only seemed to make Road Rage *even angrier*. She sprinted forward and hit Big Chew with an I Can Make This

Yellow If You'd Just Go Kick that dropped him to his knees. Which was exactly where Road Rage needed him to be to smack him with a Merge Already Chop.

"Now *that's* what wrestling should look like!" yelled Road Rage as Big Chew lay on the mat. "But all of you speed-limit junkies think you know better." She turned her attention to the booing crowd. "They should really hand out licenses for being in the audience, since you obviously have no idea how a wrestling match is supposed to be enjoyed!"

"I think Road Rage could use a copy of my bestseller, *How Being Famous Solves Everything*," said Penelope. "In chapter five, I talk about my experiences hanging out with celebrities who taught me that focusing inward—"

"Don't tell me how to live my life," shouted Road Rage.

The match was getting out of hand. If Big Chew wasn't going to tag Game Over in, there was only one option left. She'd have to do it herself.

Game Over hopped the ropes and landed in the ring.

"What are you doing?" asked Big Chew as he pushed himself off the mat. "I'm not done yet."

"Yes, you are," said Game Over. "And so is she."

Before Road Rage could argue, Game Over swung a Vile and Villainous Fist that shut her opponent up. Road Rage was dazed. Game Over struck her with a series of Eternal Darkness Strikes that toppled the raging wrestler right out of the ring.

"I'm pulling you over and giving you a ticket." Game Over put her hands on the ropes so she could launch herself down toward Road Rage. "A ticket to your own defeat!"

But before she could, she was spun around.

Mack Truck glared at her. "End of the road." He threw a Fast Lane Haymaker Punch.

But Game Over grabbed his fist before it even hit her.

"Oh dear," she said in a mocking tone. "Looks like you just hit a pothole!"

She tossed his hand aside and hit Mack Truck with a Diabolical by Nature Kick straight to his chest. With Mack Truck stunned, Game Over jumped into the air, grabbed his head, and tossed him to the mat with a Good Guys Finish Last Bulldog.

This was the rush Game Over had been hoping she would have felt during her face match. The restraints were off and there was nothing that could stop her.

But Big Chew stepped in front of her, blocking her way.

"I told you I got this," he said. "And besides, I didn't even tag you in."

"Since when do we care about the rules?" she asked. "I'm taking my turn. Deal with it."

"Game Over! Game Over! Game Over!" shouted the crowd.

The fans clearly wanted her to wrestle as much as she wanted to. Heel or not, why couldn't Ollie see that?

"Beep, beep!" yelled Road Rage from behind.

Game Over felt Road Rage's knee slam into her back. Unable to keep her balance, she tumbled up and over the ropes.

She'd been tossed out of a match. Again.

"Stay there," said Big Chew from inside the ring. "I got this."

This was not playing out the way Game Over had thought it would. Heels certainly felt more right than faces had. But being heels was causing more harm than good. And *not* in the way it was supposed to.

CHAPTER 27

OLLIE

HOW is this happening again? thought Big Chew as he ran across the wrestling mat toward Road Rage.

He was certain he was being an excellent heel. But just like their first match with Birds of a Feather, their strategy was *not* working. In fact, they were close to losing the match because of it.

Big Chew slammed into Road Rage, who locked him in a Traffic Jam Hold.

"It's so nice to see people sharing a hug," said Penelope, oblivious to the peril Big Chew was in if he didn't break out.

Road Rage sneered as she held Big Chew in place. "Give it up, bubble butt. We all know you don't have the gas to stand up in a fight."

Big Chew knew any number of illegal moves could free him. But he had a better idea. One taken straight out of his brother's playbook.

"See, Road Rage. That's where you're wrong. Very wrong."

Desperate times called for desperate measures. Big Chew raised his leg and let one rip. It was loud. It was proud. And it forced Road Rage to loosen her grip.

"Someone needs to clean out their exhaust pipe," said Road Rage, coughing.

The crowd laughed.

Big Chew hoped they were laughing with the Ragtag Team and not at them. Being laughed at wasn't exactly heel of him.

Wham!

Something very large collided into him. Big Chew barely managed to stay on his feet.

"Pay attention, Ollie—I mean Big Chew," he heard Game Over shout from outside the ring.

Big Chew turned and saw that Mack Truck had been responsible for the collision. Road Rage must have tagged him in while Big Chew had been distracted.

"Do you smell that?" asked Mack Truck from across the ring. "That, my friend, is the sweet smell of pain." Mack Truck sniffed the air. "And maybe a hint of pine. But mostly pain!"

"Roadkill! Roadkill!" chanted the crowd.

Big Chew knew that Roadkill was one of Mack Truck's signature clothesline moves. Much like its namesake, it involved running over a helpless creature, flattening them, and leaving them for dead. Or, in the case of wrestling, pinning them.

Mack Truck held his hands out. He mimed sticking a key in the ignition and turning it.

"Vroom! Vroom!" he bellowed.

"He's revving the engine!" yelled Road Rage from the ropes. "Everybody make sure your seat belts are fastened because this crash is going to be intense!"

Mack Truck sprinted forward with total disregard for the arena speed limit.

Before Big Chew could dive out of the way, Mack Truck rammed into him. The result wasn't quite roadkill, but it wasn't pretty.

Big Chew fell to the mat. Before he could get up, he saw Mack Truck towering above him.

"Recalculating route," said Mack Truck. "Your defeat is now directly in front of you."

"Stay away from my partner," he heard Game Over shout.

As Mack Truck bent down to pin Big Chew, Game Over appeared and hit him with an I Follow My Own Rules Power-slam. Mack Truck stumbled away.

"You know what we should do?" asked Penelope. "Check my social media feed. That's where the *real* action is. Wait, only one million likes? I spent hours getting that woke-up-like-this photo perfect!"

Big Chew pushed himself off the mat and climbed back to his feet.

"Thanks for that," said Big Chew. He cleared his throat. "I mean, what are you doing? I totally had this."

"You got nothing," said Game Over. "Let a hard-core wrestler like me take a few cracks at 'em."

Heel or not, Big Chew needed a breather. So he tagged her in and hopped over the ropes as the crowd began to chant.

"Game Over! Game Over! Game Over!"

Big Chew watched as Mack Truck ran to his corner and tagged in Road Rage. She crashed into Game Over with a Your Blinker's Been on This Whole Time Diving Headbutt.

Game Over hit Road Rage with a Big Bad Backbreaker. That left Road Rage stunned. And angry.

"Forget what my anger management coach says," yelled Road Rage. "I'm going to put the pedal to the metal. Except the pedal will be *you*, and the metal is going to be the mat!"

Road Rage jabbed Game Over with an illegal In My Blind Spot Double Eye Poke that sent Game Over to her knees. It hurt Big Chew to even watch something so dirty. But she wasn't done. Road Rage climbed up onto the top rope, gave two thumbs-down to the crowd, and plowed Game Over with an I've Been Waiting at the DMV for Hours Diving Spear.

"And then he told me I was the best interviewer he ever spoke to," said Penelope as she finished her boring story. "Oh, and apparently Road Rage and Game Over are working out their anger issues or something. It's an emotional, sweaty sport."

The referee walked over to Road Rage, wagging his finger. Big Chew was certain she would get a talking-to. But Road Rage grabbed the ref by his striped shirt and sent him through the ropes and onto the floor.

"Road Rage just threw that man straight out of the ring!" yelled Penelope. "That's what happens when you aren't on the guest list. Speaking of exclusive guest lists—"

This is madness, thought Big Chew.

He knew as a heel that he shouldn't care. But attacking a ref? That wasn't just dirty. It was *wrong*. This charade had gone on long enough and he knew what he needed to do.

Big Chew sprinted over to the referee and helped him off the ground.

"Don't worry," said Big Chew. "I'm going to end this. *By the book*." The book he was referring to was the rule book. "Time to win this match fair and square."

Big Chew flung himself over the ropes and into the ring.

"Hey, Road Rage," he shouted. "You sure could use a car wash after fighting so dirty."

Road Rage laughed. "You're nothing but a bump in the road. And unfortunately for you, my shock-resistant costume can handle that kind of off-roading."

Road Rage sprinted toward him, but Big Chew hit her with a Rules Are Great Clothesline. She toppled down to the mat and Big Chew rushed over to Game Over's side.

"Playing dirty isn't getting us anywhere. But I have an idea," said Big Chew.

Across the ring, Mack Truck entered and helped Road Rage to her feet.

"We can't wrestle at the same time," said Big Chew. "It's against the rules."

"You know how I feel about rules," said Game Over. She charged forward and crashed into Mack Truck with a Bad to the Bone Spear. "This is a two-player game and I'm booting this fool from the match!" The impact toppled both wrestlers over the ropes.

Big Chew, now alone in the ring with Road Rage, turned his full attention on his opponent. He was going to win this match his way. As a face.

"It's time to send you back to the assembly line," shouted Road Rage.

Big Chew put his hand to his ear. "Wait a minute. Do you hear that?" He paused. "That's the check engine light. And you're way overdue for a tune-up. Let me help fix that!"

He flung himself off the ropes and sprinted down the mat toward Road Rage. She threw a dirty Four-Wheel Drive Elbow at him. But Big Chew ducked and landed a Squeaky-Clean Slam that sent her to the mat. He turned, ran across the ring, and climbed up to the top rope.

"I'm going to win this match fair and square!" he yelled.

He launched himself off the rope, twisting and turning in the air, before hitting Road Rage with a Heroes Never Lose Splash. The weight of his body held her to the mat as he reached over and lifted Road Rage's leg high in the air. The referee slapped out the pinfall.

"Eight! Nine! Ten!"

Ding! Ding! Ding!

"I can't believe it!" shouted Penelope. "This is incredible. I'm trending right alongside the super-cute video of that puppy in the hot dog suit. Keep those posts coming, everyone! Oh, and the Ragtag Team won."

But instead of cheering, the crowd booed.

"Game Over! Game Over! Game Over!"

That didn't make any sense. After all, *he* had won the match.

That was when Big Chew saw that Game Over was standing on the top rope with her arms in the air, screaming and booing right back at the audience. Right back at *her* fans.

Big Chew *had* won the match. But the fans didn't seem to care. They wanted Game Over. She strutted in front of the crowd.

"Enough with these noobs," she shouted. "Game Over is ready to face the final bosses!"

The crowd continued to shout her name. No Big Chew chants. Not even any Ragtag Team ones. All anyone wanted was to cheer for Game Over. Why did he even bother showing up if everyone, including Game Over, was going to ignore him all the time?

CHAPTER 28

TAMIKO

"WHO'S the best? I'm the best!" shouted Game Over to the cheering crowd.

Nothing compared to the spine-tingling feeling she got after winning a match. It hadn't necessarily gone according to plan. Or rather, things had almost completely derailed. But hearing everyone chant Game Over's name put any worries she had to rest.

Only, she realized that she was celebrating alone. She turned and spotted Big Chew already making his way up the entrance ramp toward the locker room.

"Why the sad face there, Big Chew?" asked Game Over as she joined him. "Can't say that it was pretty, but hey, a win's a win. Great work out there."

"I suppose," said Big Chew. "But ..."

But Game Over didn't hear him because right at that moment a huge wave of boos erupted for her. Not bad boos, but the heel-approved, love-to-hate-you boos.

Before exiting, she turned and grimaced at the audience, which just made them boo even more. Sure, they hadn't won the way she would have wanted to, but the Ragtag Team had clearly won the crowd. Well, at least Game Over had.

And it wasn't her fault they liked her more than Big Chew.

She made her way back to the bustling locker room. She caught up with Big Chew by their lockers, already wiping the black paint off of his face.

"Sorry, dude. What were you saying?"

"All they want to do is boo for you," said Big Chew.

"For us," said Game Over.

"No," he said flatly, "I didn't hear a single cheer for me."

"Well, it *was* kinda hard to hear over all the boos."

"Exactly! And *I* won the match," said Big Chew, shaking his head.

Game Over wasn't sure what the problem was. He'd won the match. More important, they'd won the crowd. It wasn't her fault if they liked her more. Why couldn't Big Chew see that? Or better yet, be happy for her?

"You did win the match for us," she replied, sitting down beside him, "but you also turned face. And I turned heel last week. Linton told us the crowd would be confused if we weren't unified and they probably were."

Big Chew nodded. "We have to work together as a team. But we tried being faces. We tried being heels. What else is left? We did everything."

"Everything?" asked a raspy, aging voice.

Through the crowd of wrestlers, Game Over saw Lil' Old Granny and Dentures Dan sitting side by side at their lockers.

Both were rubbing joint-relief cream on their elbows and knees for their upcoming match.

Game Over and Big Chew walked over and took a seat on the bench across from them.

"I don't mean to eavesdrop," Lil' Old Granny said, pointing to her hearing aid, "but I couldn't help but overhear you two young'uns talking about having tried everything. Ain't that right, Dan?"

Dan popped his dentures into his mouth and said, "Sounds about right, Granny. Although to be fair, I haven't had a working hearing aid in ages. But I've become a pretty good lip-reader."

He pointed to his lips and flapped them up and down like a fish.

"Sorry, Granny," said Big Chew. "We were just talking about our face and heel turns."

"Yes, Dan and I were talking about that, too. You turned so fast I almost got whiplash watching ya. But why?"

"Because Linton said that all the greatest tag teams were unified," said Game Over. "Even the Krackle Kiddos manage to do that!" She knew they were cheating their way to victory. But she had to admit they had the seamless twin thing down. How was the Ragtag Team doing worse than them when it came to being on the same page?

"Tsunami, Birds of a Feather, the Scallywags, the Terrible Twosome, Full Throttle," said Big Chew, raising a finger with each tag team name. "All those tag teams are so coordinated."

"But you're forgetting, ya whippersnappers," said Dan, "that you're looking at the greatest tag team." He jabbed his chest, then Granny's, with an arthritic finger.

That's right, thought Tamiko. She looked up at the shimmering championship belts that were hung above their lockers. They'd been the tag team champions for years now.

"Look at Dan and me. We've been wrestling together since we were about your age, maybe younger. Practically grew up together."

"Sure did, Granny. We had our ups and downs and plenty of arguments over the years."

Big Chew chimed in. "You even broke up a few times!"

Despite his deep voice, Game Over could practically hear Ollie's excited voice sneak through. It was a good reminder that her best friend was underneath all that muscle and bronzer.

"That's right, sonny," said Granny. "This boy knows his wrestling. But you know what you don't know?"

"What's that, Granny?" asked Game Over.

"Diddly-squat about being a good teammate."

Game Over hung her head. Besides her, Big Chew did the same. She felt like she was getting a talking-to from her parents. And when she hung her head and didn't talk back, that meant she knew they were right.

"The two of you are sitting here after only two matches saying that you've done everything." Dan laughed. "Why, you two sound like you're about ready to give up just 'cause things are hard. But that's all part of growing up. Trust me. I've done my growing."

Lil' Old Granny sized up both of them.

"Now, tell Granny, is Nursing Home faces or heels?"

Game Over opened her mouth. Then closed it without

saying anything. Now that Granny had asked, she wasn't sure. Big Chew's silence suggested that he didn't know the answer, either.

"That's kinda a trick question," she said after a while. "You're not really either."

Big Chew nodded. "You and Dan do your own thing."

"Granny and I are the best of friends," said Dan. "But that doesn't mean we're the same person. In fact, in some areas we're complete opposites. Game Over, you looked pretty comfortable swinging that chair. And Big Chew, you seemed comfortable playing by the rules."

Granny wrapped a wrinkly arm around Dan's shoulders and gave him a squeeze.

"Sure, we've had our differences," she said. "But what's kept us bonded all these years has been our ability to be true to who we are. Only *then* can we be true to each other. Now, if you'll excuse us, Dan and I have some applesauce with our names on it to attend to."

Dentures Dan giggled to himself and pretended not to hear her. "What's that, Granny? You're going to have to speak up." He winked at Game Over and Big Chew.

"Oh, don't tell me you've eaten it all again!"

"Fine then, I won't tell you," he said with a chuckle.

Granny and Dan shuffled out of the locker room, their arguments about applesauce growing quieter and quieter.

Big Chew and Game Over sat in silence for a moment. Other wrestlers milled about the locker room, preparing for their various matches. But they ignored them.

Finally, Big Chew spoke. "I want to be a good teammate."

"Me too. But I also want to be true to myself," said Game Over.

"Me too," said Big Chew.

"So that settles it," said Game Over. "I'm officially staying heel."

"And I'm turning face again," said Big Chew.

For the first time since she turned into a wrestler, Game Over was feeling rejuvenated. With two wins under their belt and a notebook rapidly filling up with evidence, it felt like they might actually be able to solve the mystery *and* get a shot at the championship belt.

CHAPTER 29

OLLIE

WRESTLING matches waited for no one, which is why Ollie and Tamiko transformed and sprinted up the arena stairs. Ollie planted his butt in his seat with plenty of time to spare before the next match.

"Our second victory *and* wrestling advice from Nursing Home," said Ollie. "How can this day get any better?"

"I'll tell you how," said Tamiko. "We still have one more wrestling match to watch."

Ollie looked down and spotted Hollis sitting by himself in the row in front of them. His brother shoved a helping of white truffle into his mouth and chewed it slowly.

"What's up, Hollis," said Ollie. "Had any luck talking to Breonna?"

"No," he said sadly. "Her friends told me that Breonna likes bad boys. But I guess maybe I took the whole bad boy thing a little too far." He took another bite. "Girls sure are confusing."

"*You're* confusing," said Tamiko. "Have you considered Breonna might want you to, I don't know, just be your normal disgusting self?"

Hollis spit out the white truffle. "Be myself?"

Fresh off their conversation with Nursing Home, Ollie felt inspired to help.

"Yeah, bro," he said. "If you're comfortable with you, then maybe she is, too. She liked you when you started dating. But then you went and changed. Twice."

"You're right," said Hollis. "I tried being nice and that didn't work. Then I tried being mean. Well, meaner. That didn't work, either. But maybe I could try being myself. That's just crazy enough to work! I'm a genius!"

"Well . . ." started Tamiko.

But Hollis had already tossed the plate of overpriced food onto the ground and run off.

"Never thought I'd be giving your brother dating advice." Tamiko shuddered. "I guess that face training got to me somehow."

"Now, this is more like it," said Penelope Dunnelly over the arena speakers. "Says here that the most exclusive tag team is coming up next. That's exactly the kind of people who I want to rub elbows with. Let's all cheer very loudly for the Krackle Kiddos!"

"Boo!" yelled Tamiko. "And not the good kind, either!"

The Krackle Kiddos sauntered down the entrance ramp and into the ring.

"Doesn't matter," said Tamiko. "They're gonna be good and buried in no time. There's no way they beat Skeleton Crew."

Ollie agreed.

"Now give it up for some dead guys," said Penelope. "It's Skeleton Crew!"

Skeleton Crew arrived at the top of the entrance ramp. The entirety of Skull's skin had been painted a deathly white except for two large circles under her eyes. She swayed slightly back and forth as if she were a ghost. Her partner, Bones, ambled next to her. Tombstones were tattooed all over his body, while a collection of tiny rattling bones dangled around his neck.

But Ollie knew something about the undead duo was wrong.

"They're limping," he said as he watched them walk toward the ring.

Ollie had a bad feeling about this. The wrestlers stopped a few steps into the arena and spoke into a pair of custom skeleton-lined microphones.

"This fight is dead and buried," said Skull in a pained voice. "Those among the living would say it's been canceled."

The crowd booed.

Bones struggled to stand. "It's not our fault! If you want to boo someone, boo the diabolical demon who snuck up on us backstage and attacked us!"

Attacking your opponent before the match wasn't out of the realm of possibility. This was wrestling, after all. But this was low even for the Krackle Kiddos, who Ollie was *certain* were behind this. He leaned forward, trying to read Leon's and Luna's faces.

"They were as quiet as a ghost," said Skull. "Trust me, I'd know. I didn't even have time to turn around before we were both struck by some kind of weapon. Didn't see what it was, and by the time I came to, whoever was responsible was gone. The whole thing was fishy."

"The only thing that's fishy here are your excuses," said Leon into a mic from the ring.

Luna nodded. "You're just too scared to wrestle us."

"We could send you two to your wrestling graves anytime," said Bones.

"Prove it," said the Krackle Kiddos together.

"That's not fair," said Tamiko. "There's no way they can wrestle like that."

To their credit, Skull and Bones limped slowly toward the ring, moaning and shuffling like zombies. But before they could even get halfway down the entrance ramp, the arena medic flagged them and demanded they stop. After a quick examination, she shook her head.

"You two are in no condition to fight," declared the medic.

Skull and Bones had their coffins brought down to the entrance ramp. They carefully climbed inside and were carried back to the locker room by chanting attendants in hooded robes.

"They're lying," said Ollie. "The Krackle Kiddos totally did this."

Tamiko nodded. "Doy! Who else could it be? They knew they couldn't actually wrestle Skull and Bones. So they ordered Billingsley to attack them to stop the match from happening."

This was getting out of hand. Was there nothing the Krackle Kiddos wouldn't do to cheat their way to victory?

"Well, wasn't that thrilling?" asked Penelope in a bored voice. "To think I'm missing fashion week for this. Go ahead and cheer for the Krackle Kiddos, I suppose."

"Come on," said Ollie as he leapt out of his seat.

He knew he and Tamiko wouldn't be allowed backstage. So they waited until they were out of sight to transform back into their wrestling alter egos. Big Chew and Game Over then made their way into the Wrestlers Only area. When they arrived backstage, they found nothing out of the ordinary. The hallway looked just as it had a few moments earlier.

Game Over sniffed the air. "Do you smell that?"

He did. Big Chew had assumed that the strange odor he was smelling was born from the treachery that had been committed moments ago. But the longer he smelled, the more he realized that there was an *actual* smell that didn't belong here.

Big Chew inhaled deeply. "Yeah, something smells . . ."

"Fishy," they said in unison.

"Skull had mentioned there was something fishy going on," said Big Chew. "And judging by the stench, she was more right than she knew!"

He whipped out the magnifying glass, which looked like a baby toy in his massive hands, and began to inspect the area. But despite searching every nook and cranny, there were no clues to be found. Billingsley appeared to be no fool and, like his scheme in the control room, he left no trace behind that would connect him to the crime.

"There's nothing here outside of this awful stench." Big Chew's eyes began to water. "We should head back. It's time to go home and the arena will be closing."

Big Chew and Game Over emerged from the backstage area and sucked down fresh, non-fishy air. With their investigation concluded, they discreetly transformed back into Ollie and Tamiko and made their way out into the arena entrance lobby.

They spotted Leon and Luna loitering near the front doors.

"There you are," said Leon as they approached. "We've been waiting for you."

The last thing he wanted to do was spend time with the Krackle Kiddos.

Ollie shook his head. "Tamiko's dad is going to pick us up."

"Billingsley's just outside," said Luna, as if she hadn't heard him. The Krackle Kiddos wouldn't take no for an answer. Despite their protests, Leon and Luna dragged them outside toward their limo, where Billingsley was waiting for them. "We can drive you home and we can talk about those scaredy cats, Skull and Bones. Can you believe that?"

"Ah, congratulations on your victory, children," said Billingsley.

Like you didn't just help them win, you sneaky cheat, thought Ollie.

Leon and Luna performed their customary routine of ignoring Billingsley's existence and piled into the car. Ollie, on the other hand, stopped beside Billingsley.

"Can I help you, Master Ollie?" asked Billingsley.

But Billingsley already had. There was no denying the smell coming off of Billingsley's hands. Next to him, Tamiko's eyes lit up and watered as she smelled it, too. Her gaze met Ollie's and he knew she'd reached the same conclusion he had.

"What's that smell?" asked Ollie.

"Yeah, it smells fishy," said Tamiko.

"That would be me," said Billingsley, holding out his hands for them to smell.

"You?" Ollie couldn't believe his ears. Was Billingsley admitting his guilt?

"I was preparing bouillabaisse for dinner. That's a very fancy fish stew for very fancy people. It's a Krackle Kiddos favorite, but good heavens is it smelly. And expensive."

"Come on, you two!" yelled the Krackle Kiddos from the car. "Let's go so we can celebrate our victory and maybe stop at all the ice cream places on the way home."

As they climbed into the backseat, Ollie leaned closer to Tamiko.

"That's *totally* the same smell that was backstage," he whispered.

"And bouillabaisse is totally a made-up dish," said Tamiko. "He's a liar."

Ollie shook his head. "But what could he have used to attack them that smelled so fishy?"

"I don't know," whispered Tamiko. "But we gotta find it or no one will believe us." She reached over Ollie and lowered his window. "Now, come on. We need to get some sort of cross breeze going. I'm dying here."

CHAPTER 30

TAMIKO

THAT must be Ollie, thought Tamiko as she heard the doorbell ring.

It was Wednesday evening and he was supposed to swing by her house before they went over to Krackle Manor for another training session with Leon, Luna, and Ollie's mom. As before, they planned on using the session as cover to continue their investigation.

Tamiko crossed the living room to answer the door, but was suddenly cut off by Snack Guy. Her dad planted his feet in front of her and struck a heroic pose.

"Snack Guy needs you," he shouted. He turned and opened the door, revealing a startled Ollie. "And you, too."

"Me?" asked Ollie as he walked inside.

Tamiko hoped her dad's fantasy of becoming a wrestler was just that. A fantasy. But despite it being a really bad idea, he remained set on his goal. Having wrestled herself, she knew how intense it was, and for all his enthusiasm, there was no way her dad would last two seconds in a match.

"They tried to kick me out of the fun. But they can't keep Snack Guy away from Slammyville!"

"It's Slamdown Town, Dad."

"Oh, right. Silly me. Anyway, I have some pretty remarkable *snack* talk that I need a pair of seasoned vets like you two to practice on."

This was going to be interesting. And probably painful.

"Does Snack Guy have any snacks?" asked Ollie.

"He sure does!"

"All right, show us what you got," said Tamiko.

She and Ollie each grabbed a bag of chips and took a seat on the couch.

"Snack Guy needs to inspire fear in his enemies. All the greatest wrestlers inspire fear."

"That's not necessarily true," started Ollie.

But Tamiko shushed him. "Just let him have this. It's easier than correcting him."

So they both nodded, and her dad—or rather, Snack Guy—continued.

"Let me try out a few really killer lines I cooked up. Because when Snack Guy is in the kitchen, he's cooking!"

A few moments of awkward silence passed.

"Oh, sorry. I didn't know you started yet," said Tamiko.

"Let me try again, bug." He put on a serious tone. "I hope you like a little fire in your life. Because I turned on the stove! And it's one of those gas-powered ones with flames."

Tamiko groaned.

"I mean, stoves are hot, I guess," said Ollie.

"I'm not sure you really understand how smack talk works, Dad."

"Dad doesn't. But Snack Guy has a taste for snack talk. Along with a culinary degree that he worked really hard for after his parents doubted him, but he stuck with it and now they totally respect him. And he wrestles, too. Pretty intense backstory, am I right?"

Tamiko had been wrong. This was turning out to not be interesting at all, only painful.

Bzz! Bzz!

Tamiko looked down at her phone. She had never been so happy for a distraction.

"It's Linton Krackle," she whispered to Ollie.

"I bet he's calling to schedule our next match," hissed Ollie.

Needing to make a quick exit, Tamiko made up an excuse.

"Hey, Dad. Really interesting stuff here, but Ollie and I need to head upstairs. Totally forgot about a math assignment we need to work on before we leave."

"Long division," said Ollie.

"That's some solid dedication to your schoolwork, kids. And I sure wouldn't want to *divide* your attention. That's a good one. I should write that down somewhere."

They left her dad in the kitchen and sprinted upstairs to her room. She made sure to close her bedroom door behind them. If her mom or dad walked in and overheard them, it wouldn't matter what match Linton was calling about because her wrestling career would be over.

She answered Linton's call in her no-nonsense Ms. Manager voice.

"I see you finally remembered that your best tag team needed their next big match scheduled," she said hastily.

"What are you talking about?" said Linton. "I never forget anything. My mind is like a steel box of retention. Now, seriously, what were we talking about?"

"The match."

"Oh, right, right." Linton cleared his throat. "You've managed to string together a couple of wins. Not pretty ones. But I admire a fellow winner. I've done my fair share, of course. Which is why you'll be facing my kids this weekend."

She heard Ollie take a sharp breath next to her. Their big chance had finally arrived.

"We—err, I mean my client, has wanted to face your kids since the beginning. Why the change of heart?"

"My kiddos asked for it. And what they ask for, they get. They want the best, and turns out your client has gathered quite the following. Well, not your client. More like Mr. Manager's client. Point is, the Ragtag Team's caught their attention."

It felt good to know that Game Over had become well-known enough that even two spoiled brats like the Krackle Kiddos thought the Ragtag Team was worth facing.

"But," continued Linton, "make sure to show up when you're told to. And for the love of a fresh crisp twenty-dollar bill, figure out your team unity problem. It's painful to watch."

"Don't worry," said Ms. Manager into the phone. "The Ragtag Team has sorted out all their team issues. They have personally assured me they will be ready."

Ollie nodded in agreement.

"I hope so," said Linton in a judgmental tone. "Have your

clients show up at my office before the match on Saturday. I want to see this change with my own eyes. It's my money on the line here. My precious, precious money. I'll give Mr. Manager a call later and fill him in with the details. After I count this jar full of coins that's practically calling my name."

As soon as Linton ended the call, Tamiko let out a cheer. Ollie did a funny little dance.

"This is the best day ever," he shouted. "We finally get our chance." Ollie stopped dancing. "But we need to gather as much evidence as we can against the Krackle Kiddos before we meet with Linton."

"But even if he doesn't believe us," said Tamiko, "we are totally going to own those good-for-nothing cheaters! And expose them for what they are to the whole arena!"

CHAPTER 31

OLLIE

OLLIE knew that despite his mom's constant encouragement, he wasn't very good at working out. In fact, he was downright awful at it. But, as he watched the Krackle Kiddos later that night as they trained in their private gym, he couldn't help but think that compared to *them*, he was practically the most athletic sixth grader in the whole world.

Leon and Luna's complete lack of output was quite revealing. And if Ollie was being honest, really hilarious. They struggled to complete one jumping jack. They struggled to complete one sit-up. And they struggled to not complain the whole time.

Ollie's mom marched around them. "Quit your belly-aching!"

"But that's the problem," said Leon after finally completing a sit-up.

"Our bellies do ache," said Luna. "Along with everything else!"

Leon pointed to Ollie and Tamiko. "Why can't we just stand and watch like them?"

"Because we're not the wrestlers," said Ollie.

"That's right," said Tamiko. "You are."

Leon sighed and nodded. "The truth hurts."

"But not as much as these push-ups," said Luna.

Tamiko excused herself to giggle in the bathroom without anyone hearing.

"Can we take a breather?" begged Leon. "We've been training for hours."

"You've been training for five minutes," said Ollie's mom.

"Well, it feels like hours," said Luna.

The Ragtag Team is going to kick their butts, thought Ollie.

Leon and Luna could afford the best. Whether that was a personal trainer, the latest workout clothes, or every exercise machine known to man. But what money couldn't buy was talent, and it was painfully obvious that when it came to talent, the Krackle Kiddos were bankrupt.

"It'll feel like days when I'm done with you," shouted his mom in a firm but encouraging tone as she jogged in place. "Besides, I like what I'm seeing here. Now, push-ups! As many as you can do. Go, go, go!"

The Krackle Kiddos huffed, then puffed, then pushed. And then they fell face-forward onto the floor after barely managing to complete two push-ups.

"A new record," cried his mom triumphantly. "Well done, both of you. I think you've earned that breather now."

The Krackle Kiddos remained on the floor, panting and gasping for air as if they'd finished a marathon. Ollie walked past them to talk to his mom privately.

"Mom, can't you see that they're not very good?" he asked once he was out of earshot. "And don't you think that's weird?"

"Ollie! That's not very nice." His mom gave him a disappointed look before gesturing to the Krackle Kiddos. "All I see from them is maximum effort. You know, some athletes save all their energy for the big moment. And their record doesn't lie! Now if you'll excuse me, I need to run around the block a few times before we start up again."

As Leon and Luna gulped down water, all Ollie saw was two kids who had cheated their way to every victory they'd claimed.

"It's over?" asked Tamiko when she reappeared. "I was only gone for, like, two seconds."

Ollie shushed Tamiko as the Krackle Kiddos crossed the room toward them. The last thing they needed was for Leon and Luna to catch on to what they were doing.

"Open these," said Leon before shoving a box into Ollie's hands. Tamiko received an identical box from Luna.

"What's this?" asked Ollie.

"I'm not opening your mail for you," said Tamiko. "You can get Billingsley to do that."

Luna laughed. "They're for you, not us. Open them."

Ollie wasn't sure what the Krackle Kiddos had in store. Maybe this was some sort of trap. But his curiosity got the better of him. He opened his box to find an official Slamdown Town Krackle Kiddos T-shirt inside. And what was more, Leon and Luna had signed it. He glanced over at Tamiko and saw that she had received a matching shirt.

"A shirt with both of your faces on it," said Tamiko, confused. "Just what I always wanted," she added with a hint of sarcasm.

"Why did you give us these?" asked Ollie.

"Because we're best friends," said the twins.

Had Ollie heard correctly? All the Krackle Kiddos had ever done was boss them around. Now suddenly, they were handing out gifts and calling themselves best friends. Of all the strange circumstances involving Leon and Luna, this one might have been the strangest.

"You guys are, like, the first friends we've ever had," said Luna.

Leon nodded. "Our parents are always fighting and busy with their own stuff. Daddy loves money more than anything and Mommy loves spending it more than anything. And they'd both push a little old lady out of the way if they spotted a penny on the ground."

"Then over argue who saw it first," said Luna. "We sort of get lost in the shuffle. And sure, we get everything we ask for. Because we're worth it and everything."

"But you can't buy friends," they said in unison. "Even though Daddy tried one time."

Ollie wished the Krackle Kiddos would stop talking. Every word they said made him feel sorry for them. And that was exactly the opposite of what he wanted to feel toward the two most spoiled brats he'd ever met.

"He's the whole reason we're doing this," admitted Luna.

"Your dad is making you wrestle?" asked Ollie.

Leon shook his head. "No. At least, not really. We're only wrestling to impress him."

"He loves wrestling because wrestling makes him money," said Luna. "So we figured that if we won, he'd make a fortune, and then he'd *have* to care about us."

Leon sighed. "Or at least notice us. But we were wrong. He doesn't care at all. He's never even bothered to show up for one of our matches."

"But we're glad we decided to wrestle because we were able to meet you two," said Luna. "It's good to have people that actually want to be with us."

"After each match we look up in the stands and see you," said Leon. "It feels good to have people notice us. I mean, why wouldn't you? We're the best wrestlers to ever step foot in that arena," he added quickly in a thinly veiled effort to make the situation less sentimental.

To say Ollie felt conflicted was an understatement. On the one hand, Leon and Luna's gesture was nice. And admittedly a bit weird and self-centered. They clearly liked him and Tamiko enough to consider them really good friends. On the other hand, the Krackle Kiddos were self-indulgent cheaters who were ruining the arena and had caused Tamiko's dad to lose his job and, apparently, dive headfirst into a snack-themed midlife crisis. Their entire friendship with Leon and Luna rested on the need for evidence to out them. That *needed* to happen.

So why did he feel so bad all of a sudden?

His mom entered the room, a thin layer of sweat sparkling on her forehead. "Nothing like a quick jog around the entire neighborhood three times to get you pumped for working out!"

The Krackle Kiddos groaned, but made their way back to the mats. Tamiko caught Ollie's attention and motioned for the two of them to slip away. As Ollie followed her out of the gym and into the hallway, the guilty feeling remained.

When they snuck into the empty living room for a private chat, it became clear that Tamiko was just as disturbed by what had happened as he was.

"Why did they have to go and do that?" she asked. "I figured they didn't care about us! Now we're telling each other deep emotional secrets and giving gifts? That wasn't part of the plan!"

"I know," said Ollie. "All that stuff about their dad and why they're doing this. It doesn't excuse the cheating, but—"

Tamiko shook her head. "No! Don't do that! They're the bad guys, remember? We're supposed to feel bad for them because despite getting everything they want, their dad loves money more than them? Look around! They can literally buy anything, whether that's winning or happiness."

As Ollie looked over the various trophies and plaques lining the walls, he wondered how much power money *actually* had. The Krackle Kiddos admitted that money was incapable of buying friendship. If friendship couldn't be bought, maybe happiness also wasn't for sale.

Suddenly, something caught Ollie's eye. Or rather, a lack of something caught his eye. Above the mantle, he saw a dusty outline of a giant fish. Ollie remembered that this was the living room where Linton had shown them the krackle fish.

"That's fishy," said Ollie as he pointed to the vacant wall.

"Actually, it's not," said Tamiko. "Looks like the krackle fish is—"

Ollie's eyes lit up as he understood.

"Missing!" they shouted together.

"Wait," said Ollie, taking out his evidence notebook and flipping to the most recent entry. "Didn't Skull and Bones say they were attacked with a weapon?"

"Yeah," said Tamiko. "And then there was the fish smell. In the locker room *and* on Billingsley."

Ollie paced back and forth. "Billingsley said he was cooking dinner, but in reality he was attacking Skull and Bones backstage with the krackle fish so that they wouldn't be able to wrestle the Krackle Kiddos!"

"That fish is massive," said Tamiko. "I wouldn't want to be whacked with it."

Ollie's mind raced. This last piece of evidence, coupled with all prior proof, didn't paint a good picture for their "friends." "But of all weapons to use, why the krackle fish trophy?"

"What are you looking at?" asked the Krackle Kiddos as they entered the room.

"A crime scene," said Ollie as he spun to face Leon and Luna.

They were covered in sweat and guzzling down energy drinks.

Luna nearly spit her drink out. "Crime? What crime?"

"The case of the missing krackle fish," said Tamiko.

Leon laughed. "You're both acting so weird. And not just today, either."

"Yeah," said Luna. "You were, like, really, really good in class for one week and then you were really, really bad in class the week after. And now you're detectives or something?"

Ollie pointed to the mantle. "But there was a fish trophy up there, right?"

"Yeah, our krackle fish trophy," said Leon. "Daddy and Mommy took us on a fishing trip a few years ago before they got divorced."

Luna smiled at the memory. "Together, we caught the krackle fish that was on the mantle. The fisherman who took us out said it was the biggest krackle fish ever caught and that we should take it home as a memory of that day."

"It was a fun day, actually. With Daddy, Mommy, and both of us ..." said Leon wistfully. He looked lost in the memory.

"A seagull pooped on Daddy's head," said Luna, "but it was such a good day that he wasn't even mad. We all laughed, together ..."

"As a family," said Leon.

"So where is it now?" demanded Tamiko.

"Oh, who knows. Daddy probably sold it to make a quick buck. He doesn't care about good memories," said Leon.

"Just pebbles, like the krackle fish," said Luna.

"You mean money," said Ollie.

"Whatever," said Leon. "Anyway, what are you guys doing?"

"And what's that?" asked Luna, pointing to the evidence notebook.

The Krackle Kiddos moved forward, and before Ollie could process what was happening, snatched the evidence notebook straight out of his hands.

"No, wait," said Ollie as he tried to grab it back.

But it was too late. The Krackle Kiddos were already leafing through the notebook. Every clue, every accusation, laid bare. Not a word was spoken. Ollie hardly dared to breathe. Now that they knew they were caught, would the Krackle Kiddos confess?

"Why would you write this stuff about us?" asked Leon. His face was red and his voice was harsh. It reminded Ollie of how they always talked to Billingsley.

Luna tossed the book back to them. "This is preposterous," she said, her voice betraying her rising anger. "Why would we have Billingsley fix the matches? We're the best wrestlers Slamdown Town has ever seen."

"You don't need to cheat when you're the best," said Leon.

"Leon. Luna. Just listen to us," stammered Ollie, but they cut him off.

"You're jealous. Both of you. You wish you could wrestle like us."

"No," said Tamiko. "That's not it."

"Yes, that's exactly it," said Leon. "Not everyone can be a great wrestler."

Luna looked like she might cry. "We thought you were our friends. We even went out of our way to make all those changes to the arena because you wanted them. But you only wanted to hang out with us because we're the first family of wrestling. You're just like our parents. You don't care about us. Just yourselves."

"But everyone's going to get what's coming to them," they said together. "Our workout is over, as is this friendship. Now, get out of our house. Your mom's waiting for you in the car."

There was no wiggle room. No chance to plead or argue.

"Why do *I* feel bad just because we called them out as cheaters?" said Tamiko as they made their way down the hallway.

Ollie didn't have an answer for that.

Everything had happened so quickly. He never meant to hurt the Krackle Kiddos, only expose them. But they'd forced his hand. Now there was only one person who could help.

CHAPTER 32

TAMIKO

IT was Saturday before the first wrestling matches, and Game Over and Big Chew stood in Linton Krackle's cramped office as he flipped through the evidence notebook.

"This is ridiculous," he shouted from across his desk. "This is preposterous. This is . . ." Linton paused, looking up at the two of them. "What is this?"

"Evidence," said Game Over. "That your kids are cheating."

Linton's face dropped as he flipped through the notebook.

"Paying people off? Hiring a fake referee? Attacking an opponent?" Linton grew more and more flustered the further he read. Even the bald spot on top of his head was beet-red.

"Well?" asked Big Chew.

Linton closed the notebook. "They're just kids! Not criminal masterminds."

"It doesn't take a mastermind to see that they can't wrestle," said Big Chew.

"Which is why they have Billingsley fix the matches for them," said Game Over.

"Billingsley? Billingsley's just a simple butler who does whatever he's told."

"Exactly!" said Big Chew and Game Over.

"Seriously, Linton. Work with us here." Game Over leaned forward, using her impressive size to offer a bit of intimidation. "I know they're your kids, but it's clear that the Krackle Kiddos have been up to no good the minute they arrived in Slamdown Town."

"They got rid of all the wrestling posters and replaced them with a gigantic one," said Big Chew.

"They got rid of my dad—err—" Game Over cleared her throat. "I mean the snack guy, and replaced him with a chef."

"And they got rid of Screech Holler and replaced him with a TV personality."

Linton waved his hands dismissively. "All improvements. Expensive improvements."

"But where does it end?" asked Game Over. "Slamdown Town is the best place ever invented. And the Krackle Kiddos are ruining it."

Big Chew nodded. "There's nothing we love more than the arena. And these changes spit in the face of everything that makes it great." He pointed at Linton. "Besides, what's next? Replacing you?"

Linton snorted so hard that he had to find a tissue before continuing.

"Don't be ridiculous," he said as he wiped his nose clean. "I'm the CEO. They can't replace me. Now look, I understood you're both scared to face my kids—"

"We're *not* scared," said Game Over.

"Good. Because this hogwash"—Linton motioned to the book—"proves nothing. Now you two get out of my office, get in that ring, and do what I don't pay you to do: wrestle."

Game Over reached for the evidence notebook, but Linton snatched it away.

"Nope," he said, tossing it into his desk drawer. "This piece of fiction stays with me. I'll pull it out whenever I need a good laugh."

Game Over and Big Chew left Linton's office feeling defeated.

Big Chew sighed. "Well, we tried to do it without embarrassing them. If Linton doesn't believe us, he will after we kick their butts today!"

They headed backstage toward the locker room with plenty of time to hang out before their match. But on the way, Big Chew spotted Hollis waiting outside the Wrestlers Only entrance. And to his surprise, he saw that his brother was wearing his Lil' Chew outfit, a knockoff Big Chew costume complete with winter gloves, rain galoshes, and a bedsheet draped over his shoulders. Hollis even sported a golden pair of briefs on the outside of his pants.

"Hey, Big Chew!" shouted Hollis as they approached. "It's me, Lil' Chew!"

Game Over crossed her arms. "So, this is the infamous pipsqueak who wouldn't leave you alone after matches."

"I can't believe Game Over knows who I am," said Hollis as his eyes went wide.

"Where you been, buddy?" asked Big Chew.

"Well, I haven't quite been myself lately." Hollis took a deep breath. "But I've grown a lot over the past three weeks."

Game Over slapped her forehead.

"First I messed up by being too nice," said Hollis.

"Been there, done that," said Game Over. "Being a face is overrated."

"Then I found myself being too mean," he continued.

Big Chew shrugged. "I made the same mistake last week. The heel turn wasn't for me."

"But my brother—the little pip-squeak that he is—said I should be myself and maybe I'd get my girl back. So here I am, back to being me." Hollis leaned in toward Big Chew. "But don't tell him I took his advice," he whispered. "Don't want him to know . . ."

"Your secret is safe with me," said Big Chew.

"And part of myself is being your number one fan!" Hollis handed him a marker and an autograph book. "Can I get your autograph, for old times' sake?"

Big Chew leaned down and signed the book before tossing the marker to Game Over. She ignored the book and signed her name across Hollis's forehead.

"Wow," said Hollis. "Two for the price of one! By the way, I have to ask. When you disappeared, that was because you were abducted by aliens, right?"

Big Chew was spared having to answer when Breonna walked by, drawing Hollis's attention.

"Hey, good luck out there, guys," said Hollis. "There's something I gotta do."

"Good luck," said Big Chew.

Game Over shoved a finger into Hollis's face. "Don't mess this up, ya nitwit, or I'll kick your butt."

"That would be awesome," said Hollis as he sprinted away. "But I promise I won't!"

Linton hadn't listened, but at least Hollis did.

When they finally reached the locker room, Big Chew and Game Over suited up for their match against the Krackle Kiddos. But this time, in the spirit of staying true to themselves, Game Over pulled on her original costume: the solid-jet-black singlet, sleek leather jacket, knee-high combat boots, and her retro controller necklace.

Big Chew emerged wearing his original costume, the one he and Tamiko had made together: his purple singlet, shiny gloves, big red cape, and shiny gold briefs.

"Nothing is going to stop us," said Big Chew.

Game Over smiled. "We are going to kick some cheating Krackle Kiddos butt."

A buzzing crowd forming around the schedule board drew their attention.

"Crickey!" yelled Aussie Outback, the crazed wrestler from down under. She removed her buffalo hat and wiped her forehead. "If I'd known I wasn't going to wrestle till later, I would have tossed a few more shrimps on the barbie!"

"What's all this about?" asked Big Chew as they approached.

"New schedule," grunted The Giraffe. He had to crouch down to avoid hitting his head on the locker room ceiling.

That didn't seem right to Game Over. "A schedule change? This late?"

At first glance, it looked like no dramatic changes had been made. A few matches had been swapped due to injuries. Everything looked routine, until she saw that their match had been rescheduled.

"Our match has been rescheduled!" said Game Over.

"To when?" asked Big Chew.

Game Over nearly fainted. "Five minutes ago!"

"What? But we were in Linton's office that whole time," said Big Chew. "There's no way we would have known. We'll be disqualified for sure."

Wrestlers who were a no-show automatically forfeited their matches. The Krackle Kiddos must have known that Big Chew and Game Over were in Linton's office and had Billingsley swap the schedule. She couldn't believe that they'd had the nerve to do that.

"Ah, I'm devo for ya mates," said Aussie before plopping her hat back on her head. "But what can ya do? G'day! Although it sounds like yours won't be very good."

There wasn't a second to lose. Game Over took off toward the wrestlers entrance. She heard Big Chew in pursuit. But by the time they set foot on the entrance ramp, it was too late.

"Slamdown Town," said Penelope Dunnelly, "give it up for your match winners due to no-show, the Krackle Kiddos! They certainly win a lot, don't they?"

A smattering of boos and hisses rained down from the crowd.

"No, no!" shouted Game Over. "We're right here."

"We're ready to wrestle," confirmed Big Chew.

"Ah, finally worked up the courage to show up?" said Leon from the ring.

"Well, it's too little, too late," spat Luna.

"Because we just won and there's no takesies backsies," they said together.

No! Game Over refused to allow this to play out. She'd worked too hard to have the Krackle Kiddos take the match away from her.

"You swapped the schedule so we didn't have to wrestle you!" she yelled.

"Just like how you got out of every other match!" shouted Big Chew.

"Making excuses now, are you?" asked Luna.

"We've been here the whole time," said Leon. "The entire arena saw us waiting for you cowards. There's no way we could have swapped the schedule."

"You're disqualified," said Luna mockingly.

"And we're the winners," declared Leon.

"Deal with it," they said together before bursting out with laughter.

This was a nightmare. There was nothing either she or Big Chew could do to undo what had happened. The Krackle Kiddos had managed to defeat them without raising a hand.

"We were too late," said Game Over quietly.

"Yes, you were. But you did get here just in time for our big announcement." Leon and Luna leaned into their microphones. "Oh, Daddy! We need you!"

Linton emerged from the wrestlers entrance and hustled right past Game Over and Big Chew. She was tempted to snag Linton in a Game-Breaking Bug Lock.

He clambered into the ring next to Leon and Luna.

"Yes, kids?"

"Our championship match is going to be the biggest wrestling event in the history of wrestling," said Luna. She shoved a piece of paper and a pen into his hands. "Which is why we need you to sign this contract so we can hire a production crew to film it."

"A movie deal? I can practically taste the profits," said Linton, smacking his lips.

"I'm sure you can," said Leon. "We would have asked you earlier but you weren't here to watch us win. In fact, you weren't there to see any of our victories."

"Well, I'm here now." Linton signed his name with a flourish. "And I'll sign any piece of paper that will make you two happy. There. Are you happy?"

"Yes," said Luna, smiling. "We're very happy."

"By the way, did you have plans for next Saturday?" asked Leon.

"Nothing outside of wrestling," admitted Linton. "Well, and counting my money, of course, but that's every day on the hour, as you know."

Luna smiled. "Well, congrats. You now have a free Saturday. Because you're fired."

"Oh, that's very thoughtful of you," said Linton. And once the reality of what had just been said sunk in, he replied with a much louder, "Wait, what?!"

"Slamdown Town is ours now," they declared together.

"But you can't do that," insisted Linton.

"Actually, Daddy. We can."

"Says who?" asked Linton.

"Says *you*," said Luna. She waved the paper he'd signed moments earlier in front of his face. "This isn't a contract at all. It's the deed to Slamdown Town, which we found in the pile of messy papers on your desk. And you just signed the arena over to us."

The crowd gasped.

This has to be some kind of joke, thought Game Over.

Leon laughed. "Joke's on you, Daddy. We got the idea from watching wrestling on TV. On that show the CEO's kids kicked him out of his arena. We know how much you love it and the money it makes you and now it's ours."

"I only wanted you to be happy," said Linton as he slowly climbed out of the ring.

"And as the new CEOs and owners," said Luna, ignoring her father, "we declare that next week Nursing Home will face us for the tag team championship belt!"

Game Over had seen enough. She marched back to the locker room.

"We warned him," she cried as she vented some of her anger by bursting open the locker room door with a well-placed kick. "That's it. We've been beaten. It's over."

"We can still investigate," said Big Chew. "There's got to be some way to prove that Billingsley switched the schedule. Maybe we can compare it to his handwriting."

"It doesn't matter." Game Over sank onto a nearby bench, completely and utterly defeated. "Leon and Luna are in charge of Slamdown Town now. *They* would be the ones we'd show the evidence to. You really think they're going to bust themselves?"

Big Chew opened and closed his mouth several times, but no words came out.

"It's just like *Brawlmania Supreme*," said Game Over. "The final boss is rigged. You can try a thousand times and maybe— *maybe*—if you get lucky like me you can beat them."

"You didn't get lucky," said Big Chew, "you got good. We can get good."

"And then what?" she asked. "Even if we do beat them it won't matter because they make all the rules. They'll continue to 'improve' the arena until they've changed everything that we love."

"So what are you saying?" asked Big Chew.

"I'm saying, 'What's the point?'"

But admitting that didn't make Game Over feel any better. In fact, it made her feel *much* worse.

CHAPTER 33

TAMIKO

TAMIKO smashed the buttons on her controller.

It had been an entire day since she and Ollie had resigned themselves to a Krackle Kiddos victory. But despite being in her own living room, she still felt trapped in the arena.

Leon and Luna had already made so many changes. Now that they'd ousted their father and were running the show, there was no telling what Slamdown Town would become.

She was doing everything she could to distract herself, and playing *Trash Bin Terror: Garbage Day* was always good for turning off her brain for a few hours. But, as she threw out moldy vegetables and recycled plastic bottles, she realized she couldn't take her mind off of what had happened.

"Hey, bug!" yelled her dad from the basement. "How about you put the controller down for a second and come help your favorite dad?"

She sighed, tossed the controller to the floor, and headed down to the basement. She wondered what Snack Guy shenanigans her dad would have up his sleeve today.

"Ah, there you are," said her dad from behind his makeshift curtain. "No peeking. It'll spoil the surprise. Take a seat over there on the couch."

Tamiko took a seat.

Her dad stuck his head out from behind the curtain and smiled. "Excellent. Prepare to be amazed by Snack Guy's awe-inspiring, death-defying, super-crazy, snack-inspired moves!"

He leapt out from behind the curtain, decked out in his ridiculous Snack Guy costume. Tamiko couldn't help but giggle.

"First, I'm going to deliver a Cheesy Clothesline!" He lifted his leg as high as it could go, which admittedly was not very high, and kicked his foot forward.

"That's not a clothesline," said Tamiko.

"It's not?" he asked. "But I researched it and everything."

"Trust me. I know. That's more of a Ketchup Kick."

"That's a good one!" He wrote down her suggestion on a piece of food-stained paper. "Well, I know you won't be able to withstand my Hot Dog Piledriver!"

He brought his hand dramatically into the air and slowly chopped across his body.

Tamiko waited a moment before asking, "Are you going to do the move?"

"Oh, I must have been moving too fast for the human eye. Observe once more."

Her dad repeated the same motion. But this time he made sure to do so even slower.

"Um, Dad. That's not even remotely what a piledriver is. I guess you could call that a Soda Pop Chop or something. But even that might be a little generous."

"How about a Diet Soda Pop Chop?" he asked, writing down the suggestion.

Tamiko was starting to regret coming downstairs. Her dad's lack of wrestling knowledge rivaled only Penelope Dunnelly's. But Tamiko had told her dad time and time again what the correct wrestling terms and rules were. How could he *still* not know?

"Listen, Dad," she said as she slid off the couch. "I should really get back to my game."

"Hold on there, bug. I can't let you leave without sampling my extra-salty, extra-crispy . . . French Fry Finisher!"

He leapt onto the couch, lifted his hands to his mouth, and silently roared back at the nonexistent crowd. Then he raised his arms high above his head and leapt off the couch.

Tamiko wasn't sure exactly what type of move he was attempting. She guessed he was trying to do a front flip, but instead he landed smack on his belly.

Her dad groaned. "More like the French Fry Belly Flop, am I right?"

"You're supposed to finish your opponent, not yourself," said Tamiko.

"That actually makes a lot more sense, now that you say it," admitted her dad. He groaned and slowly made his way back onto his feet. "Now I understand."

"But that's just it, Dad. You *don't* understand wrestling. I get that you're trying to be a wrestler now, but you're really not that great at it, you know?"

Her dad took a seat on the couch, his cheeks red with embarrassment. "Oh yeah, I guess I was probably being silly. Just trying to have a little fun . . ."

"Maybe you should stick to something you know better. Like your cosplaying. You're really good at that."

"I am, aren't I?" said her dad. He smiled, but something about him seemed sad.

"Tamiko!" yelled her mom from upstairs. "Can you come up here, please?"

Her dad pulled Tamiko into a hug. "Don't worry, bug. I won't be bothering you anymore with any of my silly wrestling stuff. I release you back to your video games."

Tamiko didn't wait for a second invitation. She headed upstairs to discover her mom had taken up residency on the living room couch. She patted the cushion next to her.

"Seat's empty," said her mom with a smile. "And I find myself in need of a copilot. Climb aboard."

Tamiko smiled as she leapt onto the couch beside her mom. She booted up *Gnarly Cosmos*, a celestial skateboarding game where you could grind across streaking comets and do kickflips off of rocky moons.

"I heard what you said to your dad," her mom said as she landed a heelflip into a gravity well.

"Hopefully he took the hint," said Tamiko as she fought to keep up with her mom by grinding on a derelict satellite. "I don't want him to make a fool of himself out there."

"You mean you don't want him to make a fool out of *you* out there," corrected her mom.

Tamiko shrugged. "I mean, yeah. Is that so wrong?"

The sounds of the game filled the awkward silence.

"You know that your dad would gladly make a fool out of himself if that meant it made you proud of him."

Tamiko didn't have an answer for that. Or, more accurately, she knew the answer but didn't want to say it out loud. Because she knew that there was nothing her dad wouldn't try in order to impress her.

"He told me that he really liked his snack job at the arena," said her mom.

"He was *really* good at it," Tamiko admitted. "He can't remember anything about wrestling, but when it came to everyone's orders he remembered every detail. And he never judged anyone. Not even when Big Tuna asked for anchovies on his ice cream. That was cool."

"Sounds kind of gross, if I'm being honest," joked her mom. Then more seriously, she added, "I think more than the snacks, he enjoyed hanging out with you."

Tamiko let out a cheer as she *just* managed to land a backflip to pull ahead of her mom and come in first place.

"Yeah!" yelled Tamiko. "I totally beat you! I am the best!"

"I have been bested," acknowledged her mom. "Forever will I bear this shame."

"As you should." Tamiko paused. "You really think Dad went through all that trouble to hang out with me?"

"I think he might actually like you or something." Her mom playfully nudged her arm. "He's not good at video games, he doesn't know anything about wrestling, but he did put in a lot of effort to try to find something special that you guys could have. And I know that, personally, he felt like he had found it with your shared love of junk food. It's too bad that he was let go."

"Yeah. Too bad . . ."

For a brief moment, Tamiko had forgotten about the Krackle Kiddos and all the trouble they'd caused. But it seemed like, no matter how far away she got from it, even in her own living room, there was no escape.

CHAPTER 34

OLLIE

OLLIE didn't know what to do.

Typically a wide-open Sunday meant gaming with Tamiko, talking about wrestling with Hollis, or thinking about gaming and wrestling instead of doing his homework. But with Leon and Luna now fully in control of Slamdown Town, all those things felt pointless.

He'd been lying in bed staring at the ceiling for what felt like hours when, suddenly, he heard his mom's workout music waft into his room.

Ollie remembered the Krackle Kiddos saying that they never spoke to their parents. However, speaking to his mom always made him feel better.

So he leapt out of bed and followed the sound of the thumping bass.

He found his mom working out in her home gym in the garage. "Rules Are Cool (And Meant to Be Followed)" blasted out of a vintage speaker as she bench-pressed to the beat of the song.

"I thought today was a light workout?" asked Ollie as he watched the bar sag under the massive stack of weights. "You do know what light means, don't you?"

"It is," she grunted, lifting the bar up. "And I do, but everyone needs an easy day every now and again." She added more weight onto the bar. "Even me."

"You call that easy?" he asked.

She smiled and began her routine. Ollie watched in silence, unsure how to start the conversation. After a minute, she placed the bar gently on the rests and reached for her towel.

"You want a go?"

"Really?" asked Ollie. "I won't be able to lift much."

She wiped down the bench. "You can lift the bar. I'll spot you."

If his mom believed he could do it, Ollie was willing to try.

"Everything all right with you?" she asked as she tossed the weights to the ground. "You seem like you want to get something off your chest. Speaking of which, here you go."

His mom carefully lowered the bar down toward him. Even without the weights, Ollie struggled to hold on to it. But his mom was there to keep a close eye on the bar.

"I'm going to tell you something," he began, "but I'm not sure you'll believe me."

"Try me," she said.

Ollie sighed. "Tamiko and I are pretty sure the Krackle Kiddos are cheating." His arms began to shake as he lifted the bar, which refused to go any higher, despite his efforts.

"That's a pretty serious accusation, Ollie. Do you have any proof?"

"Loads," he said, struggling to speak. "We wrote it all down in my evidence notebook. They used their butler to pay off the Terrible Twosome. He dressed up as a guest referee and threw their match against the Scallywags. He dropped the shark cage on top of Tsunami as they walked out. He attacked Skeleton Crew backstage and, worst of all, rescheduled our—I mean, the Ragtag Team's—match so that they would miss it and have to forfeit."

"Wow," she said, still spotting the bar, "it sounds like you've been doing your homework. And I don't mean for school. But I just have one question."

"What's that?"

"Why would they do all that?"

"Because they can't actually wrestle. I mean, look at them!"

The bar felt like it was made out of solid lead. Ollie gulped down air and tried with all his might to lift it higher. But nothing happened. He sighed and lowered the bar to his chest.

"Now, I admit that two twelve-year-olds wrestling is strange," she said, grabbing the bar, "but I've got a good nose for sniffing out cheaters, and I don't think they smell funny. Sure, they complain a lot during our workout sessions and they're spoiled rotten, but they really do try."

"So you think they can actually wrestle?" he asked.

"Anyone can wrestle, Ollie." She smiled at him. "Where's your evidence notebook now?"

"In Linton's desk drawer. We went and showed him everything."

"And?"

"He said that they weren't cheating, and if they were he wouldn't allow it."

"Well, I don't know about that. If there's anyone at Slamdown Town who smells funny, it's Linton. Can't trust a man who loves money more than the sport he makes it from."

Ollie nodded. "It doesn't matter, anyway. We both know he's gone and that the Krackle Kiddos make all the rules now." He tried to push the bar again but gave up. "Phew. I don't think I can do this."

"Yes, you can," she assured him.

She began to gently lift the bar upward. Not very much, but enough to get the process started. With his mom's help, Ollie felt that maybe this *wasn't* impossible. He channeled his renewed confidence into one huge push.

He grunted. He groaned. He did it.

"I did it!" shouted Ollie triumphantly.

"Good job, Ollie," said his mom. She plucked the bar out of his hands and placed it up onto the rest as if it were a toothpick. "I knew you could. And remember, you and Tamiko have gotten through difficult situations before. If you work together nothing can stop you two."

Ollie gave his mom a sweaty hug. "Thanks, Mom. You're the best."

"Well, I *am* a champion." She kissed Ollie on the cheek.

Ollie headed back up to his room. But he had only made it to the bottom of the staircase when he felt his phone vibrate in his pants pocket.

Bzz! Bzz!

He dug it out of his pocket and discovered the culprit was none other than Linton Krackle. He sprinted up the stairs and closed his door before answering.

"Linton?" asked Ollie.

"How did you know it was me?" demanded Linton.

"The caller ID told me."

"Foiled by technology! That's what I'm always saying. By the way, who is this?" asked Linton, suddenly suspicious. "I thought this was Big Chew's number. Are you his kid or something? Go get your dad for me."

Oh right, thought Ollie. Big Chew's voice was different from his own.

"Hey, Dad," said Ollie in a voice he hoped was convincing. "Phone call!"

Ollie shot over to his nightstand, yanked the gum out of its wrapper, and chewed it.

"Big Chew here," he said in Big Chew's gravelly voice. "Sorry about that. My, umm, son really likes to answer my phone."

Big Chew groaned. Even with all his heel training, he remained absolutely awful at lying. Linton either didn't notice or didn't care because he moved right past the obvious fib.

"Wasn't aware you had a family," said Linton. "But that's good, actually. Means you'll understand my situation better. I need your help."

"My help? Now isn't really a good time."

Linton completely ignored Big Chew. "Let's meet. Face-to-face. Somewhere"—he struggled for the right word—"discreet. It's not safe to do this over the phone."

That got Big Chew's interest.

"I couldn't risk contacting Ms. Manager," continued Linton in a panicked tone. "No, I have to speak with you directly. No middle people, no matter how skilled in negotiations she is. You have to come alone. Tell no one."

What on earth could Linton need Big Chew for that he couldn't tell him over the phone? He seemed downright scared. Desperate, even. Maybe he'd misplaced his wallet and needed Big Chew to rough up some people. Whatever it was, he was curious.

"All right," said Big Chew. "Where should I meet you?"

CHAPTER 35

TAMIKO

GAME Over made her way up the escalator, past her favorite used video game store, and toward the mall food court. When the phone rang earlier that day, she'd been expecting Ollie. Instead, she'd received an urgent call from Linton asking Game Over to meet him immediately.

"Meet me immediately," he'd said.

"Where?" she'd asked.

"The food court in the mall. Come alone."

So, after transforming into Game Over, she made her way into the food court and immediately spotted Linton sitting at a table. He was wearing a fedora, a trench coat, and sunglasses. If he was trying not to be seen, he wasn't doing a very good job of it.

Game Over took a seat opposite him. "Hello, Linton."

"Shh," he said, leaning in. "Not so loud. Was I really that easy to spot?"

"Yes. Why the secrecy?" she asked.

"Because I have something super-secret to tell you."

"I'm all ears."

"Not yet, we're waiting for another pair."

"Another pair of what?" she asked.

"Ears. Oh, here they are now."

Suddenly, Big Chew sat down in the chair beside her.

"Tamiko? I mean, Game Over," he corrected.

"Ollie? I mean, Big Chew. What are you doing here?"

"I could ask you the same thing."

"Okay, you two, let's get down to business," said Linton.

Linton tossed the evidence notebook onto the table.

"I have a confession to make. I lied to you when you confronted me in my office. My kids, the Krackle Kiddos, have only been winning because the matches have been fixed."

"We knew it!" said Game Over, snatching the evidence notebook.

"Yeah, they were ordering Billingsley to cheat so they could win!" said Big Chew.

"No," said Linton. He sighed. "It wasn't Leon or Luna or Billingsley. It was me."

"*You?*" asked Game Over and Big Chew in unison.

"Yes. And the worst part about this is that Leon and Luna don't know anything about it. My kids actually think that they've been winning their matches, bless their greedy, selfish souls."

"But, why?" asked Game Over.

"And how?" asked Big Chew.

"The why is complicated, but the how is pretty straightforward." Linton sighed again and shoved a handful of greasy fries into his mouth. "The first match was easy. I paid off the Terrible Twosome to take the fall and give my kids an easy victory. Werewrestler and Sasquat are some of the dirtiest wrestlers around, and were happy to take a dive for the right price."

"But what about Billingsley?" asked Game Over.

Linton leaned in. "What about him?"

"Werewrestler came to your house and we saw him and Billingsley talking."

"Yeah, he handed him an envelope," said Big Chew. "Probably filled with cash."

"You're right, but for the wrong reasons. Leon and Luna asked Billingsley to get signed posters of the Terrible Twosome. Do you think he's going to sign and give out posters of himself for free? Werewrestler and Sasquat came by to drop them off. Billingsley was paying them for the posters, not for throwing the match. Also, when were you at my house?"

"Never mind that," said Game Over.

"I didn't know that Leon and Luna were fans of theirs," said Big Chew.

"They're not. They used the posters as target practice for their new bow and arrow and then took what was left, tore it up, and sprinkled it in the litter box. The cat seemed to like it."

"Okay, but what about the match against the Scallywags?" asked Game Over.

"Yes," said Big Chew, grabbing the notebook and flipping to that page. "Billingsley dressed up as the referee and called the match in their favor."

"We even found a fake mustache as he was fleeing the scene."

"And all those costumes in his room," said Big Chew. "How do you explain that?"

"Billingsley? He's part of several local theater groups. He's got a costume for every performance and, apparently, a fake mustache. Also, when were you in Billingsley's room?"

"Never mind that," said Big Chew.

Linton rubbed his mustache. "No, it was I who dressed up as the referee."

"But the referee was tall. Like, really tall," said Game Over. "And you're . . ."

"Short. Like, really short. I know. Rub it in, why don't you? Ever heard of stilts? Dressing up as the referee was a surefire way to ensure my kids won, but it was too risky to use again. My costume fooled everyone once, but I doubted it would a second time. That's when I got the idea to drop the shark cage on top of Tsunami. I'd remembered that it was faulty, as most things in the arena are, and figured that everyone would assume it was an equipment malfunction."

"But we saw Billingsley snooping around by the shark cage on the security footage."

"Nope, it was me. Leon and Luna had asked him to hang their victory banner from the ceiling. In fact, he nearly caught me. Which is why I had to delete the security footage. Unfortunately, I've never been good with technology. Fortunately, my coffee spilled all over the computer and deleted it. But my luck almost ran out when I tried to pay off Skeleton Crew."

"But they said that they were attacked with a weapon."

"They were, but not intentionally. I kept a small emergency fund hidden inside the krackle fish trophy that only I knew about. I was on my way to bribe them when I tripped and whacked Skull and Bones in the back of the head with it. I didn't mean to hurt them, but when you accidently hit a pair of wrestlers like Skeleton Crew with a giant fish, you don't stick around. You ditch the evidence and run! Which was exactly what I did."

"And Billingsley smelling fishy . . ." began Game Over.

"Was just him preparing bouillabaisse. That's a very fancy fish stew for very fancy people. It's a Krackle Kiddos favorite, but boy is it smelly. And expensive."

Big Chew cut in. "So it was *you* who switched the schedule at the last second?"

"You left me no choice. Originally I was going to try to bribe you to throw the match. I tried my best to stall, but the two of you wanted to face my kids so badly and prove that they were frauds. Getting in the ring would have confirmed your suspicions. And revealed the truth to the entire arena. I couldn't let that happen, not after you came to me with your evidence."

"You mean . . ."

"As a short-term, immediate solution I altered the schedule while I came up with a long-term solution."

"Which was?"

"Firing you. And, as I sat there trying to come up with a clever way to both fire you *and* make money off of it, I was tricked into signing over the arena and fired myself!"

Game Over couldn't believe it. As she flipped through the

notebook, trying to poke holes in Linton's story, she came to only one conclusion: He was (finally) telling the truth.

"So now you know the how. But as to the why . . ." Linton trailed off.

Game Over could see that he was searching for the answer himself.

Finally, he said, "Let's just say that it's not easy being a father. You know, Big Chew."

"What?" asked Game Over.

"I have a son," said Big Chew. "Who likes to answer my phone. Remember?"

"Oh, right," said Game Over.

"I want my kids to be happy," Linton continued, "but the only way I know how to do that is by buying them things. And then they think that the only thing I care about is money. It's not the *only* thing I care about, it's just one of three things, the other two being my kids and wrestling. I thought that by letting them wrestle we'd be able to connect in a different way. But it didn't turn out how I'd expected . . ."

Game Over thought about her own dad and the recent conversation they'd had. Maybe her mom was right. Maybe the only reason her dad wanted to be Snack Guy was so that they could spend more time together. She suddenly felt guilty, but she pushed it aside.

"So why can't you just talk to them and tell them what you told us?" asked Big Chew.

"Yes," said Game Over. "*Everything* you told us."

"I've tried, but my kids want nothing to do with me. Which is why I need your help."

"Why should we help you?"

"Maybe you don't understand. Leon and Luna *truly believe* that they are great wrestlers. If they step foot in that ring without my protection, Nursing Home will destroy them, and I'm not just talking about their egos. Nursing Home, the geriatric terrors, may *actually* destroy them!"

Game Over didn't love the Krackle Kiddos, but she didn't hate them, either. And, after getting to know them for a few weeks and hearing what Linton had to say, she actually felt bad for them.

She turned and looked at Big Chew, and wordlessly, he nodded. She'd known Ollie long enough to know when they were on the same page, and now was one of those times.

"I can pay you," said Linton, taking out his checkbook.

"We don't want your money," said Game Over.

"Oh, thank goodness," said Linton.

"We want everything back that your kids took away," said Big Chew.

"Everything?"

"We want the wrestling posters back in the entrance. We want my dad—err—I mean, Mr. Tanaka back at the concession stand. We want Screech Holler back as the announcer. And we want you back as CEO."

Linton gasped. "Me? But, why? I cheated, I lied, I . . ."

"Because those are the things that make Slamdown Town the best arena in the tristate area," said Big Chew. "No, the world. And we wouldn't change them *for* the world."

"Plus," continued Game Over, "if we convince them to tear up that deed and bring you back as CEO, we know you'll keep things the way we like them, mostly because you're cheap."

"I'll take that as a compliment . . ."

"So what do you say?" asked Big Chew.

Linton considered this for a moment. "You've got yourselves a deal. But if, and only if, you get into that ring, defeat Nursing Home, and . . ."

"And?"

"Ensure that my kids aren't pulverized."

"Well, that'll be the hardest part," said Game Over.

CHAPTER 36

OLLIE

"WE'LL have to invade," said Ollie as he grabbed his lunch box from his locker.

He'd spent the entire evening coming up with different scenarios in which the Ragtag Team could get themselves into the ring to protect the Krackle Kiddos from Nursing Home. But it wasn't until this morning when he'd come up with his brilliant plan.

"That's your brilliant plan?" asked Tamiko through a mouthful of food. She'd already opened her lunch box and was halfway through a turkey sandwich. "Invade the match?"

"Linton isn't there to schedule us and there's no way the Krackle Kiddos would allow it. So we'll have to take matters into our own hands."

Tamiko nodded. "Okay, I'm always down for an invasion. But what about when we get in the ring? We can't outwardly defend Leon and Luna, remember? Which means that . . ."

"Yes," said Ollie as they entered the lunchroom. "We need to make it *look* like it's Nursing Home versus the Krackle Kiddos versus Ragtag Team."

"Wow," said Tamiko, taking a seat at the lunch table, "that is brilliant. It will be nearly impossible to pull off. It's hard enough beating one team, let alone two. But it is brilliant."

"Think of it less about fighting the Krackle Kiddos and more keeping them out of harm's way. The hard part will be selling it not only to the audience but to the Kiddos, too."

Ollie locked eyes with Leon and Luna across the cafeteria. They quickly looked away.

He and Tamiko tried to talk to them earlier this morning, but, as with Linton, they wouldn't even hear them out and, when the Krackle Kiddos spotted them approaching, they glared at them and walked in the opposite direction.

"I almost feel bad for them," said Tamiko. "Actually, I do."

"Me too," said Ollie. "It must be hard to go back and forth between your parents. Their mom seems more interested in spending money than spending time with them."

"And their dad seems more comfortable showering them with gifts than showering them with love. Okay, so I feel a little less bad for them. I mean, have you seen the size of their TV?"

Ollie laughed. As he unwrapped his sandwich and Tamiko started on her second, he realized that in the flurry of activity they hadn't addressed the elephant in the room.

"I'm sorry for what happened," said Ollie.

"*What* happened?" she asked.

Tamiko actually stopped eating. That meant she was really listening.

"I was jealous," he admitted. "I wanted to be the best. And when everybody loved Game Over more than me, I felt like I was the worst. Which wasn't really fair to you. I had my time to wrestle on my own and you didn't and I guess I was just getting used to sharing the stage."

"No, it wasn't fair. But I get it." Tamiko smiled awkwardly. "But I wasn't being so great of a friend myself. Kinda let the attention get to my head, you know? I wanted what you had, but I wanted it all to myself. I wasn't a team player. And we are a team. So, sorry for that."

Hearing Tamiko say that made Ollie feel a lot better.

"I suppose we both messed up, then," said Ollie. "But we still won two matches!"

Tamiko smiled. "All we have to do is bring *us* into the ring. Just like Nursing Home said, remember? You and me. We're best friends. We can be the best teammates, too."

"Well, so long as Nursing Home doesn't kick our butts first," he said doubtfully.

"Did I hear someone say something about Nursing Home kicking butts?" asked Breonna. She walked up to their table carrying a lunch tray. "My granny's secret recipe for kicking butts in the ring is the best there ever was!"

"Hey, short stacks, quit hoggin' my Breonna-kins," said Hollis, who appeared behind her carrying two lunch trays of his own. "Grabbed you a chocolate milk, babe."

Tamiko held out her hand in warning. "Hold it right there, eighth grader. Which version of Hollis are we in the presence of?"

"She has a point," said Ollie suspiciously. "You may look like the brother I remember, but I've been tricked before. Are you the one *true* Hollis?"

Breonna giggled. "You're both so cute. Don't worry." She locked her arms around Hollis. "Hollis learned that I like him because he's him. He doesn't need to be a goody two-shoes or a big, bad boy. *This* is the Hollie-poo that stole my heart in the first place and the one that has it again."

"And forever?" asked Hollis hopefully, burping up some chocolate milk.

"Don't get ahead of yourself," said Breonna. "But for today, yes."

"Turns out, some people had some pretty all right advice about being true to yourself or whatever," said Hollis, pretending to be offhand about it. "Not that *you* two would know anything about that. And if you did, you'd be smart enough to know to keep your sixth-grade mouths shut or else I'd feed you a knuckle sandwich. *If* that were the case, of course."

"Yep, that's Hollis," said Tamiko.

"We're actually going to celebrate tonight over at my granny's place," said Breonna excitedly. "Dentures Dan is even going to stop by. We get to use the TV trays and everything!"

That gave Ollie an idea. "Hey, Breonna, I don't suppose there would be TV trays available for me and Tamiko? We'd love to meet her." He turned to Tamiko. "Be great to *find out* some *things* about her and Dan before the big match this weekend, wouldn't it?"

"What? No way," stammered Hollis.

"Yeah," said Tamiko, catching on. "Ain't no house like Nursing

Home. I hope I'm as cool as Granny when I'm that old. That old lady's got the moves!"

"That sounds lovely," said Breonna, her voice cracking with excitement. "Oh, this is going to be such a good time. I can't wait to introduce you both to her."

Hollis shook his head. "I thought this was a date, babe. Just you and me."

"It's my grandmother's house, Hollie-poo. Plus, I'd love to hang out with Ollie and Tamiko and get to know them better now that we're back together. And Granny would, too! The more the merrier, she always says. I hope you both haven't eaten big lunches." She leaned in. "You *can't* say no to Granny's cooking. Otherwise she puts you in a headlock."

***

From the moment Ollie set foot inside the house, he was overwhelmed with the smell of flowery perfume, baking food, and the distinct scent that all old people's houses have.

"Ah! Fresh stomachs," said Granny with excitement when he, Tamiko, Hollis, and Breonna entered. "You two must be Ollie and Tamiko. Wonderful to meet you." She turned to Hollis. "And I see *you* finally got your act together, young man. Don't you go breaking my granddaughter's heart again or you'll regret it!"

She flexed slightly, her muscles bulging.

Hollis gulped. "Yes, ma'am. Understood, ma'am."

"Good." She pulled Breonna into a hug. "So wonderful for

you to stop by, sweetie pie. Speaking of which, I hope you all like dessert, because I baked five sweet pies this morning. But don't ruin your dinner. We're having meat loaf! Ground the beef myself with these fists. Worked up an appetite. You all look hungry. Here, have some candy!"

She shoved a mysterious assortment of candy toward them.

"Is this candy from when it was first invented?" asked Tamiko as she looked it over.

Granny shrugged. "Maybe. I haven't been able to have any of that for years now, on account of needing to watch my sugar intake."

Granny's house was filled with half-finished craft projects and workout equipment. Each room had cream-and-pink fine china lining the walls. Ollie kept almost accidentally knocking over porcelain cat figurines that were strewn haphazardly in every nook and cranny.

"You break it, you break Granny's heart, and that has no price," warned Granny.

Ollie made sure to keep his elbows tucked in for the rest of the tour. They found Dentures Dan snoozing in the training room in the basement with the television turned way, way up.

"Dan!" shouted Granny as they approached. "Get up! We have guests over!"

Dan startled. "I wasn't sleeping. I was resting my eyes."

"That's what the kids call sleeping these days, Dan."

Dan squinted at them. "You kids and your fancy new words. Back in my day, we only had a few words, and even then we used 'em sparingly!"

"Dan's a little cranky after his nap," whispered Breonna. "And before it, too."

Granny made her way over to the mat. "Let's show these young'uns how it's done."

"Don't push yourself too hard, Granny," cautioned Breonna.

Watching Nursing Home up close and personal was a master class in tag team wrestling. They executed each move with precision. There was power behind every throw, control in every hold, and arthritis in every slam. Old age had not slowed them down.

Ollie was beginning to think they had no weaknesses at all.

"And now for our all-powerful finishing move," shouted Granny, "the Geriatric Gutbuster. This move's been known to bust guts. Stand back, everyone!"

"No, not you," said Dentures Dan, motioning for Hollis to come onto the mat. "We need a volunteer from the audience."

"I'm about to get destroyed by Nursing Home," said Hollis, his voice full of awe.

The Geriatric Gutbuster dominated the tag team division, ending the run of countless challengers. Its appearance meant two things: the end of the match was only a few seconds away and the bust-ee on the receiving end of the buster was about to get busted.

Lil' Old Granny grabbed Hollis from behind, rooting him to the spot.

"Hit it, Dan," she shouted.

Dentures Dan prepared to charge. And that's when Ollie noticed it. Being so high up in the stands, he'd never caught the slight wiggle of Dan's famed dentures before he charged. But wiggle they did. A fitting tell that signaled the exact moment before he raced forward.

That's when Ollie heard Granny's hip pop. The second part of the Geriatric Gutbuster was when Granny flipped her opponent straight onto her knee. The timing was important, as the victim never knew exactly *when* she was going to perform the transition to get bowled over by the stampeding Dan. Clearly, Granny's hip had performed the move many times, and the constant use had worn down her joints enough to make the small yet noticeable sound.

Granny gingerly spun Hollis around and placed him gently on her knee. Before he reached Hollis, Dentures Dan made sure to (unfortunately) not use any actual force on Ollie's brother as he collided into him. Hollis played his part, pretending to be in crippling pain.

Everyone cheered loudly for Nursing Home, but none louder than Tamiko.

"Again! Again!" she insisted. "And don't hold back this time!"

Sure enough, the tells were present every time the move was performed. The action only stopped when both Granny and Dan needed to pause for their hourly prune juice break. That gave Ollie and Tamiko time to retreat into a corner and discuss what they had seen.

"This is going to be really tough," said Ollie, making sure to not hit any of the fine china.

Tamiko shook her head. "Tough? There's the understatement of the century."

"I can see why Linton was worried. The Krackle Kiddos would be in serious danger if they fought Nursing Home one-on-one. Thankfully, they'll have some backup."

"All we have to do is beat the greatest tag team that Slam-down Town has ever seen while defending the biggest frauds in the history of wrestling. Oh yeah," said Tamiko sarcastically. "It's going to be a piece of cake."

A loud ringing drew their attention. Granny entered the basement from the top of the stairs, clanging a cowbell. "Dinner's ready!" she cried. "Dan, you better get those dentures back in. My meat loaf's been known to fight back!"

CHAPTER 37

TAMIKO

IT was the night before the Ragtag Team's big invasion and Tamiko's mind was racing. She had brushed her teeth, put on her pajamas, and turned off the lights, eager to rest up for the big day. But, of course, the second she got into bed she was wide awake.

She rolled over, fluffed her pillow, and rearranged her stuffed animals, but nothing could get her to relax. Finally, her eye caught the video game console sitting on her bedroom floor.

Tamiko crossed the room, turned on the TV, and booted up *Revenge of Kragthar*.

"Take *that*, you crazy goblins," she shouted.

Slaying fantasy creatures and stealing all their loot always put her mind at ease.

"Crazy goblins?" asked her dad as he walked past her bedroom door. "That sounds like *Kragthar* shenanigans to me."

Tamiko couldn't believe her ears. "Whoa, Dad. That's actually right."

"Your old man remembers a few things, ya know! Sometimes." He smiled. "I was there when you and Ollie finally beat that game, remember?"

"Oh yeah. It took us forever, but we did it."

He motioned to the space on the floor next to her. "Is that seat taken?"

"Yeah," she said. "By you!"

He plopped beside her. "Ah, you almost got me there."

Tamiko paused the game.

"Listen, bug," he said, rubbing the back of his head. "I'm sorry."

"For what?"

"For Snack Guy. I kinda went a little overboard with that."

"Kinda? A little?" teased Tamiko.

She knew he was being serious. Maybe that's why she was joking with him. It was unlike her dad to talk to her like this.

Thankfully, he laughed. "True. I just . . ." He nudged Tamiko playfully in the arm. "I liked hanging out with you, kiddo. Even if that meant working at the same time."

"Well, I really liked it, too," admitted Tamiko. "I really wish that Leon and Luna hadn't replaced you. It's not fair."

Even thinking about it made her cheeks glow red with anger. Maybe she'd let Nursing Home get in a *few* hits before saving the Krackle Kiddos in the ring.

"That's how it goes sometimes," said her dad. "And then I thought—incorrectly, I now know—that if I could sell the snacks, maybe I could be a wrestler."

"It wasn't your craziest idea ever, but it was up there."

He shrugged. "People do crazy things for their favorite people. I know how much you like wrestling. I figured if I was a wrestler, you'd want to spend time together. Maybe you'd even think I was cool."

Wait, what? she thought. Did her dad really think she didn't want to hang out with him?

Her mom was right. This whole time, becoming Snack Guy hadn't been some crazy, deluded fantasy of his. Far from it. This had all been his way of trying to make her happy.

Tamiko tossed her arms around her dad, squeezing him harder than she'd ever squeezed, even when she was Game Over.

"Goodness, you're strong," he said as he gargled for air.

"I don't need you to be some wacky wrestler to think you're awesome. Because you *are* awesome, Dad. I don't care that Mom and I can kick your butt in video games. And you don't have to know every single fact about wrestling. You're fun to be around just the way you are."

She couldn't believe that her dad had gone to such great lengths to become a wrestler just to impress her. A wave of guilt washed over her as she recalled all the times she'd gotten upset when he got confused. Learning anything new was hard. And yet, her dad had given up his Saturdays and tried his best to understand wrestling, all for her.

After one last squeeze, Tamiko relinquished her dad from her bear hug.

"A little dusty in here," said her dad as he sniffled slightly.

Tamiko giggled. "Plus, I'm not the only one who thinks

you're awesome. Everyone loved you at the arena. You remembered all the orders and always knew exactly what would brighten someone's day!"

It was good to see her dad smiling so big. She missed that smile. The big goofy one that crept over his face whenever he was *super* excited about something.

"Aww, thanks, bug." He sighed loudly. "I miss it."

"Me too," admitted Tamiko. "But who knows? Maybe things can go back to the way they were. I have a good feeling about it."

Bzz! Bzz!

"Not it!" she shouted.

"It's for me," said her dad as he fished the phone out of his pocket. "It's someone named Linton Krackle. Probably a spam call."

Tamiko leapt off the floor.

"Dad!" she yelled at the top of her lungs. "Answer it! Linton Krackle is the CEO of Slamdown Town! Remember?"

"The CEO?" he asked in a panic. "Why would *he* be calling *me*?"

"That's why you have to answer it! To find out! Quick!"

He fumbled with the phone and answered it before the call went to voicemail.

"Hello?" he said as he ran into the other room. "Yes, I can talk."

Tamiko waited anxiously for her dad to return. She of course knew what Linton was calling about. Well, *Game Over* knew. Which is why she feigned ignorance when her dad reentered her bedroom, grinning from ear to ear.

"What did Linton say, Dad?" she asked in an innocent tone.

"Oh, it's *big* stuff, bug," he said happily. "Huge, even! But it's also a *big* secret. What I can tell you is . . ." He leaned in close and whispered for dramatic effect. "You're going to be super-duper happy about it."

"Spoiler alert, Dad," she replied, smiling.

CHAPTER 38

OLLIE

THE muffled din of the waiting arena echoed around the locker room as Big Chew and Game Over made their pre-match preparations. Saturday had arrived and with it their chance to put their plan into action, stop the Krackle Kiddos, and bring Slamdown Town back to normal.

After enjoying the opening matches (which included a surprise victory over the Unbeatable Rowdy Russell, who was then renamed the Beatable Rowdy Russell), he and Tamiko had snuck away to transform into their wrestlers and wait for the championship match to start.

And now the wait was over. Well, almost.

"Nursing Home has nearly completed their long, arduous stroll down the ramp in eight minutes and forty-three seconds." Penelope Dunnelly's voice echoed around the locker room. "I'm being told that is record time for the Geriatric Duo. Well done!"

"The Krackle Kiddos will be entering next," said Big Chew.

"Give it up for the Krackle Kiddos," said Penelope Dunnelly. "I don't care about wrestling, but I always pretend to when I call their matches. They pay the bills, after all."

Game Over pounded her fist into her palm. "I'm ready to kick every butt in that ring and take back what's rightfully ours! The posters, the snacks, the announcer, and the belt."

"And Linton," said Big Chew.

"Sure," said Game Over.

"Don't forget, we're here to protect the Krackle Kiddos. Remember what Linton said. Defeat both Lil' Old Granny and Dentures Dan while keeping Leon and Luna safe."

"Right. Exactly what I said earlier. Kick all the butts. You don't have to worry about me," she said, standing. "I'm just hoping that sleazeball sticks to the plan like we discussed."

Linton had called the Ragtag Team that morning to outline his master plan. Apparently, he'd gotten a "brilliant" idea after speaking with Screech Holler and Mr. Tanaka.

The Ragtag Team would invade the match, protect the Krackle Kiddos, and defeat Nursing Home. But they wouldn't be the *only* ones invading.

Mr. Tanaka, Screech Holler, and yes, Linton Krackle himself wanted in on the action.

"Why?" Big Chew had asked him over the phone.

"Because it's our arena, too," Linton had said, "and we want to do our part."

"Can your part be staying at home and waiting till it's all over?" Game Over had asked.

But there was no convincing him otherwise. So now they weren't a ragtag team of two.

They were a ragtag team of five.

"Although, really," Tamiko had said after they'd hung up, "we're the ones who have to do all the work. They just want to be involved so they can hog all our glory. Well, except for my dad, who wants his job back so he can hang out with me more."

"They'll stick to the plan," Ollie had said. "And if they don't, you can kick Linton's butt."

With Big Chew trusting that Game Over would behave during the actual match, the two wrestlers made their way into the arena. They set foot at the top of the entrance ramp just as the referee cleared both Nursing Home and the Krackle Kiddos for the championship match.

Big Chew raised a microphone to his lips. "Well, well, well. What have we here?"

"Looks like a party to me," said Game Over. "Our invites must have gotten lost in the mail. But that's okay because we're crashing this get-together."

"I don't have this in my note cards," said Penelope. "If I remember correctly, it seems like the Rugtug Duo is here. Maybe they got lost on the way to the bathroom?"

Big Chew sighed. "It's Ragtag Team. And we aren't lost."

"Then what *are* you doing here?" demanded the Krackle Kiddos.

"Maybe you two need some reading glasses," said Granny. "You can borrow mine. Because the schedule clearly doesn't have you two on it."

"The nerve of these young people," cried Dentures Dan.

"Shut it, Gramps," said Luna. "And you Ragtag chumps can beat it! You wasted your chance to wrestle us last week."

"We aren't going anywhere," said Big Chew.

"What are you going to do? Grab a front-row seat?" joked Leon.

"A front-row seat to beating all four of you? Absolutely," said Game Over.

"It seems we have a few more horses in this race," said Penelope. "Can you really have three teams facing off against each other for the championship belt?"

"You can when someone invades the match," said Game Over.

With that, Game Over and Big Chew charged down the entrance ramp at full speed.

"And they're off!" screamed Penelope Dunnelly. "I'm talking, of course, about my fake eyelashes, which just fell onto the floor somewhere. Did anyone see where they went?"

"I'll boost you up," shouted Big Chew as they approached. He knew Game Over was raring to go. While he may have wanted to get into the ring first, he was a face. And being a face meant putting the Ragtag Team's best pair of feet forward.

Big Chew knew those feet belonged to Game Over. And so he cupped his hands together and used them to springboard her over the ropes and straight into the ring.

"You all need some more experience before facing a level-ninety-nine wrestler like me," said Game Over. "Too bad you can't reload to your previous save."

Ding! Ding! Ding!

The bell sent Game Over and Lil' Old Granny colliding into each other.

Game Over unleashed a blistering combo of strikes that sent Granny reeling. But within a heartbeat, she regained her balance and landed her good knee straight into Game Over's gut. Game Over countered by Powering Up, a throw that started by pounding her own chest and then tossing her opponent into the air. But Granny, surprisingly spry for her age, recovered midair and caught Game Over with a diving Why Haven't You Called Spear.

"Just like food at Grandma's house, these hits keep coming!" yelled Granny.

While Game Over kept Granny busy, Big Chew had a mission of his own. He snuck around the ropes to the corner where Leon and Luna were about to charge into the fray.

"Okay, you take Granny and I'll take Game Over," he heard Luna saying.

"What?" Leon scoffed. "No way. I want Game Over. You take the hag."

"What about me?" asked Dentures Dan, who suddenly appeared before them.

Big Chew's stomach dropped. Dentures Dan charged toward Leon and Luna to deliver a Cardigan Chop. Big Chew needed to act now or else the Krackle Kiddos could be in serious danger.

So he dove forward and, in one smooth motion, safely scooped the Krackle Kiddos into his massive arms, rolled behind Dan, bounded off the ropes, and came barreling back toward him with a Bubble-Bursting Flying Kick that sent Dan tumbling backward onto the mat.

"Hey!" said Luna, trying to wriggle free. "Put us down!"

"Yeah, get lost, Big Chew," said Leon. "You know, like you did before?"

He chose to ignore that. The Krackle Kiddos may have been spoiled, pretentious jerkfaces, but he needed to occupy their attention long enough to prevent them from stupidly charging into the fight. They wouldn't last long, considering how ferociously Game Over and Granny were going at it, and with the invasion, all rules were off.

"Things that go away tend to have a way of coming back," he said as he hung them from the turnbuckles by their underwear. "Like me. And the guy who used to do the snacks."

"We fired that small-town loser weeks ago," said Leon, struggling to free himself.

Big Chew pointed to the stands. "Well then, how do you explain that? And don't call him 'loser'!"

There, way up in the crowd, was Snack Guy. Or, as Big Chew had known him for years, Mr. Tanaka. He handed out snacks in all his costumed glory to fans who were eager to gobble up sweet and salty food from their appetite savior.

"Snacks!" yelled Snack Guy. "Get your snacks here! Actually affordable and delicious snacks, made to order by yours truly!"

"Hey, you," shouted the Krackle Kiddos. "You aren't Slamdown Town official. Where is security? Where is Jean-Pierre? Get that Snack Man out of our arena!"

"It's Snack *Guy*," said Snack Guy proudly.

But suddenly, Jean-Pierre appeared in the stands behind him.

"Look out," shouted Big Chew.

"This is my kitchen now," said Jean-Pierre.

"No," said Snack Guy, turning to face him. "I may not know how to work an oven, but I am the master of the microwave and I've come back to claim what is mine."

Jean-Pierre scoffed. "You and what army?"

Suddenly, a crowd of eighth graders surged forward to defend Snack Guy and urgently demanded their snack wishes be fulfilled by the appearance of this mysterious purveyor of tasty morsels.

"At least those eighth-grade menaces are good for something," said Big Chew.

Back in the ring, Big Chew saw Game Over was now fighting Dentures Dan. She pursued him into the corner and followed up with a Pass the Controller Already Beatdown, a series of rapid haphazard blows that threatened to end the championship match right then and there.

But Dan wasn't some newbie. He was a tag team champion with decades of experience.

"You know what you need?" asked Dan. "A good old-fashioned history lesson!"

"Oh, that's not good," muttered Big Chew under his breath. He stretched out his hand. "Hey, Game Over! Tag me in!"

Game Over smiled. "I think I've softened them up enough for you. Let these geezers have it!"

She slapped his hand before rolling out of the ring.

"And don't worry," she said, pointing to the Krackle Kiddos, who still dangled by their underwear on the turnbuckle. "I'll make sure nothing happens to these pip-squeaks."

Luna swung her arms wildly. "And I'll make sure something *does* happen to you!"

"Yeah," said Leon, "just who do you think you are? Hey, Granny!"

"Yes, deary?" asked Granny from across the ring.

"Let us down!" said Luna.

Granny grinned. "With pleasure . . ."

"I'll handle this, you handle Dentures Dan," said Game Over.

Big Chew turned his attention back to the ring. "I hope you brought an extra cup of applesauce," he shouted as he leapt over the ropes and landed on the springy mat, "because you're going to need the metabolism boost when I'm done with ya!"

Dentures Dan rattled his teeth. "Quit yer yapping and get over here."

Big Chew sprinted toward Dan, who immediately struck him with a Senior Discount Slam. But Big Chew popped right back up and countered with a Sticky Situation Suplex that bounced his opponent off the mat and into a grapple. That proved costly, as Dentures Dan got him with The Good Old Days, an armlock that trapped his opponent in a hold while he quietly (and without any signs of stopping) reminisced about how great things used to be.

"Back in my day," started Dentures Dan, "people used to take their time and enjoy the simpler things in life. Like rock chucking and taking long drives to the middle of nowhere."

Big Chew knew he needed to shock Dentures Dan into releasing him.

"Do you know how people will get around in the future?" he asked. "Self-driving cars!"

"B-b-but the machines will take over," sputtered Dentures Dan.

Big Chew used Dentures Dan's irrational fear of technological advancement to break free.

"Here," said Granny as she broke free of Game Over's grapple from across the ring and sprinted toward Dan. "Let Granny show you how it's done!"

Big Chew successfully defended a Grandma's Warm Apple Pie Grapple attempt from Granny and launched an Elastic Elbow at her gut. But she blocked the attack and pushed Big Chew backward.

"Wow, you're strong," he admitted.

"You think you've seen Granny at her best? Watch this!"

Big Chew was scooped up by Granny's muscled arms in one fluid motion that he never would have believed her little old legs could support. He knew the Bunion Bruiser was coming.

Lil' Old Granny lifted Big Chew above her head, ready to bring their combined weights plummeting down on his unfortunately very easy to hit big toe.

Or she would have if Game Over hadn't collided into both of them. Granny's knees buckled as Big Chew was sent hurtling to the mat below.

"Ollie—er—Big Chew," shouted Game Over. "We got a Dentures Dan problem!"

Big Chew shook his head. When his vision cleared he saw Leon and Luna, who had freed themselves from the turnbuckles, had both leapt onto Dan's back in an attempt to grapple him. But the aging wrestler was too strong for them and easily tossed them both to the mat.

"I got them. You take Granny," said Big Chew.

As Game Over charged at Granny in the ring, Big Chew dove in between Dentures Dan and the Krackle Kiddos, holding back the middle schoolers with ease.

"How strong are all of you?" demanded Leon as he struggled to free himself.

"No one's been able to stop us," grunted Luna. "So what gives?"

"This is the most shocking event I've ever witnessed," yelled Penelope. "And I used to be a weatherperson for the Thunderstorm Channel!"

"Can she talk about anything other than herself?" asked a familiar voice.

Finally!

Big Chew spotted Screech Holler approaching the announcer's table, no, *his* announcer's table. The lights shimmered off his bright orange suit and made him appear almost angelic. He quickly flattened his electric-blue hair to look more presentable.

"Sorry it took me so long, folks," he said. "Without my parking validation, I had to walk here. I don't suppose anyone has some water they can spare?"

"Don't you know that you've been replaced by a fancier model?" demanded Penelope.

"Right." Screech shook his head. "Well, that's a shame. I'll have to tell that big-time movie producer who I saw in the parking lot earlier that you *aren't* interested in hosting that huge award ceremony. Mentioned something about blue ribbons, kibble, and kittens?"

"You mean the International Kitty Kibble Eating Competition?" asked Penelope, her voice quivering with excitement. "It's my life's ambition to host that show. Here, loud man. Take this."

Penelope tossed the microphone to Screech and sprinted toward the exit.

He took his seat. And, for the first time in weeks, brought the mic close to his lips.

"Well, Slamdown Town," he shouted. "What do you say? You want good old Screech Holler to add some much-needed commentary to this match?"

The audience roared their approval. Leon and Luna, on the other hand, were irate. They stopped trying to outmaneuver Big Chew and instead made their way toward the ropes.

"You can't be here!" cried Leon. Spit flew from his mouth as he spoke.

"We got rid of you," said Luna with a pouting face. "You aren't famous at all!"

It was time.

"Now!" shouted Big Chew.

Just then, the shark cage dropped from the ceiling. But, unlike Tsunami, Big Chew was waiting for it. He grabbed it out of the air, opened the door, and gently tossed the Krackle Kiddos inside. With a smile, he slammed the door shut and made sure it was firmly locked.

"What are you doing?" asked Luna.

"You can't do this to us!" said Leon.

"Well, that's too bad, kids, because I say he can."

Boos rained down as Linton Krackle made his grand appearance in the arena. He came to a stop at the top of the entrance ramp and lifted the microphone to his lips.

"That's right," said Linton with open arms. "Let the boos come. I feed off your boos! Saves on grocery bills."

"*No! No! No!*" shrieked the Krackle Kiddos. "We fired you. We fired all of you!"

Linton sighed. "You did, kids. You did. But we're here to take back what's ours. Besides, I wouldn't miss your big match for the world."

"You're messing *everything* up!" yelled Leon.

"Just like you *always* do!" screamed Luna.

The Krackle Kiddos were in full meltdown mode. They yelled at the top of their lungs, angry tears streaking down their faces. Their predictably fragile tempers had shattered. But with them locked safely in the shark cage, that meant the Ragtag Team could focus on one thing:

Defeating Nursing Home.

CHAPTER 39

TAMIKO

BEING in the ring was exhilarating. Game Over had never felt more alive as she did trading blows with Granny, who definitely knew a thing or two about wrestling. And one of those things was slamming a Bed Before Seven Haymaker straight into Game Over's gut.

"Granny thinks it's past your bedtime, young lady," said Granny.

"Speak for yourself, old-timer," said Game Over. "I can go all night!"

She managed to keep her lunch down and landed a No Scope Flying Punch on Granny. She followed it up with a You Should Uninstall Your Game Knee, which Granny dodged and countered with a What?! I Didn't Hear You Bull Rush.

Game Over toppled past the shark cage, over the ropes, through the barricade, and right into an unfortunate fan sipping an unfortunate jumbo-size soda.

"That's why you pay extra to sit in the splash zone and even more for ponchos!" yelled Screech as he zipped up his poncho.

The ref began his count for her to get back in the ring.

"Nobody messes with Nursing Home!" said Lil' Old Granny. "Now, somebody fetch Granny a nice bowl of room-temp broth."

Dentures Dan wagged a finger as he motioned to be tagged in. "Oh, that reminds me of the time I once ordered room-temperature broth, back when I was still a young whippersnapper!"

"Folks, you better run out for a bathroom break," said Screech. "This could take a while."

Big Chew rushed over to Game Over. "Tamiko—umm, Game Over, I mean. Are you okay?"

She accepted his hand and got back to her feet. "I'm fine. Trust me."

"I can go in there if you need a break," offered Big Chew.

Game Over knew that Big Chew could dish out some serious punishment on Dentures Dan. But she *needed* to do this. She had to prove to herself and to everyone that she could rise up and win while being true to herself.

That being said, she was part of a team. And she owed it to Big Chew to let him have his shot, too.

"I want to do this," she admitted. "But I understand if you want to wrestle."

"Someone from the Ragtag Team needs to get back in that ring," shrieked Screech. "Or they'll lose the match here and now!"

The ref continued his slow count. There wasn't much time left.

The Krackle Kiddos howled with laughter. "They're scared of us even when we're locked in a shark cage. How funny is that? But seriously, someone let us out right now."

Big Chew looked into the ring and then back at Game Over. "I think the best wrestler should go in there," he said.

She sighed. "I agree."

"So then, get in there," he said with a smile. "And let me know when it's time to finish this match. Together!"

Game Over pulled Big Chew into a backbreaking hug.

"I won't let you down, dude!"

With a second to spare, Game Over shot back into the ring. Every hair on her body stood on end. This was it. This was where they won it all.

"Time to dole out some justice to you hooligans!" yelled Dentures Dan.

"You selected Extra Hard Mode, and guess what?" Game Over leaned in menacingly. "There are no cheat codes for *this* game."

The two wrestlers met in the center of the ring. Dentures Dan synched in a Have You Seen My Glasses Choke. Game Over raised her arm and hit Dan with an illegal Power-Up Eye Poke. Dan reached for his eyes, releasing his hold on Game Over.

"That was definitely dirty there, folks," said Screech. "But Game Over escaped what looked like certain defeat."

Suddenly, she felt a titanic hand grab her and pin her to the spot.

"Didn't your parents ever tell you to respect your elders?" asked Granny.

Game Over felt her stomach drop. This was not going to end well.

"She's setting up the Geriatric Gutbuster," warned Big Chew from outside the ring.

"Goodness, folks," yelled Screech. "This surely is the end for the Ragtag Team. No wrestler has survived Nursing Home's iconic finishing move!"

"I can't wait to see this," said the Krackle Kiddos.

"Remember the tells," yelled Big Chew. "You can do this!"

That's right, Game Over thought. *I can do this.*

She watched, held firmly in place by Granny, as Dentures Dan prepared to charge.

"Let Nursing Home drop some age-old wisdom on you," whispered Granny.

Game Over took a deep breath. And then another. She tuned out everything: The crowd cheering. Screech screaming about how everyone could start heading to the parking lot. The Krackle Kiddos taunting her from inside their locked cage. Nothing else mattered except Dentures Dan's teeth.

They wiggled.

Pop!

And there was Granny's knee. Game Over put all of her energy into pushing as hard as she could off Granny as she lifted her high into the air.

"What in the name of tapioca pudding?" uttered Granny in surprise.

"Gotcha," said Game Over.

Granny had not been expecting her to push back at that moment. And instead of Game Over being brought down on her knees, Granny shot forward and collided straight into the stampeding Dentures Dan.

"Nursing Home has gone and gutbusted themselves," shouted Screech.

The moment of victory had presented itself. Now they needed to act on it.

"Let's finish this," she shouted to Big Chew. "Together."

He nodded. "I'll set 'em up, you knock 'em down!"

As Big Chew jumped on top of the ropes, Game Over dove under them. She searched underneath the ring and found what she was looking for.

A single, illegal folding chair.

"What in the name of Slamdown Town am I witnessing here, folks?" asked Screech.

Nursing Home wobbled on their feet in the center of the ring, still woozy from their collision. But that's *precisely* where they needed to be for this tag team takedown to work.

Big Chew balanced on the top rope as Game Over climbed back into the ring, chair in hand. "It's now or never," she shouted. "Ragtag Takedown!"

Big Chew corkscrewed into the air and flung himself toward the center of the ring.

"It's Bubble-Bursting time!" he yelled.

The aerial attack sent the elderly duo teetering backward.

"Batter up," Game Over shouted as she swung the chair with all her might.

Thwack!

They teetered. They tottered. And with a resounding thud, Nursing Home fell to the mat.

"An unbelievable takedown, folks," yelled Screech. "I think we have witnessed the birth of the Ragtag Team finishing move! That was a thing of beauty!"

"That was impressive," said a pair of voices from behind. "But that's only one team down! And there's no way you can stop the awesome might of the Krackle Kiddos!"

Game Over turned to see that the Krackle Kiddos had finally used their scrawny twelve-year-old frames to their advantage and had wriggled their way through the shark cage bars.

CHAPTER 40

TAMIKO

LEON and Luna charged at Game Over and Big Chew. The scrawny middle schoolers ran smack into them and had the audacity to look shocked as they fell to the mat.

The arena went silent.

"That was a fluke," said Leon, shaking his head.

Luna jumped back up to her feet. "This time you're going down!"

"I wouldn't do that," said Game Over.

But they didn't listen to her. Instead, the Krackle Kiddos charged at them again. Apparently, they hadn't learned their lesson the first time. Or the second time. Or the third.

Leon and Luna struggled. But against actual opponents, there was nothing they could do.

"All right, let's end this charade," said Game Over as she gently lifted Luna and placed her next to Granny on the mat. Game Over laid her massive body on top of them both. Across from her, she saw Big Chew did the same for Dentures Dan and Leon.

The ref blinked, unsure of what to do.

"What are you waiting for, a signed invitation?" asked Game Over. "Count them out before we toss *you* on this pile, too."

That was all the encouragement he needed.

"Eight! Nine! Ten!" counted the ref.

Ding! Ding! Ding!

"Slamdown Town," yelled Screech, his voice teeming with unbridled excitement. "Give it up for your match winners and your new tag team champions. The Ragtag Team!"

"We kicked every butt in that ring!" screamed Game Over. "And we're the champs!"

"I couldn't have done it without you," said Big Chew.

"I know," said Game Over. "Thanks for being the best partner a girl could ask for."

They soaked in the cheers of the crowd. That is, until Werewrestler and Sasquat appeared at the top of the entrance ramp. They looked angrier than Game Over had ever seen them.

"You lied to us, Linton," snarled Werewrestler as he grabbed the sweating CEO, who at that moment was trying to run away, and lifted him high into the air.

"Lied? Me?" squeaked Linton. "I would never do such a thing."

Sasquat spat on the ground. "Save it for someone who cares. The only reason we threw our match was because you promised payment. So explain to me why you paid us in toy money. Do you think dealing with us is some kind of game?"

Gasps were heard around the arena. Even Screech was shocked.

"Toys? Money? What's he talking about, folks?"

"Yeah, Dad. What *is* he talking about?" demanded the Krackle Kiddos.

"W-w-well, you see," stammered Linton.

"This old cheapskate's been paying people off so you'd win," said Werewrestler. "What? You thought you could *actually* beat *us*?"

The Terrible Twosome howled with laughter.

"Now, that's not true," said Linton. "I didn't pay *everyone*. Just you two. Took care of the rest of the matches myself." He turned toward the Kiddos. "But trust me, kids, everything I did, including locking you in the shark cage tonight—I did it so you wouldn't get hurt."

"That was you?" asked the Krackle Kiddos.

Linton sighed. "That was me . . ."

"For someone who never bothered to show up to one of our matches," they said, "you sure seem to be showing a lot of interest all of a sudden."

"There was a reason I was never there," began Linton.

Then, in true wrestling melodramatic fashion, Linton confessed everything to the entire arena. He admitted to rigging every match, down to the last detail. By the end, Werewrestler let him drop only after Linton coughed up the money in cold, hard cash. *Plus* ten percent.

"Listen, kids," said Linton, straightening his cheap suit. "I know you don't want to be here. With me, that is. And that you only came to avoid going back to reform school. But when you said you wanted to take up wrestling, I figured it was something we could bond over. I guess I was wrong."

Leon and Luna had sat in silence, listening, throughout their dad's entire speech. The arena waited with bated breath. Game Over was certain the tantrum they were all about to witness would be spoken about for generations. Finally, the twins raised the mics to their lips.

"You're saying you did all that—pretending to be a referee, taking out wrestlers, even paying off opponents—so that we would win?"

"I sure did."

"But you love money more than anything in the world," they stated, confused.

"Not *everything* in the world," replied Linton softly.

Game Over felt nauseated. Or maybe oddly emotional? The two were hard to distinguish sometimes. Either way, she hoped this would wrap up soon. She wasn't sure her stomach could take it much longer.

"You two come first," Linton clarified. "But money is definitely second."

Leon and Luna looked at each other. Game Over was certain they were forming a devious plan. They always knew how to come out ahead.

"You were willing to buy our love?" asked Leon.

"Just so we'd be happy?" asked Luna.

"For you two, and you two only, you betcha. And I'd do it all over again."

"That's awesome," the twins shouted in unison.

Game Over shouldn't have been surprised at the Krackle Kiddos' response. Maybe she'd held out hope that those two spoiled brats would finally learn some big lesson. Instead, it appeared that the only thing they'd gained was a more direct path to their dad's wallet.

"We love you, Daddy," they said as the three embraced in the center of the ring.

"Aww," said Screech, "doesn't that just melt your heart, folks?"

"You know," said Leon with a sickly sweet voice, "there are *way* cooler things than wrestling that would make us even happier, Daddy."

Luna batted her eyelashes. "I hear there's a six-month astronaut camp where they launch you into space!"

"That sounds expensive," said Linton with a strained voice.

Leon and Luna pouted their lips, quivering them for extra effect.

"Puh-lease, Daddy," they begged.

"All right, fine," said Linton. "If my kiddos want outer space, they get it."

The Krackle Kiddos leapt up in the air.

"Space! Space! Space!" they cheered.

"Guess we don't need this anymore," said Leon as he pulled the deed from his pocket.

"To be honest, I've never even *liked* wrestling," said Luna. "You can have it back."

And together, they tore the deed to pieces and tossed them into the air.

Game Over breathed a sigh of relief. Not only had the Ragtag Team managed to keep Leon and Luna safe during the match *while* defeating Nursing Home for the championship belt, now the Krackle Kiddos were officially departing Slamdown Town for the foreseeable future.

Linton handed Game Over a shining gold belt, one of two that had belonged to Nursing Home for what seemed like forever, but was now hers.

"I believe these now belong to you," said Linton. He gave Big Chew a matching belt. "And remember, you scuff it, you bought it. And I charge triple what it's worth."

Game Over ran her hand over the musty leather belt, the metal cool to the touch, before hoisting it high above her head. Besides her, Big Chew did the same.

This night could not have turned out more perfectly.

"Folks, I've never seen an emotional roller coaster of a match like this," admitted Screech. "You had drama, you had excitement, you had an invasion, and new champs to boot! Why, that was so much action that I've just been informed by Linton that he will be charging everyone extra on their way out. No freebies!"

"Ah, classic Linton," said Game Over.

Big Chew looked around the arena. "So, what do we do now?"

Game Over laughed. "What do you mean, what do we do now? We're champions! And I could *really* use some celebration sour gummies."

"That sounds great," said Big Chew with a massive grin.

The Ragtag Team headed back to the locker room as champions. They left the locker room as eleven-year-old Tamiko and Ollie, still riding the high of their victory.

CHAPTER 41

TAMIKO

THE following weekend, Tamiko strolled across the mildew-riddled carpet of the arena arcade toward *Brawlmania Supreme*. She passed beeping machines and screaming kids. And, as had become all too common, some fresh-faced wrestling fan had the audacity to be playing it when she arrived. She watched as he battled the Buff Boss. But, as had happened to her so many times before, the kid couldn't avoid his Briefcase Beatdown and received the dreaded message:

GAME OVER

For years, she'd hated those words. Now she viewed them as a rite of passage. Anyone who wanted to see their initials at the top of the high-score list would need to see them a lot.

"Get used to it, dude," she said as the kid kicked the machine and stormed off.

"What do you think happens if someone takes your spot?" asked Ollie from behind. He'd been waiting in line for the bathroom and had gotten back faster than Tamiko thought he would.

"Hmm," she said, walking up to the machine and patting the side of it. "I don't know, but I don't think we're going to find out anytime soon."

"Why's that?" asked Ollie.

She patted a pocketful of quarters. "I plan on crushing my own high score so no one gets close. But enough games for now. We have a title to defend."

✳✳✳

Tamiko's shoes made the familiar, welcome pop as she and Ollie walked across the sticky arena floors. "Do you smell that?" she asked. "That's the smell of normal."

He sniffed. "And Hollis's dirty underwear."

Tamiko took a deep breath. "Exactly the way things should be."

Two familiar voices drifted over the din of excited guests entering the arena.

"We were hoping to bump into you two," said the Krackle Kiddos.

They were dressed in what Tamiko only assumed were real (and very expensive) space suits. The Krackle Kiddos removed their helmets simultaneously.

"I see your dad kept his word about sending you to space camp," she said, desperate to move the conversation along. The

Krackle Kiddos had avoided talking to them all week. She guessed they were still mad at them for saying that they had cheated, when in reality they had been none the wiser.

"He sure did," said Luna.

"Since Daddy is willing to buy our love, we figured we'd push it as far as it can go," admitted Leon.

"And what's higher than space?" they said in unison. "By the way, we looked for you during the championship match and couldn't find you. Where were you?"

"We must have both been in the bathroom at that time," said Ollie. "All that fancy food really goes down hard."

A moment of awkward silence passed.

"Sorry about accusing you of cheating." The words tumbled out of Tamiko's mouth. "That was pretty uncool."

"It certainly was," said Luna. "But you technically weren't wrong."

Leon nodded. "The matches *were* being thrown. By Daddy, of course. Not us."

"We're incredibly awesome and would never need to do that."

"Sure," lied Ollie, "but it still wasn't cool on our part. I know we never really got to know each other all that well, but I did have a good time hanging out at your dad's house."

"Yeah, you two aren't all that bad, either. Not completely, anyway," admitted Leon.

"You're not really *great* friends," said Luna. "But you're *our* friends, so that means you're great by association. Krackle friendship is premium friendship."

"But unless you also happen to have tickets to the moon, we're leaving you both behind. Maybe we'll send you a moon rock or two."

"That'd be cool," said Ollie. "We'll keep an eye out for it."

"Make sure mine's got an alien in it!" said Tamiko.

With a noncommittal shrug, Leon and Luna Krackle placed their space helmets on their heads. They snapped their fingers, and Billingsley appeared with their luggage.

"Hey, Billingsley!" called Tamiko as he trailed the Krackle Kiddos.

"Yes, Master Ollie and Mistress Tamiko?" he said, turning around.

"We're sorry for thinking that you were a criminal mastermind."

"No need to apologize. I live to serve, whether that be as a butler or a red herring."

And with that, he bowed and followed the Krackle Kiddos out of the arena.

"Do you think they allow butlers in space?" asked Tamiko as she watched them leave.

Ollie shrugged. "If they don't, that space camp is going to see one galaxy-size tantrum."

Tamiko and Ollie snaked their way through the crowd before spotting Ollie's mom on her way to prepare for her own title-defense match against Malachi McButtkickin, the mythical leprechaun turned professional wrestler whose luck they were all certain had run out after deciding to face The Referee.

"Before I go, I want to say what a good job you both did,"

she said to Tamiko and Ollie. She placed a strong hand on both of their shoulders. "You knew something was up and you followed it through to the end. I'd say if wrestling isn't in either of your futures, I'd be proud to write you both letters of recommendation for careers as referees."

"Thanks, Mom," said Ollie, his face red with embarrassment.

Tamiko laughed. "Appreciate it, Mrs. Evander. But I don't think ref life would agree with me."

"I thought that too, but now look at me." Ollie's mom smiled. "Now, you two have fun tonight. I'll try not to win *too* fast to keep things entertaining."

Leaving Ollie's mom to her pre-match exercises, they navigated the hallways until they reached the snack area. At the counter, her dad's Snack Guy outfit drew the attention of everyone that passed. And to Tamiko's delight, people seemed very impressed.

"Back at last," said her dad as he spotted them approaching. He cupped his hands around his mouth and shouted, "And do not fear, Slamdown Town, for Snack Guy is here to defeat your nefarious hunger!"

The fans around the snack counter cheered and jumped for joy.

"No one will go hungry on Snack Guy's watch," he declared boldly. Then he leaned down and lowered his voice. "How am I doing, bug?"

"You're doing great, Dad," whispered Tamiko.

He beamed at the compliment. "I'm glad we get to do this again."

"Me too. I like having you here."

Hollis appeared and pushed his way to the front of the line.

"Outta my way!" he yelled. "I need snacks and I need them now!"

"A jumbo-size chocolate-dipped cotton candy with sprinkles and two hot dogs with extra ketchup," Tamiko's dad replied.

"Yes! But wait, I also need—"

"A cup of tapioca pudding, a bag of prunes, and one club soda to wash it all down."

"Right as usual, Mr. Tanaka," said Hollis. "Or is it Snack Guy? Either way, this time the hot dogs *are* for the nostrils. The Walrus is back, baby!"

Breonna appeared as if drawn over by Hollis's body odor.

"Oh, Hollie-poo! You ordered for me already?"

"Of course I did," said Hollis, placing a few dollars on the counter. "Paid for it, too."

"Hey, isn't that my lunch money?" asked Ollie.

"Just being me," said Hollis.

"Everything's back to normal," said Breonna. "But make sure to pay your brother back."

Hollis cracked his knuckles. "Oh, I'll pay him back."

Ollie gulped.

"Sorry to hear about Granny," said Tamiko. Being the champion was awesome, but she felt bad knowing that meant Nursing Home (and their fans) had to lose.

Breonna sighed. "That's okay. I know she'll get her belt back one day."

"I'm not so sure about that one," said Hollis, shoving a pair of hot dogs in his nostrils and looking down at his Lil' Chew outfit. "Big Chew and Game Over are hard to beat."

"Attention, Slamdown Town!" Hearing Screech Holler's voice ring out over the speakers made Tamiko feel right at home. "We've got a fantastic night of wrestling ahead of us brought to you by our newly reinstated charismatic and extremely attractive CEO, Linton Krackle. I was paid to say that, folks. Left a bad taste in my mouth, though."

Boos floated up and down the hallways of Slamdown Town. Linton may not have been the best CEO. Or even a good one. He wasn't even a good *person*, really. But Slamdown Town under his reign had brought Tamiko some of her favorite memories. And at the very least she could give him that. But she—of course—booed along with everyone else.

"Come on," said Tamiko, grabbing Ollie's hand and leading him away from Hollis and Breonna. "We should head back to the locker room. It's almost time."

They pushed their way through the chattering crowds and headed to the locker room. They were ready to spend their Saturday doing their new norm: not just watching wrestling, but wrestling together in the ring. They each transformed, suited up, and prepared for their first match as Slamdown Town tag team champions.

But before they made their way out for the title-defense match, Game Over had one tiny surprise for Big Chew. She rummaged through her pockets and pulled out a permanent marker.

"These lockers are like our new seats," she said, opening her locker door and writing her name—*Game Over*—on the inside. "You're up, dude."

He grabbed the marker and added his name to the inside of his locker, as well.

"How does it look?" asked Big Chew.

"Perfect. These are ours now," declared Game Over as she admired their handiwork. "Remember how we said we were the king and queen of Slamdown Town?" She grabbed the golden tag team belt hanging in her locker and put it on. "Well, I think that's for real now!"

Big Chew smiled and put his own belt on. "Yeah. Things are back to normal. Mostly. But they're also a little different. And that's okay, because we're in it together."

Game Over nodded. She wasn't sure what other secrets she or Ollie or maybe some other kid would discover at Slamdown Town, but she was certain there were more to be found. And she knew that as long as she had Ollie by her side, she'd be down for any challenge.

"Come on," she shouted. "We've got belts to defend!"

Game Over and Big Chew made their way into the arena. They walked onto the entrance ramp to the roar of the crowd. Cheering fans brandished signs and yelled from the stands. All the hairs on her arms and legs stood on end. If this was how she would be spending her Saturdays from now on, she could definitely get used to it.

"Slamdown Town," shouted Screech Holler. "Give it up for your tag team wrestling champions: Big Chew and Game Over! The Ragtag Team!"

ACKNOWLEDGMENTS

Maureen Smith, Gary Nicoll, Patty Nicoll, Lauren Palette, Olivia Smith, Lindsey Tews, Ryan Nicoll, Don Palette, Barb Palette, Jessica Palette, Anne Heltzel, Jessica Gotz, Mary Marolla, Megan Carlson, Brenda E. Angelilli, Monica Burton, Lena Buzzetta, Joseph Buzzetta, Jillian Vanek, Jess Landau, Steve Landau, Morgan Rubin, Michael Krouse, Joshua McHugh, Maya Carter-Ali, Amir Ali, Marielle Carter, Andrew Moriarty, Courtney Hindle, Dwight Hahn, Will Morrison, Steve Miller, Elizabeth Miller, Maddie Miller, Sean Humphrey, Rita Place, Rick Place, Jack Place, Maria Losada, Rachel Jackson, Rob Domingo, Patricia Melendez, Melinda Carr, Steve Palette-Nicoll, and Kitty Meow.